DESPERATE DOGFIGHT

Savage looked behind him. He could see two holes in the fuselage fabric only a few inches behind the cockpit. There were probably others he could not see.

For the next few minutes, there was a wild scramble as the Boche tried to get on his tail and he tried to avoid them while at the same time getting just behind one of them. Then, during one of the maneuvers, Savage did have a Pfalz dead to rights in more than one sense. But both of his machine guns jammed at the same time. This happened very rarely, and it would not have happened at all if he had had time to caliper his ammunition before takeoff.

Savage did not curse easily. He had been taught to express himself otherwise. This time, however, he vented his frustration and rage with some blisterers, though in French and Italian. He finished with a single Arabic word.

There was no time to try to unjam the guns. The enemy was too close. He fled, climbing toward a distant cloud. . . .

Don't miss the next original Doc Savage novel,
Python Isle by Will Murray,
writing as Kenneth Robeson,
coming in October 1991.

ESCAPE FROM LOKI

Doc Savage's First Adventure

by Philip José Farmer

BANTAM BOOKS
NEW YORK • TORONTO • LONDON • SYDNEY • AUCKLAND

ESCAPE FROM LOKI

A Bantam Falcon Book / August 1991

ISBN 0-553-29093-2

Published simultaneously in the United States and Canada

PRINTED IN THE UNITED STATES OF AMERICA

RAD   0 9 8 7 6 5 4 3 2

To Norma and Lester Dent, Will Murray, Bob Sampson, Bill Colby-Newton, Alberta Camus, and to all those who loved and love Doc and his five aides, Pat Savage, and the splendid villains.

Also, to the Golden Age of the Great Pulps.

I

Spiders, men, and Mother Nature make trapdoors.

This trapdoor was Hers. It was made of air and water, but the springing mechanism was confusion in the mind of the man who had ventured onto it. What seems Up may be Down.

Like a young god who had stepped onto a trapdoor, Lieutenant Clark Savage fell from the heavens into hell.

He had not known that he was flying his airplane on its back. Cloud-wrapped, unable even to see the instrument panel before him, he had been as ignorant of his danger as a hog freighted to the slaughterhouse.

His chaser biplane plunged nose-down out of the dark mists. The bright French afternoon sun of March 31, 1918, dazzled him. Not until then did he know that his senses had tricked him. He had been upside down, for how long he did not know. His Nieuport 28 was heading vertically for the earth at two hundred miles per hour and picking up speed far too rapidly. He had to bring it out of its dive, but not too abruptly. The Nieuport shed its upper fabric if it was put beyond a certain stress. Once a piece of fabric parted from the others, the propellor slipstream got under the covering. Then all of it was ripped off.

He had no parachute. The Allied commanders had decreed that parachutes were for sissies.

If the wings did crumple, then he would cry out: *"Mon Dieu! Peste! Sacre bleu! Merde! A mon secours!"*

Or similar phrases in ten other languages which he spoke fluently though he was only sixteen years old. At the moment, he was thinking in French because he had been speaking only that for several months.

That the wings could collapse did not disturb him. He was very young and bursting with spring sap, exploding hormones, and headlong optimism.

However, unlike most of his age, he did not live just for the moment. He had plans for the rest of his life. But an Allied combat flier, regardless of age, had to be keenly aware at every second of what was happening around him. If he daydreamed, he would go to the Land of the Permanent Nod.

Today was Easter. He hoped he would see at least eighty-four more of the days on which the Resurrection was feted and, in America, rabbits laid eggs. But he knew the aerial warfare statistics. Here today and possibly gone today, too.

Just as he eased the Nieuport out of the dive, he noted that it was, at this second, at 5,500 feet altitude. He also looked behind, above, below, to the right, and to the left.

No aircraft in sight. So far, he eluded the two German fighters pursuing him when he had taken cover in the cloud.

Below was the wasteland of the battlefield. It looked as if a frantic leprechaun had been digging in it for days, trying to find the pot of gold stolen from him. High-explosive shrapnel-filled shells and mustard-gas-filled shells had blown thousands of holes in the earth. Then more shells had blasted holes in the holes and in the spaces among them. And then these holes had been moved around again and again. If holes had ghosts, the field would be covered with a thick gray ectoplasm. Phantoms in a traffic jam.

To the south were the half-wrecked trenches of the French Sixth Army. They were occupied by half-wrecked men who had somehow survived the apocalyptic bombardments or by bottom-of-the-barrel reserves rushed up from the rear.

To the north were the German trenches. Behind them, several miles or so, the Gallic sun of the Picardy region glittered on Teutonic cannons, rows on rows, at the moment silent.

Savage had a peculiar feeling then. It was as if he had been seeing with blurred vision, and he had just put on spectacles. Where he had thought there was nothing unusually significant five miles behind the Boche artillery, there now was a German observation balloon.

The Drachenballon, "dragonballoon," was tiny at this distance. But its yellow semisausage shape with, at one end, three inflated stabilizers like fat short wings and a swollen rudder, and the basket below it were unmistakable. The ropes suspending the basket were invisible, as were the anchoring cable and the telegraph line from the basket to the ground. The flat-bedded truck holding the winch to which the cable was attached was not too small to make out. Nor were the rings of antiaircraft cannons, called "Archie" or "ack-ack," and the sandbagged emplacements for the heavy machine-gun pits.

Savage again glanced around, up, and down. Eternal vigilance helped keep you alive. But it also gave you a stiff neck.

The wind was, as usual, from the west. To fly home, he had to buck it, though it pushed him sideways, not straight on. His fuel gauge told him, "There's enough gas, if you switch soon to reserve, to get us to our aerodrome. But don't dillydally around! Get going!"

Later, recalling this moment, he knew he had not had to decide what he was going to do. Without thinking about it, he had turned north.

And in that direction, to his right, were two other tethered yellow sausage-shapes marked with black crosses. These were spaced about three miles apart. He should have spotted them at the same time as he did the first one.

By now, the defenders around the nearest aerostat must have seen his plane. They would be aiming their weapons at this lone plane even though they would not expect it to be a foe. What pilot would be stupid enough to attack now that he knew he was detected and at such a distance?

There were two recommended courses for balloon busting. Come in low and fast before the enemy was aware of you. Or drop out of a cloud or the blinding glare of the sun in a steep dive with your engine turned off so that you would give as little warning as possible. He did not have the time for either approach.

It was more dangerous to attack an observation balloon than a combat plane no matter whether you came in at low level or from on high.

There were no trees for miles around here. They had all been blasted to bits and the roots blown out long ago.

If he came in at ground level, he would be getting the concentrated force of rifle and machine-gun fire between him and the balloon. On the other hand, Archie's 77-millimeter cannons could not be depressed enough to shoot at him until he gained altitude. That would be when he climbed to get close enough to the sausage to shoot his incendiary bullets.

By now, the Germans knew, or thought they knew, that he was French. Thus, he was crazy enough to attack. Above, below, and ahead of him, black puffs with scarlet fire in their centers sprang into being like genies out of bottles of air. Then the blackness seemed to be solid.

The Nieuport vibrated slightly. Whatever had struck it did not stop it from continuing its steep dive.

He leveled out, the engine roaring, the wheels a foot from touching the churned mud, the much-dented landscape flashing past him. Now and then, he came to a mound of earth, an abandoned cannon, a fire-scorched tank, barbed-wire barriers still not fragmented by exploding shells, or an overturned gun carriage. When these barred his path, he flat-arced the Nieuport over them. He also zigzagged, a wingtip almost scraping the mud whenever he banked to change course.

He could see ahead the white-hot flames jetting from the mouths of the machine gun.

Then he was past the first line of trenches, past the second line, past the maze of the third line, and was bringing the plane sharply up.

The balloon was being swiftly winched in. Black smoke poured from the gas engine on the truck bed as it labored to get its ward down from the sky.

The outer ring of machine guns was busy. Their barrels swinging to anticipate his path, they spat at him. Then he was above them, a position he did not like at all but that was unavoidable if he would hit the sausage. It was now down to about five hundred feet from the truck.

The plane trembled twice as it was hit hard somewhere on the frame. He was sure that the bullets were colandering the Nieuport, but he could feel their impact only when they struck that part of the fuselage near him.

He whipped the plane steeply upward, and the right half of the instrument board splattered into fragments which struck his goggles and face. The left lens was starred, though he could still see through it. If his face was bleeding, it did not pain him.

Abruptly, as the aerostat grew larger, small, black, and expanding clouds appeared ahead of him. A second afterward, like dazzling greenish crimson-hearted beads on a string, "flaming onions" burst around him. They were rockets as dreaded as the ack-ack, and the Nieuport shook each time they exploded.

The lovely but sinister kaleidoscope of smoke and fire vanished. He was too close to the balloon. The protectors did not want to risk hitting it.

The biplane shuddered three times like a wader stepping into the Arctic sea.

If it had been struck fatally, it showed no sign of it. Not faltering, the rotary engine roaring at full throttle, the angle of its ascent almost vertical to the earth, the Nieuport sped upward toward the balloon. It was close to hanging on its propellor.

He could see above and ahead of him the two observers leaning out of the gondola, their rifle muzzles flaming.

Not for long. Their heads disappeared. Then one climbed up onto the edge of the gondola and leaped out. Whether his parachute opened in time or what happened to the other man, Savage did not know.

The twin Vickers machine guns, one mounted forward of the cockpit and the other forward to his left, quivered noisily like two hungry cats that had just seen a fat mouse. Their streams of bullets, tracers burning to show him the missile path, leaden missiles and incendiaries, struck the basket. It flew apart like a bird nest struck by a tornado.

The two white-hot lines of his bullets plunged into the underside of the sausage. Its hydrogen contents gouted redly. The blast hit his Nieuport so hard that it seemed to stop dead in the air. But it did not. And the burning balloon began to fall at once.

The left wing of the plane narrowly missed being severed by the suddenly lax cable, and Savage felt the heat of flames as he passed just above the balloon.

At the same time, the Nieuport fell off to one side. Savage righted it but could not slow its dive. Only because the other side of the observation site sloped steeply was he able to keep from smashing into the ground. Even so, its wheels struck the ground hard as the plane bounced high and almost out of control.

He thought he had lost the wheels, but he could not check them yet. He was too busy fighting to keep the craft straight. Keeping it level was another thing.

It dipped. He was so close to the still downward-inclining earth that he knew now that his wheels had been torn off. He expected the whirling tip of the propellor to dig into the mud an inch or so below it.

Then he was rising again, and Archie was placing his shells too close to him. Black smoke appeared ahead of him, and the left side of the windshield suddenly had a big jagged hole in it. At the same time, his scalp burned on its right side. Glancing around, he saw that he was west of the second balloon but obliquely approaching it. The flame-hearted black puffs, a school of self-destructing fish around him, were coming from its defenses. He pushed down slightly on the control stick. The ack-ack could no longer reach him. But the rifle and machine-gun fire could.

To make it worse, a mob of soldiers to his right, several hundred yards away and fifty feet below, was firing its Mauser rifles and Maxim machine guns at him.

Oily smoke from the fire under the engine cowling

wrapped his head. He was half-blinded. His nostrils stung. He started coughing, a most dangerous reaction just now.

At the same time, he felt the wind cool against a trickle down the right side of his face. That burning on the scalp must have been caused by a piece of shrapnel cutting through his fur-lined flier's helmet and ripping through his scalp. The fluid on his face was blood, absorbed by the fur at first but now flowing out of the helmet and quickly evaporating from the wind.

He looked behind him. Flames writhed like the bloodied tentacles of a wounded octopus from the rear part of the fuselage. The Nieuport could explode at any second. And now, despite the smoke from the engine and the oil film on his goggles, he could see a new danger.

Diving down above and behind him were two Pfalzes. They would be shooting at him within ten seconds.

He pushed his goggles up onto his forehead because the oily deposit from the engine smoke had filmed them. He had to squint then, and his eyes burned.

Something knocked his right foot upward from its position on the rudder bar. His right shoulder suddenly burned. The edge of the cockpit was torn apart.

What happened after that filtered through a twilight screen in his mind. He was vaguely aware that the left side of the instrument panel had exploded from bullets fired from behind him. Equally vague was how long it was after this that he had seen a river about forty feet below him. Later, he was to remember hazily that he had fumbled with the buckle of his crash belt.

Time ceased then to exist for him.

II

When he partly regained his senses, he was crawling on mud. His face was only a few inches above it. The mud stank of fish long dead and dissolved into the water-soaked earth.

Suddenly, a tiny crater appeared in the mud several inches ahead of him. He could not hear very well but knew, vaguely, that he was being shot at. He kept on crawling, feeling cold wet earth on his right knee where it came through a tear in his flying suit. His right leg dragged a little.

Somehow, he had survived the crash and had swum to shore in his heavy clothes.

The riverbank sloped upward slightly. If he could get to its top and to the ground beyond, he might be out of the line of fire.

He seemed to take a long time. Meanwhile, other craters of mud appeared ahead of him. By the time he had scrambled over the top of the bank and rolled away from it, he had almost regained the full power of his hearing. Rifles were indeed banging away at him.

Just ahead was a muddy and much-rutted road. Beyond it was a shattered forest, stumps sticking out, fallen trunks scattered like matches from a spilled box, very few limbs, these having been blown to bits.

He turned and crawled, slid, rather, to a mound of mingled brown weeds and mud. He looked with one eye from one side of it. The river was about two hundred feet wide at this point. It should be the Verse, a tributary of the Oise. He must have come down near Noyon, now held by the Germans.

The crackle of gunfire came from soldiers on the opposite bank. Suddenly, it ceased.

In the middle of a river were three vessels. One was a tugboat pushing a dozen open barges piled with coal. Its pilothouse lacked a roof.

The second craft was upstream of the tug. High and fierce flames covered it from bow to stern. Its shattered hull looked as if it had been a patrol boat. As his gaze lingered on it, something exploded amidships, and the front section sank, followed a moment later by the aft section.

The third vessel was a steam-powered patrol boat flying the flag of the Kaiser's Empire. Its machine guns were pointed toward where he had gone over the bank, but they were now silent. It was headed in his direction.

The patrol boat would soon be landing men to chase him. And vehicles loaded with soldiers eager to shoot a refugee would be coming down this road if they did not get stuck in the mud.

There was neither sound nor sign of the two Pfalzes that had tailed him until he had crashed. Their pilots must be satisfied that they would share credit for another victory. Or perhaps their first victory.

He turned and crawled to the road. Wobbly, his right leg feeling weak, he rose then and crossed the road. His feet sank deep and made sucking sounds when he pulled them out. Reaching the other side of the road, he straightened up from his half-crouch. He was beyond the sight of the enemy. For the moment, anyway.

The forest, now no more than a widely scattered pile of half-burned wood, did not make a good hiding place. But he began trudging through it, detouring where charred stumps or piles of burned trunks barred his way. While doing this, he wondered about what had happened after he had blacked out. He should be dead. What had torn off the pilothouse roof? His airplane, of course. It must have hit the top of the pilothouse on a very shallow slant and then bounced off. At the end of its arc had been the patrol boat. The Nieuport had smashed into it and exploded.

He should have been jellied by the impact and then burned to ashes by the exploding gasoline.

During the very short time in which the Nieuport had ricocheted from the roof of the barge and had smashed into the patrol boat, he had been catapulted out of the cockpit. That was a miracle in itself since he was a big man and had had to jam himself into the cockpit. It had constricted him as if he had gotten into a coffin built for an armless woman. Maybe he had been spat out when the plane bounced from the barge pilothouse. Or perhaps he had just fallen out because the fuselage had broken apart at the first impact.

When he struck the water, he would have been hurtling at least a hundred miles per hour. He should have been as flattened as if he had hit a concrete wall. Could a man survive that?

Proof that he could, if he entered the water at the correct angle, was that he was now on land and able to walk. Certainly, his slipping unhurt into the water at that speed had been a matter of luck only.

By then, he was deep in the forest that was no longer a forest. Though he struggled over piles of half-shredded and flame-blackened tree trunks and walked over some and jumped to others, he left footprints behind him in many places. Presently, he was out of the leveled woods. Before him was a road as muddy as the first. Beyond it was another forest. This one was untouched by war, though many trees had been chopped down. Fuel was scarce in France. Trees that would have been spared in peacetime now had to go.

The clouds had been building up to a complete overcast, dark and angry-looking with distant lightning. Rain came without the warning of a few drops. At the same time, the west wind struck as if it had burst from a bag. He crossed the road, leaning slightly to his left against the gale. The rain, if it kept up for long, would wash out his footprints.

Deep into the woods, he took refuge under the overhang of a sandstone ridge near a steadily rising creek. He removed his gloves, goggles, helmet, and flying suit. With a handkerchief, he cleaned off the film on the goggles. Then he took two chocolate bars out of a leg pocket of the suit. He was hungry, but he might need the bars later. Better to hang on to them for now.

After putting the bars back in the pocket, he checked out his wounds. To do this, he had to undress. His scalp bore two shallow but painful creases. His face was pitted with tiny wounds. The outer part of his upper right thigh had been slightly creased by a bullet. Moreover, there was a vaguely blade-shaped bruise about five inches long, pointing downward, on his right calf. That injury had weakened his leg and was making him limp slightly.

The inner part of his left thigh, near the groin, had been ripped open, though not deeply, by shrapnel or a bullet. His right shoulder, which had been strained severely, pained him the most. His neck hurt almost as much. He also bore small wounds on his back and several on his feet. His right elbow was burned on the outside as if it had slid hard across concrete. The backs of his hands were covered with dried blood. Shell fragments had pierced his heavy leather gloves, and the tiny red-hot particles had fried his skin as they cooled off. From just above his left knee, he pulled out a fragment of shell casing, triangular and the size of a dime.

No one else was around, so he permitted himself a gasp of pain when he removed the fragment.

Despite the many wounds, he had not lost a dangerous amount of blood.

His helmet and suit were serviceable, though they had four large holes and a dozen small holes in them.

He was getting cold. He shivered even more when he put his underwear and socks back on. The river water had gotten under his garments and soaked him. Not until he was completely dressed and body heat had built up under the thick leather and fur inner lining of the flying suit did he feel partly warm again. His feet, encased in the fur-lined leather boots, were still icy. Though the boots had been held upside down to drain, they had retained much water.

He removed his .45 Colt New Service revolver from its holster and dried it off with one of two handkerchiefs he carried. He inspected the hunting knife carried in a sheath sewed onto the right leg of the flying suit. There was a depression halfway down the weapon and between the two edges. A bullet or shrapnel had struck there and bounced off. Now he knew what had caused the blade-shaped bruise on his right calf. If it were not for the knife, he might have been badly wounded there. Still, the bruise pained him.

The rain poured like a waterfall from the edge of the overhang above him to a line near his toes. He doubted that anyone standing on the other side of the creek could see him through the cataract, especially since the sky was now solid with very dark clouds.

However, he would have to move soon. The creek level was rising so swiftly that it would be lapping at his feet in about twenty minutes.

Out there, between him and the French lines, were several hundred thousand German soldiers. A hundred or more troops were undoubtedly looking for him right now. He could go northwestward toward Holland, a neutral country, but that was a long way off. Besides, he would have to elude the German military and get help from the French civilians and then the Belgian civilians while sneaking through all that territory. After all that, he would have to evade many sentries and a triple barrier the Boche had erected along the Dutch border.

The Ludendorff Offensive, launched March 21, had brought the French and the British to their knees. They had been there before, but, this time, there was deep doubt that they could get up again. The British might have to evacuate via Dunkerque and go to England. The French were considering asking for peace terms, though that was not in the newspapers. The first American troops had arrived in France, but they were not yet well organized. The First Pursuit Group of the U.S. Air Service, Savage knew, was at Toulon. But these aviators were waiting for machine guns to put on their airplanes. It would be some time before they and the American ground troops would be effective.

Unless the Allies somehow held the lines and then pushed the Germans back, they would lose the war. The U.S.A. would have declared war on the Central Powers too late.

Savage had hoped to be in the 94th or 95th Pursuit Squadrons at Toulon. But Colonel Billy Mitchell had assigned him, temporarily, he said, to a French aerial combat unit. Mitchell wanted Savage to get experience as early as possible. Also, he was to make a thorough report on French combat and maintenance methods.

"You're young," Mitchell had said. He had added, smiling, "Eighteen, I believe."

Did Mitchell know his true age?

"I'm impressed by your record as a flier, an officer,

and your perfect French. You may be disappointed because you won't be with your fellow Americans. But this appointment will reward you in the end. Regardless, GHQ, for some unfathomable reason, has ordered you sent there. Good luck. You'll need it."

That had been all. Savage had left two hours later for his new post.

Like all youngbloods, Savage had dreamed of becoming an ace. Or, if the war lasted long enough, of perhaps matching or exceeding the victory record of Baron Manfred von Richthofen, whose all-red plane led the German Flying Circus, the terror of the Western Front.

He was not to plunge into action at once. His immediate commander, Captain Henry Joseph de Slade of the Spad 159 chaser squadron, fought as if he did not care what the odds were. But he was not going to subject the fledglings under his care to combat until they had had some preparation.

Today, Savage had gone out on his sixth flight, a dawn patrol, to seek blood. He was disappointed. Perhaps because it was Easter and the furies of war had quit raging for a day to celebrate the rise from the dead of the Prince of Peace. Or perhaps it was because the Huns had lost so heavily during the offensive. The only visible foes in the sky were some observation airplanes too far away to catch.

The afternoon flight had been different.

After Savage had returned from the morning sortie and parked his machine, a Spad belonging to another flight had come in with its pilot wounded. Just after landing, he had passed out, and his plane had crashed into Savage's craft. Both were wrecked, though the pilot survived. The only planes handy were some Nieuports recently and hastily flown in to replace Spads lost in combat or accident. The Spads ordered had not yet arrived.

Savage had not liked that. He kept his own craft in first-class order himself, better than any mechanic could do. Also, he calipered every bullet to be fired from his machine guns. Any that did not fit exact specifications was rejected. He did not want his guns to jam during a crucial moment. Or anytime, for that matter.

Yet, he did not want to miss out on this mission. And de Slade, a reckless man, would not understand his passing it up. Just before they climbed into their planes, de Slade said, "Lieutenant Savage, you may or may not be ready. We'll find out. But it's time you got your nose wet. To the attack, my little one! *Bougez les barbariens!*"

Whether he could or could not trust his machine, Savage had to join the hunting expedition. The abstract of honor overcame the concrete of practicality. During the climb and after leveling out at 16,000 feet altitude, he had acquainted himself with the flying characteristics of the Nieuport. It was a good machine, though he still preferred his Spad S.XIII. Also, his face froze while his legs and lower torso sweated heavily. The LeRhone rotary engine radiated tremendous heat which penetrated the cockpit. Moreover, the lubrication for the engine was castor oil, and inhaling the fumes often led to highly inconvenient, very uncomfortable, and exceedingly embarrassing results.

Far to the west, immense black thunderheads were building up. The sky over this immediate area, however, was a patchwork of scurrying thin or heavy clouds with occasional breaks among them. His flight was above most of them. He was alert for enemy fighters above, behind, and, when the clouds separated, below them.

Then, as they flew above an especially large break in the clouds, de Slade waggled the wings of his plane to attract the attention of his group. He pointed ahead and downward. It took Savage several seconds before he saw what his leader was indicating. Twelve large two-seater biplanes in V-formation had just left the cover of a cloud. They looked like Rumpler C.IV long-range reconnaissance-observation craft. They were at approximately 12,000 feet altitude.

Above them at 15,000 feet, just issuing from the same cloud, was their escort, twenty Pfalz D.IIIa fighters. Since the French were in the sun, the Germans probably did not see them.

De Slade signaled for attack and at once dived steeply. Savage, his heart beating more swiftly, followed him with the twelve others in the *chasse*. At last! Action!

III

The French were greatly outnumbered. It did not matter. Their captain had ordered them to charge the enemy. His often-uttered phrases trumpeted in Savage's mind. "Audacity! Always audacity! Caution is for cowards!"

De Slade intended them to come in fast, put a few bursts into whichever bomber came into their sights, and then keep going. The velocity gained by the steep dive would enable them to outrun the pursuing escort fighters.

He swallowed hard and yawned as the change of air pressure made his eardrums pop like firecrackers. Then the Rumplers, so small a moment ago, swelled into craft so large that he could see the details of their construction and the faces of the pilots and rear gunners. These blurred as his field of vision contracted and only one enemy plane was ahead of and below him. Instead of coming at the Rumpler directly broadside, he was approaching it at an angle. Never mind. Though he had a very brief time to fire, he did put one long burst into the engine and into the front cockpit. He thought he saw a ticktacktoe of holes appear in the side of the craft just before he shot by it. He could not be sure. Everything was moving too swiftly.

He had noted that the Rumpler was carrying bombs and the machine-gunner in its rear cockpit was aiming his Spandau, its muzzle flaming, at him. Then the Rumpler dropped off to one side, its pilot dead or wounded. Or faking that he was.

He looked back. Smoke was pouring from under the engine cowling of the machine, and it was beginning to spin. The gunner—poor devil!—would probably burn to death before the plane crashed. The pilot would, too, if he was only wounded.

He had no time to dwell on such commendable but

15

morale-weakening thoughts. Three Pfalzes were on his tail, though still too far behind to fire at him.

Another quick look had showed him the general situation. Burning pieces of a blown-apart Rumpler were falling. Someone, probably de Slade, had put incendiary bullets into its gasoline tank.

The rest of the Rumplers were still in formation, heading toward whatever their destination was. Most of the German fighter pilots who had left the formation had decided that they could not catch up with the French machines and were returning to their posts.

But the three Huns were still on his tail.

All the French planes were going southward.

No! Not all! One had turned back and was on a course that would intercept the Rumplers if it was fast enough. Only de Slade would tackle the enemy all alone.

Three of the Boche must have looked back and seen him. They were turning to attack him. Since they were above him by several thousand feet, they could dive on him one by one and make their passes.

Savage hoped that de Slade would have sense enough to turn, to dive to gain velocity, and to hightail it for the French lines.

He glimpsed the burning and widely scattered pieces of the Rumplers on the ground. Their bombs had exploded from the impact of the crashes.

His captain's Spad was still climbing, pointed at the Boche trio, who were eager to engage him in combat. The damn fool was going to take them on.

Savage muttered, "Well, here goes another one."

He had always respected the dictum of Shakespeare's witty buffoon Falstaff: "Discretion is the better part of valor." In other words, it was better to run away if the odds were too great. You could fight on another day. But he just could not flee now. Not when the crazy Frenchman was willing to tackle an enemy outnumbering him by three to one.

De Slade was probably screaming his defiance now.

"Cochons! Salauds! Cons qui mangent la choucroute!"

Savage eased the Nieuport up from its dive, whipped it around, and began climbing. Looking around, he saw that his four comrades had also quit running away. They were turning back and climbing.

"We're all mad!"

The three Pfalzes were now in a line. They intended to fire at him one after the other. If they missed or only crippled the plane, they would swing around and come at him again.

He held his machine on a collision course. The German in the lead plane was almost as stubborn as he. But at what seemed the very last possible second, his biplane rose upward and to Savage's left. His Spandau machine guns had been flaming at the muzzles before Savage had fired his Vickers. Not until Savage estimated the combined velocity of the two planes headed straight for each other did he shoot. Then he was past the first enemy and headed straight toward the second.

This one raised a wing and dropped off out of Savage's way. The American gave the Pfalz a short burst but had no time to check if he had hit it.

The third plane fired. Savage could see the red tongues of the Spandaus straight on. His own guns replied, and the German dived.

All three of the enemy pilots were probably as pale as he felt he was and sweating as heavily.

He 270-degreed the Nieuport to head for them again. Two were turning and climbing toward him.

He yelled like a Comanche who counts coup.

One Pfalz was swooping at a steep angle for the earth. Its propellor had been shot off. That left two to deal with the American they thought was a Frenchman. One was not far away and was on a level with him and pointed at him. The other was climbing in a curve to get behind the Nieuport.

Above, to his right, bright red-orange flared out against the blue of sky. De Slade had scored a victory, but a Pfalz was jockeying around on the captain's tail.

The four speeding to their captain's rescue were still far away. The Rumplers and escorts were rapidly dwindling gnat-sized objects.

Savage's sweeping glance took all this in. Then he had time only for the situation at hand. Once more, he was going to collide head-on with a Pfalz unless he or the other pilot lost his nerve. Or used good sense.

At the very last split second, it was Savage who chickened out. Something told him that the German, having failed to outbluff his foe the first time, was determined to do so now. Savage took his plane upward to the right. The Pfalz shot past and under him. His hunch had been correct. The pilot had been ready to smash into him if he did not get out of the way.

Then Savage had to crack his Nieuport like a whip to avoid the other machine. It dived down from his right side, its guns firing. It passed over him but quickly turned. Its pilot saw a good chance to get on Savage's tail.

Savage, however, semilooped upward, the rotary engine at full throttle. He banked slightly in time to give the Pfalz a very short burst. But the German got in one, too, before Savage flashed past him.

The American looked behind him. He could see two holes in the fuselage fabric only a few inches behind the cockpit. There were probably others he could not see.

For the next few minutes, there was a wild scramble as the Boche tried to get on his tail and he tried to avoid them while at the same getting just behind one of them. Then, during one of the maneuvers, Savage did have a Pfalz dead to rights in more than one sense. But both of his machine guns jammed at the same time. This happened very rarely, and it would not have happened at all if he had had time to caliper his ammunition before takeoff.

Savage did not curse easily. He had been taught to express himself otherwise. This time, however, he vented his frustration and rage with some blisterers, though in French and Italian. He finished with a single Arabic word.

There was no time to try to unjam the guns. The enemy was too close. He fled, climbing toward a distant cloud. If he could lose them there, he could fix the trouble. He did not know what he would do after that. Go home, probably. He really did not have enough fuel to mess around.

He plunged into the cloud, his pursuers only a half-mile behind him. His plane bucked and rolled from the murderous air currents inside the cloud. He could see nothing beyond his nose. Despite this, he rose from the cockpit, his controls on neutral, and felt for the breeches of the machine guns. Then, in the dark, he hammered at their levers with a tiny wooden mallet. He sat down when they seemed to be unjammed. A short burst satisfied him that they were, for now, working. But he was lost. He did not know where he was or in which direction he was going.

It was then that the events followed which had brought him to this forest.

Now, sitting under the overhang behind the veil of water, he wondered what had caused him to attack the balloons. It was certainly not discretion. Nor had he, as usual, coolly appraised the situation before acting. Something had made him more than slightly irrational. Perhaps he had been emotionally infected by de Slade's crazed eagerness to close with the enemy. Or, perhaps, he had been rushed along by the frenzy of combat itself.

Whatever the cause, he had to control himself one hundred percent in the future. His peculiar and intense education had given him at sixteen, he had thought, more self-discipline and good sense than most people would have in a lifetime. Evidently, that was not so.

He was lucky to be alive to know this.

A man could not depend upon luck.

What would his father, Doctor Clark Savage, Senior, say and feel if he had seen him today? His father was exploring deep inside Brazil just now and did not know that his only child had enlisted in the Air Service. He would not have forbidden him to volunteer. His father only advised Clark after the boy had turned fourteen; he did not order him to do anything.

Probably, he would be proud that his son, though his only child, had enlisted. Undoubtedly, he would be worried. However, though he loved his son, he was, in some ways, rather detached and quite scientific. He would also be very interested in how his son handled himself as a soldier stranded in enemy territory. A part of Clark's training since infancy had been preparation for just such a situation.

And he would exult in his son's feat of destroying four German aircraft in one day. He would also regret that men had had to die even though they were trying to kill his son.

Clark had some regrets, too, but they were not strong.

The rain stopped, and the thin cataract before him became a dripping. The wind did not lessen. The booming of thunder became louder. Limping, he walked from the overhang, got down on his hands and knees at the rising edge of the creek, and scooped up water in his gloves. It had no odor of sewage and seemed fresh enough, though it tasted muddy. He hoped that it did not carry typhoid.

His thirst quenched, he went up the slope and got down on his knees to look over its edge. Lightning was a herd of gigantic black kangaroos bounding on flashing and twisted legs toward him. The clouds were very dark and made the day almost night. Sixty feet away, the forest stopped. Beyond was a wide field covered with dead weeds. There seemed to be a building or two near the other side.

He stayed inside the woods as he walked toward the buildings. When he had semicircled along the edge of the trees, he was near enough to see that the buildings were a two-story stone farmhouse and a big wooden barn. Both were dark, and there was no sign or sound of human or animal life. By then, the lightning was creating dozens of bridges of brightness and uproar between earth and sky. With that and the thunder, he could not be heard. But, if someone were in the house, he could see Savage during the flashes.

He ran across the weed-grown yard. His right leg was functioning better, though the bruise still hurt him. He stopped by a window. It was broken, and the rain was pouring into the house. Though that added to the impression that the house was deserted, he stayed cautious. He went completely around the house and looked into every window. He also checked the ground for footprints. There were none, but someone could have entered the house recently on the crushed stone walk to the front door. The rain would have washed off mud scraped against the stones.

After the inspection, he opened the unlocked front door. Its hinges squeaked, but he moved it slowly. He did not think that, if anyone was inside, he could hear the door being opened. The thunder and lightning were too loud.

The intermittent flashes showed him a room bare of furniture but not of litter. A child's toy, a model of a 1913 De Dion Bouton touring car, a front wheel missing, lay on its side against the base of a wall. Old newspapers and some books were scattered nearby.

The room smelled wet and moldy. He trod slowly toward the doorway to the next room, then stopped. Now he caught a very faint odor that seemed to be that of cigarette smoke. He looked cautiously around the doorway. The pale daylight plus the lightning showed him that the room was empty. But the smoke odor was stronger. And, between the thunder and lightning noises, he could faintly hear voices.

After drawing his revolver, he went across the room, sliding his feet across the floor. This was of wood, indicating that the owners had been rather more prosperous than most farmers, whose dwellings had earth floors. It did creak a little, but the sounds were so slight that he was sure that only he could hear them. The cigarette smoke was thicker the closer he got to the next door.

When he stood by the doorway, he could hear, between the storm noises, two male voices. Of course, there could be more than that number in the room. By then the thunder and bolts had passed toward the southeast, though it was some time before they would die out entirely. Listening intently, he finally determined that the two were speaking standard American English, though not that found in polite circles.

While he eavesdropped, he kept looking behind him. There was the chance, however slight, that someone else might enter the house. Nor did he forget that the Germans might be out looking for him despite the forbidding weather.

One of the men had a squeaky-clattery voice that sounded like a mouse trapped in a tin can. Once heard, Doc thought, it would never be forgotten. Its owner was complaining that he was hungry. His belly, he said, was climbing his spine as it looked for food.

"Don't you ever think about anything except stuffing your mouth and chasing skirts?" the other man said.

His baritone was authoritative and very scornful.

"There's probably plenty of rats in that barn," the squeaky-clattery voice said. "We could catch some easy. You're a big cheese. Just sit in the center of the barn as bait, and I'll club them when they go after you."

"Cheese!" the baritone said. "Cheese! Must you keep chattering away like a chimpanzee begging for bananas? Cheese! Quit talking about food!"

"Rats ain't so bad," the squeaky voice said. "I'll bet they don't taste much different from squirrels, and squirrel meat's good! What d'ya say we go to the barn and hunt them down?"

"Cheese!"

"It'd be nice if we had some ham to go with it."

"Ham! Don't you ever dare mention that word again! I'll kick you from here to Berlin!"

The other burst into laughter.

The baritone said, "You throwback to Piltdown man! Or should I say Peltdown man, you're so hairy. I know damn well you set me up!"

"Oh, ha, ha, ha!"

"It'll be my pleasure someday to throw you in the pigpen and then eat the hogs that eat you. Unless they got good taste and reject you."

Savage listened to them while he considered what to do. The men were either escaped prisoners of war or had been separated from their unit when the Germans overran this area. In any event, they were hiding from the Boche. But there were no American forces near here nor had there been. What were two Yankees doing here?

For that matter, he was American and here. Perhaps

they were aviators who had enlisted with the French. Members of the Lafayette Escadrille?

He could make himself known, and all three could try to get through the German lines together. However, he travels fastest who travels alone. He did not know the caliber of these men. The three of them might make an excellent team. Or the two might hinder him. They certainly sounded quarrelsome. And, if they were so hungry, why weren't they out in the barn at this moment and hunting down rats? The squeaky-voiced man's idea was practical. He was also right about the taste of rats. Savage had eaten enough of them to know. They had sometimes been all he could find, except for insects, when he had been sent out on survival courses by his father.

They would have to eat them raw, however. It was too dangerous to make a fire and thus possibly attract the Germans looking for them.

He supposed that the two men had not been trained, as he had, to eat uncooked meat still warm and bloody. But if they got hungry enough, they would do it.

He had by then decided that it would not be right to leave two fellow soldiers in the lurch. He could at least talk to them and find out if they needed his help.

IV

He put the revolver in his holster, its strap loose, and then stepped into the room. Its air was thick and stinking with cheap French tobacco.

The two were sitting on the floor, smoking, their greatcoats beside them, their backs against the wall, one on each side of a window. He had never seen anyone taken by surprise move so swiftly. They did not freeze for even a fraction of a second but were up and on their feet and crouched, ready for action. However, they had no weapons, and they saw his revolver and the knife hilt sticking out of the sheath sewed onto his pants leg.

"Take it easy," he said. "I'm American, and the Germans are on my trail, too."

Their cigarettes had fallen on the floor. Both stooped slowly and picked them up. The baritone said, "You scared me. If my bowels hadn't been empty, they'd be empty now."

The squeaky voice snorted and then said, "What's that mean?"

The baritone smiled and jerked a thumb toward his companion. He said, "He's the one with the empty *head*."

"But my heart is pure," the squeaky-voiced one said. "He can never claim his is. He's a lawyer."

The baritone wore the uniform of an officer of the French Foreign Legion; his insignia was a lieutenant colonel's. He was about five feet ten inches tall, slim, and had straight black hair, dark eyes, and long and thin lips. Despite his hawkish nose or perhaps because of it, he was handsome. His age might have been thirty, but, like all frontline soldiers, he had dark fatigue circles around his eyes and facial lines that only war could draw.

Savage knew that this man must be a remarkable leader and have an equally remarkable combat record. Very few foreigners attained such a high rank in the Legion.

The other man must have evoked astonishment in most people who first saw him. He was in the battle uniform of the U.S.A., clothes which must have been made special by a tailor; no general-issue garments would have fit him. He wore the silver eagle of a lieutenant colonel. The crossed rifles on his lapels showed that he was in the infantry. How he had been admitted into the military, Savage did not know. He was only five feet two inches high, if that. His shoulders looked as if they could match the span of a bison's horns. If that squat body did not weigh 260 pounds, he, Savage, was no good at guessing.

Squeaky-voice's legs were bowed and noticeably short relative to his trunk length. His arms were freakishly long, and the backs of his hands protruding from the sleeves were matted with long, thick, rusty-red hairs. The several days' growth of beard was very thick and slightly redder than the hand hairs.

That face! Savage thought at once of a reconstruction of the head of the fossil man found in 1856 in the Neander Valley in Germany. Though the skull was smaller, its forehead slanted back. The ridges above the eyes were huge, though they did not meet. His nose was large but broad. However, his jaws were straight up and down, and he had a well-developed chin. His cheekbones were higher than an American Indian's.

The eyes were light, probably a pale blue, though Savage could not be sure in the twilight of this room. He looked as if he was the same age as his companion.

All in all, a layman would think that this man looked like an ape. Even Savage, who had at his early age an advanced education in anthropology, noted the simian resemblances. But they were really quite superficial.

He must have been teased and tormented when he was a child, Savage thought. *But he looks as if he's always been able to take care of himself.*

"You're a big one, kid," the apish man said. "Good-looking, too, if you like the Gibson collar-ad type. I bet you're a lady-killer, right? Even if you do have funny-looking eyes."

"Always looking for a fight, especially with men better-looking than him, which includes everybody," the baritone said. "Who are you—name, rank, and serial number—and how in hell did you get here? You're a flier, right?"

Savage opened his mouth to identify himself, then closed it. Through the window, he had just seen the arrival of men in gray coal-scuttle helmets and long gray great-coats, and carrying rifles. They had come from the woods fifty yards to the east.

He pointed at the window and said, "The hunting party's here!"

The two men whirled. The baritone said, "Great Scott!"

"Not Scott! Scoot!" the apish man said. "Vamoose! *'Raus mitem!* Haul ass! Feets, get going! *Vite! Schnell! Rapido!* Fade away! Scramble!"

"You forgot '23 skiddoo,'" the baritone said.

"That was passe when I was a kid," the apish man said. "You are old, Father William."

During their exchange, they had picked up and put on their greatcoats. They looked wary but not scared. A cool pair of customers, Savage thought. He ran through the house more swiftly than an hour ago. The pain from the bruise on his calf still caused him to limp, though not as much. He looked out the windows of each room. There were also troops coming from the north but none, so far, from the west and south. That did not mean that they would not soon be doing so.

"The nearest and the best way is west," he said when he returned.

"We already figured that out," the apish man said. "Let's go! Devil take the hindmost!"

There was no After-You-Gaston-No-After-You-Alphonse routine. They ran past Savage to the westward-looking room and climbed through the window he had opened before coming back to them. He got quickly through it and overtook them before they had gone more than forty feet despite his being slowed down by the injured calf.

As he sped past them, he said, "Good luck! You're going to need it!"

"What I need is a machine gun!" the apish man said. Despite his short legs, he was ahead of the Legionnaire.

"Look at that kid go!" the Legionnaire said. "In a flying suit, and he *is* flying! A Barney Oldfield on legs!"

"Save your breath!" the apish man said. "Ain't that just like a lawyer? Always talking, never knows when to keep his mouth shut!"

Then Savage passed out of earshot. As soon as he was in the woods—and wishing that they bore foliage—he halted. From behind a tree, he looked at the situation. The two were about a hundred feet from him. Then the Legionnaire slipped in the mud and slid on his face.

"Out!" the other man roared. "The showers for you!"

For a moment, Savage did not know what he meant. Then he thought, Of course, it's baseball jargon. The apish man slid to a stop and helped his companion to his feet. Then the apish man slipped, and his face smacked into the mud. The Legionnaire turned back and assisted his friend.

By then, the soldiers from the north had seen the runners. An officer shouted at them to stop and surrender. A few seconds later, he gave an order, and his men began firing.

The two kept on going and dived when they got to the first trees. Bullets smacked into tree trunks and screamed past Savage's ear.

Now, the soldiers from the east had come around the house and were running toward his hiding place. Temporary refuge, that is.

The two Americans, mud-covered, rose to their feet and ran crouching to Savage. They were breathing very heavily.

"Let's give 'em a brawl the likes of which they'll never forget!" the apish man bellowed. His deep voice contrasted vividly with his normal speaking voice. It was as if his throat had shifted gears.

"Just because you're winded?" the baritone said. "No, you old stag at bay, we don't fight! With what? We run like the striped-ass ape you are."

"I'm not the only one puffing like a dinosaur in heat," the other said. "I can outrun you any day or night, drink three beers and have a catnap before you catch up with me."

"Then you better run like hell! If you get there first, tell the devil I'll give you a character reference!"

Bent over, all three ran, stumbling and slipping now and then, over the rough terrain. There were hills and depressions, some high, some deep, creeks, sudden drop-offs, fallen trees, and projecting cliffs to go up, down, across, around, or over. Clark Savage stopped when the bullets quit striking the trees around him. Sweat was pouring from him. He removed his flying clothes and rolled them into a bundle. His fellow refugees also stopped to lean against trees. They wheezed, panted, and gasped. When they got some wind and strength back, they took off their greatcoats.

"I noticed you limping a little," the baritone said. "That must be the only thing holding you back."

"No," Savage said. "I won't desert you two."

The baritone laughed, and he said, "How about that, Colonel? This kid, this callow youth, has taken us old fogies under his wing."

"Well, I don't know, Colonel," the squeaky voice said. "It's true he's only a lieutenant and a birdman at that. And he does have very funny-looking eyes. Never seen anything like them. But he's a big fellow, and he's got a gun and a knife. I think maybe we could use his help."

Savage was about to introduce himself and ask what their names were when shouts rose from the east. A second later, a rifle cracked, and a bullet whistled over their heads. Then the rifles became a chorus, and he and his companions had to hug the earth.

Savage said, "We'd better get going before they surround us."

"Teach your grandmother to suck eggs," the squeaky-voiced one said. "Of course, we know that. Here. Give me your gun. Maybe I can pot a few, make them not so fast chasing us."

"It's better to save the gun for a surprise," Savage said. "Shooting it now would be a waste of ammunition. Besides, if I fire on them, they'll execute us if they catch us."

"Hey, I'm a lieutenant colonel!" the apish man said. "I gave you a direct order!"

Savage neither replied nor handed over the revolver.

"Subordination! I could have you shot!" But the man was smiling, showing teeth like slightly yellowed white bricks.

"The kid's got good sense," the other man said. "I don't know how, but he knows you couldn't hit the Woolworth Building with a shotgun."

"I'm going," Savage said. "You coming with me or staying here so you can needle each other?"

He began crawling toward a creek at the bottom of the slope. When he reached a thick growth of trees, he rose and ran to the creek. Not looking back, he waded into the water up to his knees and strode against its icy current. A moment later, he heard splashing behind him. He did glance behind himself then. The two were making faces. Evidently, they were shocked by the cold, cold water.

A few yards upstream, the creek curved. Once past this point, the three would be out of sight when the Germans got to the creek bank, which would be soon. They would not know whether the refugees had gone east or west. They would split their party to track them in two directions. But the refugees needed to take to the woods again before soldiers came around the bend.

Savage took the north bank because some distant sandstone cliffs loomed above the bare trees. There might be holes, caves in them, somewhere to hide. He had just stepped behind a tree to wait for the others when men shouted and then rifles cracked.

The baritone fell facedown into the water.

The apish man yelled, "Ham! Oh, my God, they shot you!"

V

The gray-clad soldiers who had appeared from around the bend were standing up to the ankles of their boots in the mud of the north bank. They had quit firing but were shouting for the two men to surrender.

The one called Ham was being held up out of the water by his companion. Despite the bickering and insulting between them, they seemed to be friends. There had been agony in the apish man's cry.

Savage glimpsed the blood running from Ham's limp body as it mixed with the muddy water. Then the young flier was gone, crawling swiftly until he got to a tangle of fallen trees. He could do nothing for the colonels. Now, it was save himself who can.

He did just that. By dusk, he had kept ahead, even

out of earshot, of the hunters. He had been forced to work a zigzag and generally northwestward course. This was taking him away from the front line and deeper into enemy-held territory. If he kept in that direction, he would eventually be near the trenches again. They curved northward, forming a truly Western Front there.

Various ideas for escape means and routes marched before his mind's eye like regiments on review. None of them passed inspection. The one he liked best was stealing an airplane from a German base and getting the hell back home fast.

Far easier said than done.

He did not lack confidence in himself. If anybody could do it, he could. But he was also realistic about anything he planned. He would have to get through many guards, get to a flying machine that was warmed up and ready to take off, overcome and eject its pilot, get off the landing field before he was shot, get away without being downed by the defense machine guns, outrun pursuers in the air. Etcetera.

At least, he could get to an aerodrome, observe it, and evaluate his chances. If he could find one.

None of the dromes in this area would be permanent. They moved around as the front expanded or shrunk. He had memorized the general features of this whole area from aerial maps and the reports from French Intelligence to which he had access. Latest information had placed the nearest German fighter-craft field north of Noyon and near the Canal du Nord. It was probably still there because the exhausted and war-weary Germans had been stopped by the exhausted and war-weary French. For the moment, apathy reigned.

He took a small pocket compass from a pocket of his uniform and checked his directions again by the last light of day. After putting his flying suit on because of the increasing cold, he trudged along through the woods. He was very slow because he did not dare show a light and had no light to show anyway. He could use his matches, but they would soon be gone.

His right leg had renewed its original pain several

hours ago, and his limp had worsened. Finally, he decided that he had better rest for a few hours. He found a shallow hollow in a sandstone outcropping, sat down in it, and permitted himself the brief ecstasy of a chocolate candy bar. His stomach growled like a caged lion angry because it had been thrown a hamburger but needed the entire cow.

He woke at 2:12 A.M., if his luminous-dial wristwatch was correct. It was raining again and as dark as the inside of a night cloud. It was best to sleep until dawn, which he did. By afternoon, his chocolate bars gone, he was at the edge of a forest giving onto a broad meadow. The only living creatures in sight were cows and some birds. Beyond the meadow was a steep-sided hill on top of which were the ruins of several large stone or brick buildings. It was time, however, not war—not this war, anyway—that had pulled parts of the buildings down.

He could see a poplar-lined road several hundred yards from the west border of the meadow. He took off his heavy flying clothes, rolled them up, secured the bundle with the rope he carried in one of the bulging pockets on his suit, and hung the bundle on his back from a section of the rope around his neck.

An hour later, he had cautiously circled the meadow and climbed the almost straight-up-and-down and heavily eroded sandstone hillside on the east. He went through a gateway in a stone wall and found himself in a sort of courtyard. So far, there had been no indications of life other than an owl hooting in the nearest building. This place must be an abandoned château or monastery, he thought. Then his memory relays closed, and the maps he had studied flowed through to the Teletype in his mind.

This was the abode of some obscure order of Catholic monks. The Brothers of Pitiful Poverty? The Friars of the Abysmally Penniless? No. Something like that, though. The area in which he stood had to be an unrepaired section. His toilsome approach up the eastern slope had kept him from seeing the northern side of the structures. That must be where the monks lived, unless the occupation had driven them away. And there should be a road leading up the hill from the poplar-lined road.

Moving silently and slowly, he entered the building. Water was flowing thinly from a doorway to his right. It was not quite as broad as his shoulders. He went through it and sloshed up a tightly spiraling and very narrow stone staircase. When he got to the top, he was in the top room of a tower. Its roof and part of the walls were gone; many stone blocks and broken sheets of shale crowded its floor.

The dark sky and heavy rain made for poor visibility. Savage raised his head slowly and only to eye level above the northern rampart. Below were some buildings that had been somewhat repaired. German sentries walked along the roofs of two of these. A partial view of a courtyard showed him ten automobiles parked there, several more sentries, and a group of officers in spiked helmets. The machines had come through a gateless archway from a winding road covered with crushed white stone lined by muddy tire tracks and spotted with oil. This place must have been taken over by the German Army as a headquarters.

Two long touring cars were coming up the road. They drove into the courtyard while the sentries came to stiff attention. A chauffeur-soldier got out of the lead car and opened the left rear door.

First to come out was a tall officer in a spiked helmet and a greatcoat. If other cigars were small dirigibles, the one in his mouth was in the Zeppelin class. His nose was large and eaglish. Below it was a thick black mustache curled up at both ends. A monocle was fitted into his left eye socket.

He held out a gloved hand and helped a woman with ash-blonde hair out of the limousine. She wore an ankle-length white fur coat, white leather boots, and a Russian-type white fur hat. She was smoking a crimson cigarette at the end of a preposterously long holder. Her mouth was scarlet, and her eyes were heavily shadowed with makeup.

A real femme fatale, Savage thought.

The second car disgorged two male servants—one of them, at least six feet eight inches tall, was a Kodiak bear of a man, a bearded behemoth—and two women, obviously the blonde's maids. The men were in Russian peasant clothes. These began unloading many items of baggage from the car, probably the wardrobe of the woman in white.

The officers who had been waiting in the courtyard conducted the newly arrived officer and his lady into the building. The servants, aided by three soldiers, carried the trunks and cases into another doorway.

A big conference, Savage thought. And that officer must be a high-ranking one indeed if he's allowed to take his wife or mistress or whatever she is into the war zone.

He decided that he would try to listen in on the conference. Then he reminded himself that only yesterday he had chided himself for having too much derring-do. He had also promised himself that he would not let overenthusiasm conquer his good sense.

Despite this, he knew that he was going to do his best to eavesdrop on this conference no matter how dangerous or difficult it was. It was his duty, though he would refrain from suicidal behavior while doing it. At least, he hoped he would. After yesterday, he was not sure that he knew himself as well as he had thought he did. And he must have used up all his luck yesterday. Not that he was superstitious and believed in luck. Luck was a random, unpredictable element better called chance. If it happened to work in your favor in a certain situation, you could not rely on it again.

Luck was one of the bitch goddesses. She liked to make you feel good, special, important to her. Then she laughed as she stuck a foot out and tripped you.

Not that he believed in goddesses. But, being human, he found it impossible not to humanize abstractions. Or vice versa.

He studied the layout of the buildings and the locations of the sentries. Then he went back down the staircase, pausing at the bottom to listen and then look around the side of the doorway before venturing into the room. He prowled several corridors and a number of rooms before he smelled food. Following its savory odor, his mouth watering and his belly tightening, he came to a hallway down which voices floated. Presently, he was looking from a darkened corridor into a room full of light, heat, chatter, and the wonderful perfume of vegetable soup and frying sausages.

Four monks in long gray robes with hoods, talking rapidly in French, were working in an enormous kitchen. A German soldier, a private, was sitting at a table in a far corner and drinking wine from a bottle. It was half-empty, and the bottle next to it was completely drained. His rifle lay on the table near him.

Savage would have to cross the huge room before he could reach the soldier. But why should he attack the man? No matter how ravenous he was, he could not do anything to betray his presence here. So, he would just have to go hungry while being tortured with the sight and odor of all that food.

One of the kettles holding soup was on a support over a wood fire in a gigantic fireplace. The cook stirring it looked cautiously at the German. Then, seeing that the soldier's attention was on the wine, the cook spat into the soup.

That particular kettle held soup for the Germans, Savage decided. If he ate, he would not do so from that container. Maybe. After all, what was a little saliva?

The spitting also told him that the monks were not lovers of the enemy. At least, that one was not.

Suddenly, the soldier fell sideways off his chair. His helmet clanged on the stone floor. Drunk, of course. The monks ran over to him, not, probably, because they were concerned about him. They just did not want to be blamed if they ignored him. Or, perhaps, they were filled with compassion for all mankind, even the despised Boche.

Savage wasted no time. He ran into the kitchen, grabbed a big bowl and a spoon from a table, used a ladle to fill the bowl, seized an entire loaf of the bread, and walked out. He had kept his eye on the monks as much as possible. The soldier, glaze-eyed, mouth hanging open, was being lifted back onto his chair. No one glanced toward Savage. He went down the hall and into an empty

room. Eating slowly though he wanted to gulp his meal
down, he emptied the bowl and devoured the loaf. It
seemed like the best meal he had ever had. There was not
much beef in the soup, but he felt full. And he was ready
to take on the entire German Army. One at a time, of
course.

Yet, he told himself, he had not been discreet. What
if the soldier had seen him? Or one of the monks had
noticed him and had not kept it to himself?

He had allowed his hunger to make him reckless.

This is ridiculous, he thought. I had to take a chance.
Otherwise, I might've gotten too weak from lack of food
and not been able to fight or to run.

His father had once said to him, "You've inherited my
tendency to introspection; let's call it brooding about one's
self. You must defeat that. Introspection, brooding, is all
right if you don't have anything else to do. You're being
trained to be both a man of science and a man of action.
Neither kind broods about himself very much. Or shouldn't,
anyway."

"Right!" Savage murmured as if replying to his father.

Still, though his knowledge and experiences far exceeded
those of most men of thirty, he was only sixteen. He could
be expected to make some of the mistakes of youth.

One of these, he found out ten minutes later, was
stealing the food. A sharp-eyed monk must have noticed
the theft and complained to the Germans. Or, possibly,
the drunken trooper had glimpsed him. Soldiers with
Alsatian dogs burst into the hallway at the same time that
he heard them through the thick wooden door of the room
in which he had been eating. The windowless chamber
had only one exit. Before he could get out of it and down
the hallway, he would be exposed for at least six seconds to
their fire, almost at point-blank range.

He could not escape. Not now, anyway.

Then the dogs were leaping against the door and
barking and yelping. Above the bedlam, a voice soared,
demanding in German that whoever was in the room
surrender or be killed. Savage thought it best not to try a

shootout. He might be on the Western Front, but he was not in a Western movie.

He opened the door slowly and stood in the doorway, his arms held high. Events went fast after that.

Presto! He was disarmed and frisked. Then he was hustled along hallways and up stairs and down more corridors and up a broad stone stairway and along another hall. Near its end, he was shoved into a bleak room lit only by gray light from a small iron-barred window. It contained a cot covered by blankets and a small table on which were a large candle in a stone holder, a pitcher of water, an empty scum-ringed washbasin, a sliver of soap, and a very dirty towel. Under the cot was a chamber pot. Hanging on a peg in the wall was a monk's robe and a pair of sandals.

The heavy wooden door was slammed shut. Its big iron lock clicked.

VI

The entire procedure had taken sixty seconds. He knew because he had counted them. Very efficient, he thought, though that could be expected from Germans. The rolled-up bundle of his flying clothes had been kept by his captors. No doubt, they would examine them for hidden weapons and other devices. He hoped that they would not rip open the seams or press certain areas between their fingers. He had plans for the objects he had cached inside the outer and inner leather linings.

The room was small and doubtless a monk's cell taken over by the invaders as a temporary lockup for their prisoner. Inset in the door was a round barred opening through which he could see the face of a sentry and the wall behind him. Though the air was heavy with moisture, it was cold, and so were the sandstone walls.

An hour passed before he heard any noise from the corridor. Then a man barked an order. The door was unlocked and creaked open. A soldier with a rifle entered and motioned him to back into a corner. An infantry captain followed him. A soldier in the hallway closed the door. Savage came to attention and saluted the officer, who returned the salute wearily.

"*Vous êtes français, n'est-ce pas?*" he said.

"*Non. Je suis americain.*"

Savage thought it best not to reveal his fluency in German.

The captain was short, slim, and blond. His otherwise handsome face bore a long wide scar that began just above his right cheekbone and ended at his chin. He raised straw-colored eyebrows at Savage's revelation, then spoke in English with a heavy German pronunciation.

"You wear a French uniform."

For reply, Savage gave his name, rank, and serial number.

"You must be the pilot of the Nieuport chaser which crashed in the Verse River yesterday," the captain said. He held out his hand. "Your identity disk, please."

Savage lifted the chain from around his neck and handed it to the officer. He read it quickly, then gave it back to the lieutenant.

The captain said, "You may sit down." He indicated the cot.

"I prefer to stand," Savage said.

"As you wish."

The captain drew out a cardboard pack of *Grün Heinrich* cigarettes from a pocket inside his jacket. "Would you like one?"

Savage shook his head.

The officer questioned him about his unit, its strength, location, and morale. The lieutenant repeated his name, rank, and serial number until he did not know if he or the German was more tired of the response. After an hour, the captain growled an oath, spun around, and ordered the door opened. The door squeaked, then clanged behind him.

Another sixty minutes, seemingly glacially slow, passed. Then, abruptly, the captain was back. This time, he told

Savage to come with him. They went down the corridor and up a flight of steps so narrow that Savage and his escort of four enlisted men and the officer had to go in single file. Then they marched down another stone-walled hall to a room that differed from his previous one in being larger and having a mirror on the wall, an iron bathtub filled with steaming hot water, two huge pitchers of water, clean towels, and a new bar of soap. It was lit by four large candles in wall sconces.

"The Baron Colonel von Hessel has invited you to be a guest at dinner tonight at eight o'clock," the captain said. "If you accept, all this is yours. You will be shaved after you bathe. Your uniform will be repaired and cleaned."

It will also be inspected for concealed weapons and other devices, Savage thought. But they could force him to strip now, anyway, and probably would sooner or later.

"Two of the guests are the pilots who shot you down," the captain said. "They are eager to meet you and to congratulate you on your exploits today."

That meant that the German aerodrome was not too far away from the monastery. An hour or so of travel, Savage thought. Maybe less. That was an information item to keep in mind.

"Also present will be Countess Idivzhopu, a member of the international banker Bugov family. She is a cousin of the Tsar and also of our Kaiser," the captain said. "Though she is Russian, she is one of Imperial Germany's firmest supporters. Especially since the Bolshevik Revolution. She has expressed a desire to meet you."

Savage raised his eyebrows.

The captain smiled and said, "We know much about you. The countess is interested in talking to you."

To get information useful to the Central Powers, of course, Savage thought. But how had they found out much about him, if indeed they truly had? Why would they be inquiring about an obscure and very young lieutenant in the U.S. Air Service? Should German Intelligence for some reason have him in its files, it could not have transmitted information about him from Berlin to the front. Not this quickly, unless they had radioed it. Why would they? He was not an important person.

He shrugged. He would find out.

"May I take that movement of the shoulders as acceptance of the invitation?" the captain said.

"Yes."

Von Hessel? The name seemed to hover half-above the horizon of his memory.

Three seconds later, which was usually the maximum time it took for him to recall anything from somewhere in that fifty-ounce complex of protoplasm which was his brain, he had it. It was not much, because he had not been given much about the baron colonel, who was also a scientist. He had two doctor of philosophy degrees, one in biology, one in physics, and also a doctor of medicine degree. He was born on the ancestral estate in Brandenburg in 1888, which would make him thirty years old.

Despite his relative youth, he had an international reputation. His monograph on the mutations of the bacteria *Treponema pallidum* after bombardment by Roentgen rays while suspended in diluted *Cannabis sativa* had caused worldwide comment in scientific circles. Much of that had been unfavorable, and he had not been heard from since then.

But Clark Savage's father had once mentioned the baron to some cronies. Clark had overheard him.

"The man is a colonel in the Imperial German Army. But no one seems to know in what branch. He's a rather sinister character, if my informants are to be believed, and you can expect that he'll come up with something both devastating and inhumane if Germany should go to war."

That was all young Clark knew about him. So, what was the baron-colonel-doctor doing here? Why would he be the least interested in a mere American lieutenant?

The captain turned and bawled an order through the narrow window in the door, which swung open. A sergeant, two soldiers with rifles ready, and the Russian leviathan whom Clark had seen in the courtyard entered. The room suddenly seemed much smaller. It also stank of cheap perfume emanating from the Russian.

The captain spoke in German to Savage.

"You need no longer pretend that you don't understand our language. We know that you are fluent in *Hochdeutsch*. That is one of the many things we know about you. Now, please strip and take a bath. Zad will help you bathe and will shave you."

He indicated the huge Russian.

"I don't need help," Savage said. But he started to unbutton his jacket. When he was grabbed from behind by Zad and carried to the cot as if he were a child, Savage did not resist. He thought that the arms around him were pressing far harder than was necessary. A little more pressure would crack his ribs. A normal man's ribs would have cracked, but Savage's were extraordinarily thick.

Then the Russian shifted his grip and held Savage's 190 pounds in front of him with his huge hands only. Zad laughed as he threw the American upward with a spinning motion. Savage came down on his feet and facing the Russian. Then he was pushed back so that he had to sit down.

Zad, grinning, chuckling deep in his throat, his oversweet perfume and the understratum of long-unwashed body odor choking Savage, knelt before him. He took off Savage's boots. Then, when the lieutenant stood up, Zad unbuckled Savage's pants belt.

"I really don't want this," Savage said to the captain.

The officer smiled broadly and said, "The service is by courtesy of the countess."

To humiliate him? Or did she, and probably the baron, too, have some other motive?

"He's not undressing me," the lieutenant said, "so much as he's manhandling me. I warn you, if he persists in his boorish behavior, I'll render him hors de combat, put out his already dim lights. Also, his stench makes me want to puke. I may do it any moment now."

By then, he was getting out of his long underwear. The Russian stood back then, rolled his small, dark-brown eyes upward as if in ecstasy, and blew kisses from the tips of his enormous fingers.

"What a beautiful body!" he roared in Russian. "A

second Prince Igor Sviatoslavov, sweet hero and shining conqueror of the Quman hordes, savior of Holy Russia!"

Clark Savage understood the reference to the medieval warrior whose exploits had given rise to the first Russian epic poem. Before he could figure out what else inspired Zad's remarks, he was again seized in a bear grip, this time from in front.

Round and round he was whirled as Zad danced, hugging the American closely. His arms were pinned, and his face was buried in the thick black beard. The stink was making his gorge rise, and he was getting much more angry. The Germans, dodging out of the way, were laughing at him. Moreover, clothed only by the long underwear hanging from his ankles—he had not had time to get them completely off—he felt embarrassed and humiliated.

"My darling! Sweetmeats of my soul! You are beautiful, and you are not even Russian!"

Zad kissed Savage noisily and wetly on top of his head. The Germans screamed with laughter.

Abruptly, Zad stopped whirling, loosened his hands, caught Savage by the waist, and hoisted him high. "Time for Daddy to put baby into the bath!" he bellowed, and he lowered his arms a little. Zad was getting ready to toss him through the air, the bull's-eye being the great iron tub filled with hot water. Even if Zad's aim was perfect, Savage knew that his legs and arms and possibly his head would strike the metal.

He was held straight above the Russian. His body was horizontal, his limbs held out, his back stiff. He wanted to keep his temper under control. It would not do for the Germans to know the extent of his strength. But the Red Sea he had held back by his will, Moses-like, suddenly broke through. A scarlet deluge roared in and swept away his good intentions. He was not going to put up with this situation any longer. His reason might wish him to do so. But the ancient ape in him, the creature that saw red and went crazy, had crashed through the cage his reason had built for it.

He brought his open palms down and slammed them against the giant's ears.

Zad screamed and released Savage, who bent his body as he dropped.

Before his underwear-shrouded feet touched the stone floor, Savage had grabbed Zad's beard with his left hand and yanked on it.

The Russian, crying with pain, his hands on his ears, was pulled forward and sank to his knees. Savage had twisted his body to fall to one side. Now, he gripped the beard with both hands and slammed the giant forward. Zad's face struck the stone. Then Savage rolled away, stopped, and shucked off the underwear from his ankles.

The captain shouted at his men to hold their fire. Then he hopped out of the way as Savage rolled again before bounding to his feet.

All the soldiers stepped back against the walls. They were frightened—or at least shaken—by the fury of Savage's face.

The red mists swirling through Savage's head had not cleared. Some reason was beginning to assert itself, but it was too weak as yet.

The American stooped, lifted up the Russian by the seat of his pants and the neck of his shirt, and cast him into the tub. Facedown, Zad went into the water, much of which spilled onto the floor.

Then Savage was tearing off Zad's clothes, ripping the cloth as if it were a hundred years rotten. Zad managed to turn over while this was being done, but he did not resist. The pain in his eardrums and the shock of being handled as if he were a feather-filled pillowcase made him helpless.

Fragments of clothes flew up, followed by two boots. Zad's head went under the water then as Savage thrust him down. He came up sputtering and took his hands from his ears to try to seize his attacker. Savage knocked his hands back, shoved him under the water again, and began applying the soap and water to Zad.

Then he seized one end of the tub and turned it over on its side. Iron struck stone with a loud clang. The blubbering and sputtering Russian rolled out of the tub, along with what water was left in it.

"*Mein Gott!*" the captain said.

"*Er ist ein Siegfried,*" a soldier muttered.

"*Ein gorilla,*" another said.

Standing straight, water dripping from his light bronze skin and light bronze hair, glaring, his hands clenched by his sides, Savage shouted, "I am an officer of the United States of America Air Service, and I demand respect! I am a prisoner of war, but I won't put up with any treatment one iota less than is due me! Now, get that hulk out of here! Bring in fresh hot water, and I'll take the bath your superiors ordered for me!"

What he wanted was done. Moreover, he refused to place the bathtub right side up. He told the captain that he did not have to do manual labor because he was an officer. The captain did not like it, but he had to agree with him. He ordered two men to lift the tub back onto its bottom. They failed to budge it an inch. Three men tried. Finally, four men, red-faced, puffing, panting, and groaning, got it back to its original position.

The Germans looked at Savage with awe.

He did not tell them that he alone could not have handled the tub. But the adrenaline pumping into his muscles from his rage had given him, temporarily, the strength of four men, allowing him to dump the tub onto its side.

But he could not have done so now.

VII

After his bath, Savage was escorted to another room. Wearing only a thin and wet towel, he was cold as he walked along the dark and unheated stone corridor. His new room surprised him. It had a fireplace in which was a small wood fire. This soon went out, but he was given his uniform, cleaned and patched, an hour later. His flying boots had not been returned yet. He had only socks to wear as protection against the cold stone floor. These, however, were thick wool.

From the moment he entered the room, he was stared at through the round barred window in the door by a sentry. Savage thought that this was done to embarrass him and to lower his morale.

He, however, had spent so much time among jungle people who wore little or no clothing that his nudity did not bother him. Not in these circumstances, anyway. He would have preferred being warmer, but the chilliness was endurable. He had gone through several toughening-up courses in the snow and ice of high mountains during the past few years. The last time, a yogi who claimed to be able to control his body temperature through mental means had instructed young Clark. So far, Clark had not gotten the hang of it, but his teacher had told him that he would master it someday. That is, he would if he spent years working on the techniques.

Clark did not think that he would ever have the time to do that. But he might figure out a shortcut method to locate the psychological-biological mechanisms acting as a body thermostat.

He felt his trousers belt while putting it on. It had been taken away with the rest of the uniform and had been cleaned and polished. The areas near the buckle were still somewhat stiff, and there was no evidence that the sewing had been ripped out and resewn by the Germans.

A half-hour later, his goggles, helmet, boots, and flying suit, rolled into a bundle, were brought in. He undid the package. Then, his back blocking the sentry's gaze, he felt the lining of his suit at various places. The items inside the lining were small, but some of them were hard. They could be found easily enough if the searcher knew what he was looking for or was unusually suspicious.

But they were still there.

He put the boots on. Though they were torn and pierced in many places, they had been fixed up with tape over the holes. He wished he had his shoes. His feet would sweat in the overwarm boots. But he could not complain. He was lucky he was not barefoot. As it was, he was being treated better than he had a right to expect.

Why?

The Germans had been very thorough in their cleaning. Even the small round pocket mirror in his jacket pocket had been cleaned. It had had a thumbprint of hair oil on it when he had put it away after looking into it just before the flight took off. That was gone.

He held the mirror up in the light of three large candles in wall sconces. His eyes, tawny and gold-specked in a bright light, looked dark. As dark as his uncertain future. But futures were always unknown, and a man made his own future—to a certain extent.

Were his eyes really funny-looking? Different, yes. Strange, yes. Not, however, the kind to evoke laughter or ridicule in the viewer. Unless that person was sensitive about his own flaws and peculiarities and, hence, liable to mock others. That must be why that apish colonel had made that unkind remark about his eyes.

He shrugged, and he put the mirror back in the pocket. His father had told him that most youths were overly touchy about their appearance. It was part of adolescence. He would grow out of it. Since more was expected of him than of others his age, he would have to mature faster.

Physically, he had certainly done that, though his will had had nothing to do with that. His genetic blessings were responsible, plus a well-balanced nutrition and exercises based on modern knowledge and ancient wisdom.

Emotionally? You could only force emotional development so far. Time and experience had to do most of the work.

Clark's gold-plated wristwatch with its black leather strap had been returned to him with the clothes. He strapped it on, thinking of how things had changed because of the war. Before it had started, wristwatches were considered too effeminate for men to wear. But their practicality in the services had changed that attitude. How many other attitudes, customs, and mores would change because of this war to end all wars?

The watch was still running despite all the bangs and buffets it had undergone. The time was 6:23. His dinner invitation was for 8:00. Despite his stolen meal, he was hungry. It would help take his mind off of his stomach if he exercised. Since he was five years old, he had been spending from an hour to two hours doing the mental and physical exercises designed by his father and various consultants. He had tried to perform them every day and had usually succeeded. But yesterday and today had been too event-filled.

The sentry at the window would wonder why the prisoner, having just put on his clothes, was now taking them off. Good. The more puzzling he was to his captors, the better he liked it.

Dressed only in his longjohns, he put his body through a series of warm-ups before pitting his muscles against each other with the methods invented by his father. At the same time, he was doing mathematical problems, geometric and algebraic, in his head. Then he worked on extending the value of pi to twenty-five places. He also visualized the operation of a LeRhone rotary engine in its finest details, including the compression values in the cylinders.

He did many other cerebral exercises. These included the philosophical-theological problem of free will versus determinism and the seemingly insolvable mathematical problem of Fermat's Last Theorem. Young Clark had a theory that the two were somehow connected.

Today, though, he could not concentrate as powerfully as he usually did. Now and then, though he did not want it to, the vision of the blonde femme fatale he had seen in the courtyard flashed into his mind.

The sentry watching him knew nothing of this, of course. All he saw were the postures and attitudes Savage was taking. He must often have wondered just what the American was doing. To see him with his arms raised and bent, hands clenched into fists, the body shaking though it was not moving, and the sweat dripping from his forehead was to be mystified. Not until Savage began walking around on his hands, and then, in a crouch, making a series of leaps upward, touching the ceiling with his fingers, would the sentry have thought that he was seeing very vigorous exercises.

He would have wondered why the crazy prisoner was

working up a sweat immediately after bathing. That sequence, however, was dictated by the circumstances.

At a quarter to eight, Clark heard the tramp of marching men. The door was opened, and the same captain told him to fall in between four soldiers. His armed escort took him down the long hall, lit feebly by candles, to a broad staircase, down this for two stories, and then along another corridor. This one was well illuminated with kerosene lamps by the base of the walls. A soldier was stationed in front of a half-open door. He saluted the captain. As Savage passed the door, he glanced within. A radio operator was tapping on a code key. At the end of the hall, they halted before a high and wide oaken door before which stood two sentries. The captain ordered the door opened.

It swung out. Bright lights, the sound of voices, a gramophone playing Mozart's *Jupiter Symphony*, and the odor of food issued from the door.

"*Leutnant* Savage!" the captain announced loudly.

Savage stepped inside. He was surprised at what he saw. It was not the people who took him aback; it was the snowy-white lace tablecloth, the massive silver candle holders and candelabra, the very expensive-looking plates and tableware, the cut-quartz wine goblets, the profusion of bottles of wine, and the food.

Especially the food!

A huge bowl filled with salad, plates of carrots, celery, onions, pickles, apples, oranges, cherries, and several other fruits and vegetables. And the platters of meat and fowl: beef roast, pork chops, racks of lamb, and chicken Kiev and à la king. Dishes of potatoes, baked and mashed. Platters of rich, succulent, steaming gravy. Dishes of butter and of bread, buns, and croissants. Jams, jellies, and honey.

And hearts of palm!

His mouth watered, and his stomach growled.

At the same time, his mind growled a warning to him, though its voice was weaker than his belly's. He knew that he had not been invited to dinner just for the pleasure of his company. Seduction or trickery in one form or another was what he expected. But he had never thought of a gourmet's feast as a siren, a succubus, a Helen of Troy.

The Baron von Hessel was very clever to have set forth such a temptation. He knew that Savage, like most people in warring Europe, had not had a full meal for a long time and that that fare had been simple and monotonous. Of course, he would not expect the American to spill his guts in gratitude for his stuffing them with rich food. But he would think that Savage would be mellow, have his guard down, and might even be grateful to his host.

The baron was either a genius or very ruthless. Or both. How could anyone except the Kaiser or Field Marshal von Hindenburg have the power and influence to supply a table with such a fantastic profusion of gourmet food?

Then there was also, speaking of Helen of Troy, Lili Bugov, Countess Idivzhopu. She was walking—swaying, rather—toward the banquet table. Looking at her hips, he was reminded of the rotary engine of his Nieuport. This image was followed by that of a pendulum, succeeded by a vision of a two-stroke-cycle engine.

Her evening dress was a floor-length formal gown of scarlet silk. Though it was not, of course, skintight—only skin can be that—it looked as if it were a superepidermis, a lovely red layer above the stratum cornea.

Her narrow hips became an unusually small waist which supported a swelling rib cage. Above these were breasts gleaming as white as an Icelander baby's skin. The bare shoulders were lovely but broad. They and the large rib cage were needed to support the more than full bosom. Like twin Venuses born from the sea waves, they rose above the low-cut front of her gown.

Clark Savage was sixteen and, hence, very susceptible to female beauty. He was wide open as only the adolescent male can be, as unresisting and as immediate in response as an iron filing to a magnet. For a moment, he could almost hear the hormones raging inside him and the roaring of blood hastening to its appointed place.

This response was not approved of by the American

mores of 1918. Clark had been ashamed of it, though he
knew that he had no logical reason to be so. His experiences with some primitive societies and his recent so-
journs in Paris with French pilots also on leave had
modified his attitudes somewhat. Moreover, his lifelong
freedom from religious indoctrination, as opposed to education about religions, had softened some of the shame he
might have felt.

Nevertheless, at this moment he felt, illogically but
undeniably, that everyone in the room knew exactly what
he was feeling. His cheeks were hot.

His host, Baron von Hessel, may have been aware of
this. He did look somewhat amused. Or perhaps his usual
posture was to appear to be amused by the mere presence
of other members of Homo sapiens. It was necessary that
these inferior beings occupy the same Earth and maybe
the same room; someone had to do the work. So he might
as well accept their sometimes maddening and often irri-
tating occupation of space with a wry enjoyment and
condescension.

This appraisal of the baron's attitude did not come to
Clark Savage at once. It was to come much later, to build
up slowly during a more intimate and longer contact with
him.

From the very beginning, though, he felt that the
baron looked down on him. Well, why not? He was only
sixteen and a prisoner of war, no threat to the baron.

Von Hessel was tall, an inch higher than Savage. He
had broad shoulders and a slim waist, though a small belly
bulge showed that he ate more than was good for him.
Savage's closer view of him reaffirmed that the baron was
handsome in a thoroughly masculine way. The Roman
nose gave his regular features an aristocratic look. His eyes
were large, green, and seemed to shine with an inner
light. To Savage, an American, the monocle had seemed
foolish, an affectation, but now it seemed to give him a
superior air. It was as if it were a microscope through
which von Hessel studied the smaller creatures of this
world.

Nevertheless, he was polite enough. He clicked his

heels and bowed, speaking Oxford English in a deep bass. "No need to salute, Lieutenant Savage. This is a social party. As much as it can be under the circumstances, anyway."

He introduced the countess, and she gave Savage a small and exceptionally long-fingered hand in a black elbow-length glove. Her perfume was faint but very pleasing. Her large, dark blue eyes were as dazzling as her smile.

"Lieutenant Savage. How nice of you to accept our invitation."

VIII

Her voice was a very pleasant contralto, and she spoke in English with only a slight Russian pronunciation and intonation.

She smiled again and laughed.

"You might say you just dropped in on us. But was it necessary to make such a row about bathing? Are not Americans accustomed to taking baths?"

Clark managed to raise his eyes from her cleavage at the same time that a vision of a map of the Great Rift in East Africa appeared in his mind. No pearls or diamond necklaces draped that snowy vista. She had the good taste not to take away from its splendor with mere jewelry.

He gestured at Zad, who stood motionless as a stuffed Goliath in one corner.

"We're accustomed to giving ourselves our baths, and we don't like being manhandled."

She laughed again and said, "You must be very strong. I didn't think anyone could outwrestle that bear. And turning over that immensely heavy tub! That caused much comment, believe me! And you're so young! You must be very vigorous!"

"He must also be starving," the baron said. "Allow me to get the introductions finished, and we'll dine."

There were thirteen to be seated, including Savage. This indicated to him that his host was not the least bit superstitious. Or, perhaps, he was, but he liked to tempt the fates.

Five guests were officers of the baron's entourage.

One guest was the abbot, a tall, cadaverous, and freakishly long-faced man clad in a rough-spun wool monk's robe. He said little but ate much and swiftly, grunting and snuffling now and then. He behaved as if this was the first good meal he had had in a long time, and perhaps his last. Savage had no idea why he had been invited.

Three guests were fliers from a nearby but unspecified aerodrome. Colonel Schreider was the commandant, and the other two were very young pilots, lieutenants. They had flown the Pfalzes that had shot Savage down. They told him that they had asked von Hessel to send the Nieuport pilot to their mess. They wanted to fete him before he went on to a prisoner-of-war camp. They admired his courage and skill in shooting down two airplanes and two balloons in one day. When they had found out that he was American, they were even more eager to meet him.

Savage was sitting at the baron's right. The countess was at the other end, as befitted her role as hostess. She had seemed to have argued quietly with the baron about this seating, though not very long. Savage had felt uncomfortable about this. Though he could overhear only a few words of the conversation, carried on in German, he got the impression that the countess wanted him to sit next to her.

When she had walked away from the baron, switching her hips and waving her cigarette in its long holder, the magnet of all eyes, she had seemed angry.

Von Hessel had smiled as if he was thinking of a joke.

"You have made quite a conquest," he said to Savage. "I told her to hang her hair out of her room window tonight, play Rapunzel. Perhaps you will climb up it tonight—if you can escape. I'm sure you're thinking about that. Escape, I mean."

He laughed, then threw his half-smoked cigar into a

corner. An orderly hastened to pick it up. Instead of placing it in a waste container, he stubbed it out and put it in his jacket pocket.

Clark was too discomfited to reply, but the baron evidently did not expect one. A few seconds later, he asked everybody to sit down. Wine was poured, though most of those at the table began to eat at once. The serving arrangement was strange. Instead of having one course at a time, everything but the dessert was set out. The countess's maids, two body servants, and two enlisted men passed the dishes to those who could not reach what they wanted. Savage decided that the baron was either unconventional or he liked to upset his guests by avoiding the usual patterns. If anyone was curious about why the baron was not observing the customary method of serving, he was too polite to ask.

Savage sipped his wine slowly, determined not to drink too much. He expected questions which would be subtle but would reveal military information to the baron and Colonel Schreider. Should his share of the conversation be only his name, rank, and serial number? No. He would talk, but he would consider every word before uttering it.

Besides, he might find out something worthwhile about the enemy.

The two Pfalz pilots, eighteen-year-old Meilen and Brantweiler, wanted to talk about flying in general and Savage's exploits in particular. At the same time, it was evident from their glances at the other end of the table that they also wished they could be seated near the countess. They were balked in both desires. The baron only allowed them to talk to the American now and then, and he quite often interrupted them with his own comments on other subjects.

He plunged at once into the subject of those German munitions factories which had been spared bombing by the Allied planes.

"They are close enough to the bomber bases so that your planes may reach them easily," he said. He smiled knowingly. "The factories around them have been blasted.

Yet, not one bomb dropped by your aircraft has landed anywhere near them. Do you know why?"

"I'm sure you'll tell me why," Savage said.

"They're not bombed because your commanders have been ordered to command their pilots to avoid these munitions plants. The generals gave the commander the orders, and these generals were ordered by certain politicians to spare these plants. The politicians were told by certain very powerful industrialists, British, French, and American, to issue these orders. These industrialists have heavy investments in these German munitions factories. They don't wish to lose money because the plants have been destroyed. And they look forward to the continued production, hence, future profits, of these plants after the war is over. What do you think of that?"

Savage bit his lip.

"You do not care to reply. I would think you'd be filled with fury and resentment at these industrialists. They are traitors, though they undoubtedly think of themselves as patriots of the highest order. The bullets, shells, and bombs turned out by these German factories have slain and mutilated hundreds of thousands of French and British and will someday be killing their tens of thousands of your fellow Americans. And more British and French troops."

"I have no proof that what you claim is true," Savage said.

"If you had my knowledge of and experience with human beings, you would know that some men are quite capable of murdering millions of their own people if that will put money in their pockets."

"That doesn't mean that some men are doing that."

The baron laughed.

"Your face is red, and you look sullen. Of course, you resent what I have said about your business tycoons, as you Americans call them. Perhaps, someday, you'll be in a position to check the validity of my statements. But it'll be dangerous for you. These industrialists control the presses and the police. They will use their vast power to suppress

any revelations of their crimes. They will not hesitate to
kill you if you become too much of a threat to them.

"Your President has said that this is the war to end all
wars. He is very naive. Does he really believe that, if
Germany should lose the war, it won't wage another when
it recovers? What about the Bolsheviks? Their ideology is
dogma to them. The words of Marx and Lenin come from
on high, from the Mount Sinai of Socialism. Their godless
God has decreed that they must export their revolution
throughout the world by whatever means are needed.

"What about all the exploited and wretched masses of
Asia, Africa, and South America? Do you think they'll not
rise in arms against their European rulers someday? Of
course, they'll then be oppressed by tyrants of their own
people, but that's not relevant at this moment."

"You seem to have made quite a study of politics and
economics," the lieutenant said.

"I have studied the lust for power and the means used
to get power and to keep it," the baron said. "It's not the
atom that is at the base of human conduct. It's the desire
for power."

He sipped his wine.

"America is also fighting to make the world safe for
democracy," the baron said. "Ask your Negro citizen, your
Indian on the reservation, about democracy."

"I realize that great evils and wrongs stain the shining
shield of the world," Clark Savage said. "But I believe that
these may be righted someday."

The baron raised his eyebrows. "'Stain the shining
shield of the world'? I did not realize that you are also
somewhat of a poet."

Savage expected von Hessel to press on with similar
subjects. They were designed to raise doubts in him about
the righteousness and morality of the Allied cause. But if
von Hessel thought that his prisoner was so weak that he
would succumb to such a line, he was very mistaken.

Then, surprisingly, von Hessel pointed down the
table. He said, "Look at those men. Drooling, sniffing like
hounds around a bitch in heat. Not that they're so off the
track in their ardor. She thinks she's another Catherine the

Great, a Cleopatra, a Ninon de Lenclos. Unfortunately, she does not have their high intelligence. But who cares about that in such matters?"

Clark Savage was angered by this. A gentleman did not talk thus about women, not even his own mistress, not even if the remark was correct.

"Your face is red—again," von Hessel said, grinning over his wine.

Savage waited until he had swallowed a mouthful of delicious beef before speaking.

"Your references to her rub me the wrong way," he said stiffly.

"You think I shouldn't speak derogatorily of any woman?" von Hessel said. "But that implies that women as a group are either on a higher plane than men or on a lower one. That is the worldwide male attitude. Wrong, of course. The average intelligence of women is as high as the average intelligence of men, though that is no compliment to women. They have, in most fields of endeavor, as much mental and, usually, as much physical ability as men. Anybody not blinded by prejudice should be able to see that.

"Thus, why should I—anyone, for that matter—spare them criticism or blame? What's due to men should be due to women. That includes praise or blame, reward or punishment."

"But they're not treated as equals!"

"Exactly. And they won't be until they wage a war for equality and maybe not then. Men won't give up their power over women until they're forced to do so, and they'll fight long and hard."

He swallowed half of the wine in his glass.

"Ah, good! These monks may not know much about the delights of life, but they make a satisfactory wine. Now, my young American—that is, to say, my very naive and youthful guest—almost everything in human life springs from the fight for power! Power! Power! Power!"

"You're very cynical," Clark Savage said.

"In other words, doglike? If so, I'm the leader of the pack. Objective, clearheaded, a seer without blinders.

Which makes me what you call a cynic. See that woman down there? Of course you do; I'm being whimsical. You've been torn between your fascination with the food and her beauty—that is, her strong sexual attraction.

"She had power. The daughter of a Russian count who owned vast property and thousands of peasants, she could, if she chose, put any one of the peasants to death or to torture. She had plenty of them whipped until the blood came. Of course, she had to get her father's permission to do that.

"But the Bolshevik Revolution swept all that away. Suddenly, her parents are beaten to death by peasants who now have power over them. She is in danger of her life and has to flee her country. Her only property is some jewels and clothes and four of her servants, misbegotten and misguided creatures who cling to her through mistaken loyalty. Instead of killing her, they protect and serve her.

"But she hasn't lost all power. She still has her beauty, her sexual desirability. She uses them as a woman must use them if she is to survive and to regain some power. Fortunately for her, she met me. But what will she do if I lose my interest in her, prefer some other woman?"

Von Hessel shrugged.

"She'll find some other man with power. But when she gets old and ugly? Never mind all that, Lieutenant. Let us discuss other matters, if you care to. For instance, a subject which greatly intrigues me. That is, the efforts of your father to make you into a superman. What Nietzsche called *der Übermensch*."

Savage had just bitten into a hearts of palm salad. It became suddenly unsavory, and he came close to spitting it out. His heart seemed to be struck a blow; his stomach seemed to loop the loop.

Von Hessel smiled.

"Yes, I know much about that. Our Intelligence has a dossier on you and Doctor Clark Savage, Senior. Quite a lengthy one. I'll be frank with you. I wouldn't have invited you to dinner if you'd only been some Yankee flier with more courage than brains. We may talk about your peculiar education and your father's motives for giving it to you. That won't endanger the security of the Allied Powers."

Savage shoved his plate away. Looking straight ahead, his back stiff, he repeated his name, rank, and serial number.

"Come now," the baron said. "There's no need of that nonsense. You can't tell me anything about your movements and your role in the Air Service that I don't know."

Savage gave his name, rank, and serial number again.

The baron sighed. Frowning, he said, "You're a very stubborn young man. Not as bright, I'm afraid, as I have been led to believe."

So abruptly and vigorously that he startled everyone, von Hessel shoved his chair back and rose to full height. The loud conversation stopped, and the only sound for a moment was the music from the gramophone. It was playing "Siegfried's Funeral March" from Wagner's *The Ring of the Nibelungen*.

Von Hessel bellowed in German, "Take the prisoner back to his cell!"

Countess Idivzhopu's eyes were very wide as she gazed fixedly at the baron and the lieutenant. Her lips were open, as if she were going to question von Hessel. But she closed them without a word.

"That's right!" the baron shouted. "Don't you dare say one word of protest! Forget about your plaything for the night! He's not for you!"

He roared at the captain, who had just entered. "Kunz! Take this man back to his cell! On the double!"

Even as he was marched swiftly out of the room—two soldiers behind him, two ahead, Captain Kunz leading— Savage wondered if this event had not been staged for his benefit. The baron might have planned it, and it might not be over yet. Why else would von Hessel have spoken of the countess's having to forget about her "plaything"? That more than implied that she, and, hence, the baron, had in mind some sort of seduction for their prisoner. Just how this would unfold, he had no idea. But the baron controlled this monastery. Moreover, he seemed cynical enough, degraded enough, to use his mistress for anything he wanted.

Which, in this situation, would so influence their captive that he would reveal to the countess matters that he should keep silent about.

Or was he, Clark Savage, being too suspicious? Was he also, in his modest way, a cynic?

He was glad that he had not eaten and drunk too much. Suddenly, he decided that he would act, would do something the baron would not expect at this time. He had been waiting patiently for a chance to make a break for it. But he was out of patience. He was not logy from stuffing his belly, and he was quivering inside himself like a greyhound waiting for the gate to open and the race to begin.

IX

As he was marched to the cell in which he had first been put, Savage made his plans. The captain commanding the four soldiers was in their lead. Two of them were in front of him; two, behind. These bore rifles on their shoulders. The captain was armed only with a Luger Parabellum P08 automatic pistol.

When they got to the corridor leading to his cell, the lieutenant saw that no sentry was posted outside the door. Good! That meant that he had five to deal with, not six. What he had to do had to be done very quickly and smoothly. Overcoming five men was possible. One more would have made it very near impossible, though he would have tried it anyway.

Just as they came to the door, the captain cried, "Halt!" He started to turn around. Savage and his escort stopped. The American bent his knees and sprang upward. When he got to the level of the chests of the soldiers behind him, he straightened out on a horizontal level. At the same time, he kicked back and smote the two in front of him with his fists.

His boots drove into the solar plexuses, the upper middle part of the abdomen. Since this area contains a network of nerves, Savage figured the two behind him, hit hard there, would be paralyzed for the few seconds he needed. The two in front of him, slammed with kidney punches, would also be out of action for a little while.

As the soldiers yelled or gasped with pain and surprise and their dropped rifles clattered, he bounced off the stone floor with both feet. One of the men in front of him, his back bent backward, a hand on the spot where Savage had hurt him, was staggering into his commander. The captain, his mouth open but emitting no sound, was reaching for his holstered pistol. He was borne backward by the injured soldier. He cursed the man and shouted at him to get out of the way.

That gave Savage time to be upon the captain before he could shove the soldier to one side. Savage chopped the side of the captain's neck with the edge of his hand. Then, whirling around, he deftly plucked the Luger from the officer's holster.

The captain, unconscious, was sprawled out on the floor. The soldiers, despite their agony, were stooping to pick up their rifles.

Savage unclicked the safety of the automatic, pulled the slide back and then shot it in, and pointed it toward the soldiers. He said in German, "Don't move!"

The torchlight shone on faces twisted with pain and shock. No one tried anything.

Ten seconds later, under the lieutenant's fierce urging, a man had taken the ring of keys from the officer, slid it across the floor to the American, then helped the others carry the limp captain into the cell. One of them threw the bundle of flying clothes out into the corridor. Savage locked the cell door and pocketed the Luger.

He removed three of the five-round box-magazines from all but one of the rifles. These he stuffed into his pockets. He picked up a rifle and went down the corridor toward the outside. Before he got to its end, he heard the

soldiers in the cell yelling for help. Much good that would
do them until someone went searching for them.

The route to the entrance fixed in his mind, he
cautiously though swiftly went back along it. He assumed
that a guard had now been stationed there, and he was
right. Standing just within the doorway, out of the rain,
was a single soldier. The lightning, somewhat distant,
flashing now and then, outlined him. His back was to
Savage. His rifle was slung around his shoulder, contrary
to the regulations for guard duty. Then he turned to
present his profile, and Savage could see the glowing
cigarette in his mouth.

The lieutenant had not known until now that it was
raining or that lightning and thunder were in the west.
The thick stone walls had kept out all sound.

He waited until the guard had his back to him again.
Then he moved swiftly, hoping that the slight noise his
boots made would be drowned out by the booming and
cracking of the elements in the sky. When he got to the
soldier, who was about to cast his cigarette into the rain,
Savage hit him in the back of the neck with the butt of the
Mauser he had picked up from the floor outside the cell.
He tried not to hit hard enough to cause permanent injury
to the man's vertebrae.

He removed the magazine from the man's rifle and
threw the weapon far into the night. Then he took the
man's greatcoat off and put it on himself. When he got to
the opening in the wall through which he had first entered
the monastery grounds, he hesitated.

Should he get away from this place as speedily as
possible? Or should he go back into it, though by a
different route, and do some spying?

It took him three seconds to decide.

The dangers of being caught again outweighed any
information he might pick up. It seemed to him that von
Hessel might possess much valuable information. But how
would he get to him and how would he extract the
information from him?

He had come into the monastery like a thief in the
night, though it had been daylight then. Now, he left it

like a thief in the night. The climb down on the steep
sandstone and mud of the slope took longer than going up.
He slipped several times but caught hold of projecting
rock before he had gone far. He expected to hear at any
moment a clamor behind and above him. But he made it
to the forest beyond the wide meadow without hearing or
seeing any sign of pursuit.

The two young German fliers he had talked to during
dinner had mentioned that their aerodrome was to the
north. They had not said how far it was from the monastery. Savage had not seen it when he had climbed to the
top of the tower shortly after entering the building. It
could be beyond a range of hills to the northeast. The
poplar-lined road coming from the north probably led to
it. In any event, he was going to find out if it did. North
was as good as any direction—as far as he knew.

Stumbling now and then, walking swiftly, the rain
soaking his head and, after a while, the greatcoat, he
skirted the meadow. When he got about a mile away from
the monastery, he ventured out onto another meadow.
There was a farmhouse a hundred yards away, visible only
when the lightning flashed. Its windows were dark. He
had to wade through a ditch to get to the road. By then,
the thunder was at its loudest and the lightning at its
fiercest.

He kept turning his head as he slogged through the
thickening mud. He decided that if he were to see the
lights of vehicles behind him—his chasers—he would run
back into the woods; if, as was the case here and there, no
coppice of trees was close enough, he would dive into the
ditch. It would mean a soaking in the cold water, but it
would be worth it. At least he hoped it would.

However, automobiles would not have an easy time
getting through this mud.

The ravening elements overhead had passed to the
east by the time he had traversed three miles. No car lights
had appeared ahead of or behind him. The road had
forked once. He had taken the right-hand route. This
curved gradually, came to a range of low hills, and went

along it in an easterly direction. The farmhouses increased in number, though all were dark.

Presently, he came to a village or what was left of it. Most of the houses had been blown apart, and there were deep holes in the ground. But two comparatively intact buildings showed lights at the windows. He detoured these, climbing over debris, until he suddenly came to the village limits.

He saw a dim light ahead. As he got closer on the winding road, the lights became brighter. Soon, he saw barbed wire across the ditches on the left side of the road. It was six feet high. Behind it was another row. Both stretched into the night ahead of him. At quite a distance, inestimable because of the darkness, were two parallel lines of electric lights a few inches above the ground, running for a very long distance. On the ground between the lines was a broad, whitish, black-streaked substance.

At their end, dimly seen, were the bulks of large low structures. A flashlight danced before one of them and illuminated shadowy human figures.

The puzzling pattern suddenly shifted into a familiar shape just as the rain ceased.

This was an aerodrome, and the barbed wire walled it in. The lights were to guide night-flying airplanes in. The whitish substance was a cement landing strip splattered with mud, probably broader than it seemed to him from his angle of view. The specially made strip would be absolutely necessary for aircraft taking off or landing, especially if they were heavy bombers. Otherwise, they would get stuck in the deep mud.

However, the Germans had built only one strip, and that meant the craft would have to take off sometimes with a tailwind or crosswind. Like tonight, for instance. The wind would be behind them. But the strip was a very long one.

The big structures would be hangars, and one of the men gathered in front of a hangar waiting for the returning planes had a flashlight.

At this moment, he heard the muted roar of air machines.

He went down the side of the ditch on the seat of his pants, waded hip-deep through the numbingly cold water, managed to lift himself by an exposed tree root out of the ditch, and ran along the barbed wire back along the way he had come. When he got to the corner of the square that the wire formed around the drome, he went around it and along the wire barricade running to the north. When he was near the end of the strip, he stopped.

Several minutes passed while the thrum of many mighty motors became louder. Then the first craft, flying very low, came into his view. The lights showed him a huge plane, a Grossflugzeug, a Gotha G.V. It was a biplane bomber with two wing-mounted Mercedes-Benz motors and carrying a crew of three. A night raider. It should not have been up in this moonless and stormy weather, but the place it had bombed might be out of the storm.

He watched while three more landed after it. The undercarriage of the fifth, however, collapsed shortly after landing. The rest of the plane slid with a loud screeching along the strip, then shot off it and into the mud, its wings breaking up. There was a lot of excitement after that. Caution about maintaining a blackout was forgotten. Hot arc lights by the hangars were turned on. An ambulance, its siren whooping, sped down the strip with motorcyclists and men on foot following it.

Savage waited for a minute for the escort fighters to appear. But there were none.

He grabbed the barbed wire with gloved hands and vaulted over in one smooth and easy fashion. The second row he cleared almost as well, but one leg was caught by a point which ripped open the cloth. It also drew blood.

Ignoring it, he ran through the mud at an angle away from the strip. He was well out in the darkness, though he could not approach the hangars from the front because of the intense arc lights. Running on a curve to stay in the darkness, he got to the unlit side of the nearest hangar. By then, the Gotha bombers that had landed safely had been pulled and pushed by ground crews to face outward and were in a row in front of the hangar. The bomber crews were standing nearby, apparently watching the rescue of the crew of the wrecked Gotha. There were lights dancing around this, men shouting, and the ambulance was still waiting on the strip.

He undid the bundle and put on the flying suit, including the helmet and goggles. His rain-chilled body began to warm up.

Then he took a deep breath and, rifle in hand, walked from around the corner. He stayed close to the dark front of the hangar, crossed the space between this and the next hangar, and then angled across to the closest Gotha. After ducking under that, he scuttled on all fours under the others until he came to the fourth bomber. This was the nearest to the landing strip.

Up he went into the middle cockpit, where the pilot sat. Ahead, in the nose, was the cockpit for an observer-gunner. Behind him was the cockpit for the rear gunner. He placed the rifle against the side of the cockpit. Ducking down low, he put his head close to the controls and instruments. He could not see very well in the dimness, but there was just enough light for him to make out the controls and instruments. The function markings were just black blurs.

He studied the controls as well as he could under the circumstances. Basically, all aircraft controls were the same in function. But they varied in form from one machine type to another, and the panel instruments and other cockpit gadgets varied in location. Moreover, a pilot trying to fly a craft he was unfamiliar with was supposed to have intensive ground instruction before taking it up.

Savage could not see the fuel-supply gauge. The tanks might be almost empty.

Never mind. He was going to use whatever was left.

If he could get two mechanics to spin the propellors for him.

Another deep breath.

L'audace! Toujours l'audace!

He got out of the plane and strode up to the fringe of the crowd as if he were German-born and a zealous patriot to boot. By the light, he scanned the faces of the mechanics closest to him. Then he picked out the two sleepiest-looking ones. Like all grease monkeys in an air corps—German, British, American, Italian, what have you—they were overworked and bereft of rest. They sweated over and strained to salvage an unending flow of wrecked, damaged, and malfunctioning machines. Unsung heroes, the mechanics.

He moved close to them and spoke in German in a low but authority-impregnated voice. The tones of command were as imperative as if he were the Kaiser's cousin.

"You two come with me."

Spinning around, he walked away as if there was no question that they should obey him. He did not even look back.

The two mechanics must have wondered who he was, since they undoubtedly knew every officer on the base. But he could hear their bootsteps behind him. He did not care what puzzled looks they were exchanging.

The Luger pistol he had taken from the captain in the monastery was stuck in the side pocket of his uniform jacket. The upper part of his flying jacket was partly unbuttoned to allow him to get to the weapon quicker. Its safety was off, and it was ready to fire. That was not the recommended way to carry a loaded automatic. He was not, however, worrying about what anyone would recommend.

Ahead were the four Gothas with their double-tail ailerons by the rudder and the machine guns sticking out above the front and rear cockpits. It seemed like a long time until he got to the last machine. Then he was climbing up on the protective strip on the wing by the middle cockpit. Then he was in the middle cockpit and was putting the automatic on the floor. The rifle was ready to fire, too.

The mechanics came up to the plane and looked up at him.

"I want to start the motors," he said.

An officer—an arrogant one, anyway—would not explain to corporals why he wanted something done. So, he did not.

"Get going!" he said.

Then he added to assuage any suspicions they might have, "Special orders! Get the blocks out!"

While they removed the chocks in front of the wheels, he turned the cockpit lights on. He looked out on both sides of the aircraft. Each mechanic was standing in front of a propellor.

At his command, they spun the propellors. He had to repeat, "Contact!" three times before the motors took fire and the propellors were whirling. The mechanics stepped back out of the way. Meanwhile, a glance showed him that some curious officers were walking toward him. One thing he did not want just now was to be questioned.

Fortunately, the motors were still warm. Even if they had not been, he could not have waited for them. He started the Gotha forward, then began swinging it around toward the end of the strip. When he had straightened it out, he pushed in on the throttles. Accelerating swiftly, the huge craft rolled toward the runway. By then, the two mechanics were running after him. The crowd was scattering, some loping toward him, some hastening to get out of the way. In the lead of those advancing was an officer with an automatic in his hand.

Savage could not hear him above the thunder of the motors. However, he could lipread the shouted words.

"Halt! Stop the machine, or I'll shoot!"

The Gotha was going to pass the officer, who would have a good opportunity to empty his pistol into the man stealing the bomber.

Savage picked up the Luger from the floor with his right hand, transferred it to his left, and aimed at the concrete in front of the officer. He fired twice. Chips flew up near the officer's boots. The German fell. Struck in the leg, probably, by a ricochet. The plane sped by the writhing man.

But here was a mechanic grasping a strut on the left wing, his feet flying. And then he had hauled himself up on the wing. Now, he was making his way toward the plywood fuselage. The wings were covered with fabric, and the man put his foot through it. But he pulled it out and went from strut and wire to strut and wire.

That big hole in the wing fabric was going to cause trouble when the Gotha got into full flight and top velocity. If it ever did.

As Savage neared the beginning of the runway, he slowed the bomber down. He did not want to take the turn so swiftly that he tilted the craft and scraped one wingtip on the concrete. A groundloop, as it was called, might tear off the end of the lower left wing.

The right motor slowed down, and with the left motor unchecked in its power, its rudder to the right, the Gotha swung. When it was pointing straight down the runway, Savage matched the power of the left motor with that of the right.

He set the throttles for full speed ahead a few seconds later.

The mechanic, his face pale and distorted, had made his reckless way to the fuselage. He was near enough to the cockpit to reach out and touch the lieutenant. But he took a wrench out of the back pocket of his coveralls. Savage released the throttles. With his left hand, the other on the joystick, he picked up the Luger from his lap. The mechanic backed away.

Savage motioned with the gun for the man to jump.

Poor devil! If he did not obey the command, he would be shot. If he did jump, he would probably be seriously injured or killed.

Savage hoped that, whatever the man did, it would not occur to him to throw the wrench into the propellor of the motor nearest him.

Better make up his mind for him before that nasty thought illuminated it.

Leaning out of the cockpit, he aimed and fired. Whether the bullet struck the mechanic in the flesh of his leg, broke a bone, or he was just frightened, its effect was the same. The man collapsed and fell off the wing.

Savage had no time to look back and see what had happened to him. Ahead, the ambulance had pulled out onto the narrow runway to block it. Near it, the faces of those in front shining in the machine's headlights, was a swarm of men firing at the bomber.

The lieutenant's awareness that he was in a hell of a pickle was knife-sharp. If the ambulance did not get out of the way, the bomber might collide with it. Savage was not sure that he could lift off before he smashed into the vehicle.

But he laughed and then whooped like a Comanche. Audacity! Always audacity!

He was blazing with recklessness, exalted by the spirit of youth, ecstatic with the danger. Stealing a Gotha bomber was the high point of his life, so far, anyway, even if death would soon be taking him away. He had done what he had fantasized about, done what no one else, as far as he knew, had ever done.

The voice of his commander, de Slade, rang above the Niagara Falls roar of the motors.

Audacity! Always audacity! *Bougez les boches!*

If he had been a light bulb, he would have lit up the world. The Martians would have seen the glow. More than that, far more than that! The inhabitants of Neptune, the outermost planet of the solar system, would have seen it!

The ambulance headlights were bright, and the fire-flies born out of the muzzles of the German weapons flashed. He could put it off no longer. Now! He pulled back on the control stick. Sluggishly, the bomber rose. Would he make it?

The aircraft lurched and nosed down a little. He brought it back, knowing that, for the moment, he had survived. Glancing behind, he saw that the ambulance lights had gone out. His undercarriage had hit the vehicle and might have been torn off. If so, he would have to land this machine on its belly. A trifling consideration at this moment.

The fuel gauge indicated almost empty. That had not bothered him during those hectic moments, but it would soon be the major business to occupy him. He had better get the hell out of here. Reject the thought that he might swing back and buzz the aerodrome, maybe try to force down any fighter plane just lifting off the runway in pursuit of him. He was too exuberant. Time for a cool heart and a realistic frame of mind.

He swung to the right to get a good look at the drome. Fighter planes would be stationed there to escort the bombers, though they had not been used on this night's raid. He had not seen any until now. They had been parked in the hangars. Now a number of them were in line, their motors warming up. In a minute, they would be taking off after him.

If they could find him, they could catch him.

He would wait a little while before turning the cockpit lights off. Meanwhile, he would go due south by the compass. The darkness blinded him; no visible landmarks could be seen. The towns would be in a blackout. He would have to switch the lights on from time to time to take a compass bearing. And to check the fuel supply. That brief illumination would be enough for the fighter pilots, if any were in his area.

So far, so good, though.

He was over the eastern half of Picardy, which was bisected by the Oise River. It flowed northeast-southwest through Noyon, Compiègne, and Creil along a wooded valley. If there was enough light for the river to reflect even a pale light, he might see it. If his fuel held out long enough for him to get to it. He would have to crash-land in the river, if it was available, unless he could find a long stretch of meadow. He doubted that he had time to look for a meadow.

Unfortunately, the Gotha pilot had not left his parachute in the cockpit for his American guest. Damn inconsiderate, that.

He put the automatic pistol inside his jacket. He might have a use for it later. He threw the rifle overboard. He did not want it to be bouncing around during a crash landing.

After twenty minutes of flight, the fuel gauge showed empty. He switched on the emergency tanks. Ten minutes later, as he was about to switch on the lights again, he saw a flash of lights far away. It was intermittent, but ran a long way in a row at right angles to him. It had to be muzzle flames from artillery. A battlefront. He was still going in the right direction.

Now... if only the gasoline held out.

He did not think it would. He was surprised that it had lasted this long.

As if the Gotha had been tuning in on his thoughts and was chuckling at the joke, the motors started to cough. He lowered the nose of the plane. Time to descend, whether he wanted to or not. After some sputters, the motors quit entirely. He steepened the glide angle. The wind whistled through the struts and wires. If it had not been for the lightning of cannons far, far away, he would have felt that he was the only person alive in a vast, eerie darkness. The womb of death. About to give birth to another corpse.

Horse puckey! he thought.

I still live. I will keep on living.

Then he saw lights moving along a road. Or those of boats on a river. They gave him a reference point, though he was still so far above them that he did not know his altitude. The cockpit lights had quit functioning when the motors had stopped, thus preventing him from seeing the height indicator.

The bomber came down too swiftly and too steeply. But he saw that the faint sheen suddenly appearing was that of a river. The lights were the running lights of two steamboats. Faint flames glowed in their smokestacks.

He lifted the nose of the Gotha to lose velocity by climbing, though he did not want to lose too much. He was about three hundred feet above the boats. While he was climbing, he banked to get back to the river. Now, he was unable to do anything but land on the water. He had no more time to maneuver. The boats were ahead of him and coming fast. But he was not on a collision course with them.

He straightened the airplane out a few inches above the river. He was gambling that the landing undercarriage had been ripped off by impact with the ambulance. If it had not, the undercarriage and wheels might strike the water and cause the plane to upend nose-first. Such an abrupt and violent stopping of the craft would not be good for him, even though he was restrained by the crash belt.

On the other hand, if the undercarriage had stayed attached to the fuselage and it was now sheared off, the impact might just cause the plane to slow down somewhat before striking the water. That would be to his advantage.

Whatever happened, his fate was in other hands. Not those of the gods, but those of Chance.

He had about three seconds to contemplate what might happen. The Gotha struck the surface with a mighty jolt, soared upward a few feet, fell with a muscle-and-bone-jarring bump, slid, now turning slowly sideways and rolling to the left, the lower wing on that side tearing off from the bottom of the craft's structure, the big motor plunging into the water, the upper wing, which extended to both sides and formed a single wing, cracking in half and crashing down on him—which he avoided by ducking down—then the fuselage rolling to the right, and both the lower right wing and the upper wing ripping off with the motor.

The fuselage stopped moving. It began floating downriver. He unbuckled the crash belt. Water was up to his ankles in the cockpit and rising swiftly. If he was going to take the flying suit off, he would have to do it while in the river.

X

A searchlight blazed, its beam groping along the surface until its bright eye dazzled him. By then, the fuselage had almost sunk. He went over the side and began swimming, the searchlight following him. A man shouted at him, in German, that he should grab the rope. The boat eased up to him, its backward-spinning screws churning the water to keep from going by him. The lights showed him a manned machine gun in the bow. It was pointed at him.

There went his plan to pretend that he was a downed pilot flying for the Fatherland. There must be a shortwave radio set aboard the boat, and it had gotten the message about his theft of the Gotha.

That turned out to be just what had happened. He was treated not unkindly. He was given a cup of coffee— actually, it was chickory since real coffee was available only on the black market—and his clothes were dried out while he sat in a greatcoat with an armed guard watching him.

An hour later, he was in an interrogation room in an old and half-ruined mansion in Noyon. He was given a bowl of thin soup with a few small pieces of mutton and a small chunk of black bread that seemed as heavy as platinum. He was lucky to get that.

He spent three days in Noyon, during which he was visited and questioned by six different officers. Though these threatened to shoot him as a spy if he did not answer their questions, he refused to give them anything but his name, rank, and serial number. The last officer to interrogate him was the commandant of the field from which Savage had stolen the Gotha.

The commandant, who after an hour was nearly ready to give up his fruitless quest to get Savage to talk, finally said, "Colonel von Hessel sends you his regards."

Savage lifted his eyebrows, but he only nodded.

The commandant looked as if he had expected the American to open up. He waited a few seconds, then said, "The colonel says that you are destined either to become a general or to be executed while trying to escape."

Savage said nothing.

The commandant smiled and said, "Countess Idivzhopu also sends her regards and her felicitations. She says that she is destined to meet you again and looks forward with great pleasure to that."

The lieutenant sighed but did not reply.

The commandant shook his head. "I do not understand why she should take an interest in you, though I have heard some stories..."

He paused for a verbal reaction. When he got none, he said, "I think that when she spoke of meeting you again, she was thinking that you would probably end up in Camp Loki."

Savage frowned.

"Ah, you are puzzled by that name! I won't enlighten you. But I will tell you this—it's a promise—that you are going to the Holzminden prisoner-of-war camp. Perhaps you have heard of it?"

Savage neither spoke nor changed his expression, which was that of indifference.

"I betray no confidence in telling you this, and it will be best for you to keep it in mind. It is, as you Americans say, a hellhole. It is, in keeping with the German regard for international law, a camp that is not inhumane. But its officers are very strict, and it cannot be escaped from.

"However, if you should manage to escape en route or, by some miracle, escape from Holzminden, you will be sent to Loki. That is a newly opened POW camp, the location of which I won't reveal to you, of course. But I can tell you that its commandant will be your recent host, Colonel von Hessel! He guarantees that no POW will ever break out of Camp Loki!

"Especially since he seems to have a special interest in you!

"Any prisoner of war who escapes three times and then is caught goes automatically to Loki. You escaped after you crashed in the Oise River. You then escaped from the monastery, after which you stole that bomber. But we are being fair. The theft of the bomber is combined with the monastery escape. We count those two as just one. To tell the truth, we cannot help but admire the brazen manner in which you walked among us and took the bomber away, right under our noses. You must be part German or, at least, of Teutonic ancestry.

"So, you have two attempts to your debit, not three. But the next time you try, if you do—and Colonel von Hessel says that you will try—you will be sent to Loki."

Why would Colonel von Hessel, who was primarily a medical officer, be the commander of a POW camp? No use asking the commandant about it. However, the lieutenant told himself, he might get the answer to another question.

"Loki is for incorrigible escapees?"

"I thought I'd made that obvious."

"I like to double-check on things," Savage said. "Sometimes, the obvious only seems to be obvious. Leaping at conclusions may spring you right over the cliff edge."

"And trying to escape may get you shot!" the commandant said. He spun around and stalked out of the room.

Holzminden! Savage had heard of the infamous place. It was supposed to be the most harshly run and security-conscious POW enclosure in the territory of the Central Powers.

The camp called Loki? It must be designed to be a super-Holzminden.

A half-hour later, an officer and three soldiers came into the cell. Savage was told to pack and be quick about it. As soon as he had tied up the bundle of his flying clothes, he was handcuffed. He protested in a loud voice against the restraints. The officer told him to shut up. He was marched through the half-ruined town to the railroad station. The tracks, which had been shelled and then bombed, had been repaired. The locomotive, hissing steam and puffing black smoke, was waiting. It was connected to a long line of freight and passenger cars. Savage was escorted aboard the next-to-last car. This was used to haul cattle. The stench of crowded and frightened beasts radiated from the wood, and there were piles of manure on the floor. At least, Savage thought, the spaces between the horizontal sections on the sides admitted fresh air. On the other hand, the air outside was cold.

After the lieutenant was taken to a corner and told to sit down, he saw six other POWs climbing into the car. These were confined to the opposite corner at the other end of the car. A sergeant and four soldiers were the only Germans in the car. They were evidently farm boys. They joked about the odor and the manure, and one said it made him feel at home, but he missed his pigs.

The sergeant, a grizzled man of about fifty, missing his left ear and scarred deeply on his chin, spoke to Savage in German. Evidently, he had been told that the American could speak his language.

"You will not go near the other prisoners. You will not speak to them. You will not address us except when you have to take a leak or do something else necessary. Understand?"

Savage nodded and said, "Do I have to sit all the time? I'd like to exercise some."

"You may walk back and forth at this end," the sergeant said. "Step in the cow-flops if you want to. We don't care."

His guffaw sounded like a donkey's braying.

Savage smiled slightly.

Then the train started up with a jerk. The locomotive bell ringing, its whistle shrilling, the train began to pick up speed. After a while, Doc requested permission to put on his flying suit. The air blowing in between the slats on the side, along with acrid smoke and ashes, was cold. The sergeant did not object to the American talking, because dressing warm was something necessary.

Savage held out his hands. "I can't put the suit on unless these are unlocked."

The sergeant, grinning, said, "It's okay with me if you put the suit on. But I don't have the handcuff key. An officer in another car has it, and he won't give it to me until we get to our destination. You must be one hell of a dangerous prisoner."

Savage said nothing. He did his daily runthrough of exercises as best he could with his wrists cuffed together. But, because of his greatly lessened food intake, he cut the strenuous efforts to thirty minutes. The sergeant, watching him intently and with puzzlement for a while, finally grinned. He pointed his index finger at his temple and circled its tip. The others grinned also.

"Crazy!" one of them said.

Savage got his second meal of the day, supper, shortly before dusk. His rations consisted of another small chunk of black bread, a small and hard raw potato, and a tiny slice of onion. He also ate a hard-boiled egg which the sergeant sold him at a high price. The egg was not supposed to be for the prisoners, but when Savage saw the eggs in one of the two food bags, he made a bargain.

The sergeant, called Mixenheimer by his men, reached into Savage's jacket pocket and brought out a bundle of money, in francs, pound notes, marks, and dollar bills.

"You believe in being prepared," Mixenheimer said. "You must've expected to get captured. Or are you a black-market crook? I'll take my payment in dollars."

Which meant that the sergeant dealt in contraband currency.

Savage thought, You don't know how well prepared I am.

The sergeant took six dollars. The lieutenant ate the hard-boiled egg with gusto, but without salt. Despite that lack, it was the first tasty food he had eaten since the dinner given by von Hessel.

He was given water in a coffee mug. He asked for more but was told that that was his ration until just before sleep time.

"Two dollars for two more mugsful," Savage said.

"Make it four, and you got them," the sergeant said.

Mixenheimer removed more American dollars from Savage's packet. "What you've purchased comes from my private stock," Mixenheimer said. "I paid for it, and I can sell it to whoever has the wherewithal to pay. So, don't complain to any officer that I'm selling Army supplies."

He smiled broadly. "Besides, maybe the officer is getting his cut from me."

The rain began again. Since the train was going in a generally northerly direction, the west wind blew the cold water through the slats on that side. The miserable tenants of the cattle car moved to the east side.

Some hours later, the train stopped, and the prisoners were allowed to get out. Everybody else piled out, too. The station was very small, and so was the dimly lit village that Savage could see beyond the station. He was hustled onto a meadow behind this structure and told to do his duty, if he needed to, into the ditch. Evidently for train passengers, it had been dug for just this purpose.

The officer who had the handcuff key, a lieutenant, came up to the sergeant and told him to remove the cuffs. The light of the kerosene lamps brought from the train showed his annoyance. He stood tapping a boot toe while Savage's cuffs were unlocked and while Savage pulled down his pants and unbuttoned the flap on the rear of his longjohns.

"Hurry up, man!" the officer said. "I have to get back to the bridge game!"

"I don't have any toilet paper," Savage said, looking up.

The sergeant reached into a pocket of his trench coat and pulled out a flimsy sheet of newspaper.

"This paper's bad quality, and the ink'll run all over your butt," he said. "But it's better than nothing. Or don't you Yankees care? Haw, haw!"

"How much is it going to cost me?" Savage said.

"Two dollars. One for me, one for the lieutenant. Another dollar if you want to read it after you've used it."

Savage was getting sick of Mixenheimer's braying, but discretion told him not to reveal this.

"I'll take your kind offer," he said.

A minute later, he was done. The officer handed the key to the sergeant, who secured the cuffs again on Savage and handed the key back to his superior. Though the officer was in a hurry, he did delay going back long enough for a parley with Mixenheimer. Something—money, of course—passed from the sergeant to the officer.

Ah, well, Savage thought, there are men like those two in every armed service in the world. Just as the poor will always be with us, so will the sharpie, the hustler, and the make-a-buck-any-way-you-can dealer.

Three hours later, the train stopped again. A big wooden sign indicated the town was Mézières. They were relatively close to the Belgian border. It was here that the prisoners were to be transferred to another train, though they did not find that out until four hours later. Savage and the other POWs were held in a small room. Meanwhile,

Savage, whose whiskers had not been cropped since he had broken out of the monastery, gave Mixenheimer five dollars to shave him. While a soldier stood by with his rifle ready, the sergeant expertly used his safety razor on Savage.

"I wish I could be your guard for the rest of the war," Mixenheimer said. "I'd be a rich man."

Four hours later, the POWs were marched out from the station and across the railroad tracks to a long train lined up with several others.

Mixenheimer turned the prisoners over to a corporal. He was white-haired, stoop-shouldered, and wore round, rimless glasses. The sergeant looked dismayed when he found out that the noncom's troop consisted of one soldier—and that one fifty years old and suffering from a bad cold.

"What is the Imperial German Army coming to?" he said loudly. "You both should be home in bed and planning to make out your wills in the morning."

The corporal took the limp cigarette out of his mouth and coughed violently. When he had recovered, he said, "You know how it is, Sergeant. Things're bad—mostly boys and old men left behind the front. There were supposed to be four other soldiers with us, but they got sick with typhus. There's a regular epidemic here."

"You shouldn't be saying such things like that in front of the prisoners, Corporal Schuckheider," the sergeant said. "It'll boost their morale."

"They got eyes," the corporal said, wheezing. "Besides, from what I hear, the enemy ain't in any better shape."

"Well, hell," Mixenheimer said. "This is a fine mess. This man here, he's an American aviator flying for the French."

He jerked a thumb at Savage.

"He's escaped several times, stole a Gotha bomber from one of our airfields. I've been told he's very dangerous, though he doesn't seem to be able to hang on to his money. It'll be your ass if you let him escape again."

"He is a big fellow," Schuckheider said. "And he sure has dangerous-looking eyes. I never seen any like them before."

"You should see them in a bright light," Mixenheimer said. "They're killer eyes, tawny like a lion's hide and with golden flecks in them. I think he's crazy. He speaks German, too, better than you or me, like a Prussian baron. So watch him! If he makes any suspicious moves, shoot him! Those're my orders, and now they're yours!"

He took from a side pocket the key to the handcuffs.

"I was supposed to hand this over to the officer in charge. But there isn't any. The orders must've gotten delayed or mixed up along the line. So what's new? Anyway, though you're not a commissioned officer, you are a noncommissioned officer, and my orders didn't specify which kind of officer. My nose is clean, which is more than I can say for your snuffling buddy. Here."

The corporal took the key, though reluctantly.

"Oh, yes," the sergeant added. "Keep the American away from the other prisoners. Don't let him talk to them."

"Maybe it'd be better to shoot him now and get it over with," the corporal said. He looked at Savage and cackled. "Don't worry, Sergeant. He don't scare me none."

"I heard stories about him," Mixenheimer said. "Take my word. Watch him every second."

"Don't worry. No stupid mongrel American is going to put anything over on me."

Schuckheider ordered his charges to get onto the coach. Single file, they started to climb up. Savage was last in line. Just as he reached Mixenheimer, he stumbled and grabbed the sergeant to keep from falling.

Mixenheimer said, "What're you doing? Get your paws off me!"

He shoved the lieutenant away from him. Savage staggered back and sat down heavily on the rocks and cinders.

"Get up!" the sergeant said harshly.

"Sorry," Savage said as he struggled up. "I'm weak from hunger. I tripped on a rock. Couldn't help myself."

"Wait'll you been in Holzminden for a month," the sergeant said. Then, suspiciously, "You pretending to be weak?"

"No," the lieutenant said as he got shakily to his feet. "I've been wounded, too."

Prodded by Schuckheider's rifle, he climbed up the steps into the coach.

The locomotive, puffing and panting and sssing, was connected to a coal car and thirteen coaches. Eleven of these had taken aboard soldiers, apparently going home on leave. Many of these lacked legs and arms and wore heavy bandages around their heads or eyes. The coach for the prisoners was the third from the end. Wooden-walled and rusty-wheeled, it looked as if it had been rotting on a sidetrack for years. Only the extreme urgency brought about by a long and material-devouring war could justify bringing it back into service.

It had been a fourth-class car at its best. Its seats were wooden, its windows were streaked with dust and smoke, the floor was dirty and trash-strewn, and the only light was a kerosene lamp hanging from the middle of the ceiling. Its filthiness attested to the Germans' war-weariness and man-shortage. Under normal circumstances, they were zealously clean.

Savage was told to sit down in a front seat on the left of the car. While he was waiting for the train to start, he looked out the window. The smudged glass gave him a dim view, but he saw that Sergeant Mixenheimer was still near the car. He was talking to another sergeant, who had just arrived with five prisoners escorted by a squad of riflemen.

One of the POWs caught the lieutenant's attention. He wore an officer's cap, but of which army Savage could not make out. He was big, perhaps six feet four inches tall. His shoulders threatened to split his trench coat. His hands were the largest that Savage had ever seen. A Kodiak bear would not have been ashamed to have paws their size.

His face was long and narrow, the thick jawbone curving outward to form a chin that was round and looked like a boxer's punching bag. His expression was of intense gloom. It reminded Savage of the cartoons of the early New England Puritans. Well, there was nothing in his situation to make him smile.

The sergeant who had brought in the new group of POWs was talking earnestly to Mixenheimer. Savage cleared the glass with saliva and his glove. Now he could lip-read somewhat. The sergeant seemed to be telling Mixenheimer that the big fellow had tried to escape twice and was a real troublemaker. At least, that was what Savage thought he was saying. The darkness made it difficult to be sure.

Presently, the new group came aboard. It, like the first group, except for Savage, was seated at the rear of the coach. Three soldiers stayed aboard. That made twelve under guard and four to guard them. But three prisoners were too sick to do anything but moan and groan and ask for water now and then. They would not get any until the next stop.

Minutes passed. Smoke filled the car as soldiers and POWs puffed away.

The train started with a jerk. Mixenheimer was still standing in the same place. He was smoking a cigarette and talking to the other sergeant, who had gotten off the coach. Savage rose and started to raise the window.

"What're you doing?" Schuckheider said. He rose from his seat across the aisle, his rifle bolt clicking.

"The smoke. It bothers me. Just want to get some air. Don't worry. There're troops just outside the window."

The window came up hard. Savage put his manacled hands inside his jacket pocket and threw something out. He leaned far forward and pointed to where it lay on the ground. His voice blared.

"Mixenheimer! Your wallet! Thanks for letting me have it for a moment!"

Despite the ringing of the bell and the grumble of wheels on the track, he was heard. Mixenheimer looked startled, then felt inside his coat. He began running toward where Savage had indicated, his mouth working, obviously cursing.

The lieutenant closed the window and, smiling, sat down.

Schuckheider, leaning over Savage and blowing cheap tobacco smoke in his face, said, "What was that about a wallet?"

"Mixenheimer didn't know he'd dropped it. He'd have found out too late if I hadn't told him he had and where it was."

The corporal began coughing. Savage turned his face away. One of the few things that scared him was disease. Perhaps it didn't really frighten him; it just made him very uneasy to be exposed to deadly bacteria. That was a strange attitude for a would-be doctor, but there it was. He would conquer it. It was a mild phobia, anyway. But this fellow might have tuberculosis, and that had felled millions upon millions. He could fight men and beasts and storm and have a good chance to survive. But the "white plague" did not care how big and strong and agile and clever you were. It took the weak and the sturdy alike, swept through them like fire through a paper house.

He hoped that, someday, he would be qualified to tackle tuberculosis and find a cure for it. But this was 1918, and victory over it seemed a long way off, if it ever would come.

Schuckheider finally quit coughing. He spat a long green string into a brass goboon. He said, "That was very nice of you. Mixenheimer surely would not do that for you, not him!"

Savage looked saintly.

He had stumbled against the sergeant so that he could pick his pocket. Though he was handcuffed, he had managed to extract the man's wallet without the sergeant being aware of it. Savage's father had brought in three of the best pickpockets in the world to teach the young Savage their art. Doctor Savage had told his son that this art might come in handy someday.

Savage had taken out of the wallet half of the money he had paid Mixenheimer. The other half was a fair price for the food and water he had purchased. He doubted that the sergeant would complain to his superiors about the lifted money. He would not want an investigation.

Schuckheider went back across the aisle to a seat. He smoked another cigarette, coughing between puffs. Then he said, "You don't seem like a bad fellow. I'm sorry for what I said, about you being a stupid mongrel American. That was for the sergeant's benefit. Mostly, anyway. I shouldn't have said it. After all, one of my sons went to San Francisco, and he's become an American citizen."

Schuckheider coughed and spat some more, then lit up another cigarette. "Are you really dangerous?"

"Would I tell you if I was?" Savage said, smiling.

"No, guess not. Anyway, I'm going to be discharged when I get home. I will if the doctors have any sense. Which most of them don't have, you know."

He went into a tirade about the medical profession. The lieutenant did not tell him that he meant to be a surgeon.

Then Schuckheider started to doze off, but his coughing kept waking him up. That was a good thing for him, Savage thought. If he was caught sleeping on duty, he'd be shot.

Savage did not try to sleep. If he had, the coughing of the corporal and of the sick men in the back of the coach would probably have kept him awake, too. While the wheels clickety-clacked, he considered the map in his mind. The next town where the train might stop was Sedan. This was where the Prussians in 1870 had won a great victory leading to the fall of France, then ruled by Napoleon III. Its main industries were textiles, chemicals, medical appliances, and food processing. Nine miles above it was the Belgian border.

Belgium was occupied by the Germans. But above it was neutral Holland. It would not be easy getting through Belgium or through the triple wall on the Dutch-Belgian border and the heavily guarded and mined area around it. However, he did not want to delay another attempt at breaking free. With every turn of the train wheels, he was getting closer to Germany.

He was trying to form a reasonably workable plan when he was startled by loud voices in the rear of the coach. Turning around, he saw the big man with the ham-sized fists and dour expression face-to-face with another prisoner. He heard the huge man's voice, too, quite clearly. No escaping from it or ever forgetting it, once it was heard. It was as deep as the voice of God coming down from Mount Sinai. Well, that was an exaggeration, but it certainly was the heaviest basso profundo that Savage had ever encountered.

Now that the man's coat was off, his insignia revealed that he was a captain in the U.S. Engineering Corps.

The two were arguing violently. It seemed that the big man had spit on the other man's shoe. That fellow was short and very thin and pale. He looked like he was suffering from anemia, Savage thought. But he was certainly vigorous enough, screaming at the captain and threatening to punch him out. His insignia was that of a lieutenant in the U.S. Signal Corps.

The gob spat on the Signal Corps man's shoe may not have gotten there accidentally, Savage thought. The argument could be a ploy, a prelude to a breakout attempt. Whether it was or not, it provided him with an opportunity to do what he had been thinking so furiously about. The soldiers around the two were amused and had eyes only for the quarrelers.

Schuckheider was standing and watching them. He held the rifle by one hand.

Then the engineer pushed the other man away and turned and slammed his fist against the wall.

Savage's eyes widened.

That enormous fist had punched a hole in the side of the coach!

The wood was rotten, but it was thick. Savage did not think that he could duplicate the feat. Not without breaking his knuckles and probably his fingers.

Schuckheider jumped back and swore.

The bloodless-looking man jumped on the back of the big man and began pummeling him with his fists. Roaring, the engineer jerked his fist from the wall and whirled around with him, moving to the aisle. The soldiers laughed, and the other prisoners cheered.

Their next move was a surprise to all but Savage. The big man leaned down with the little man's legs wrapped around his trunk. He grabbed both men's greatcoats from the seat, but the anemic man snatched one coat from the huge fist. And the two, the little man riding piggyback, went through the window. Both held the coats before their faces.

The glass shattered. Everybody except Savage froze. He ripped Schuckheider's rifle from his hand and threw it through the window by his seat. He grabbed the bundled flying suit and dived out through the opening, his gloved hands holding the bundle before his face. He would have preferred choosing his own place to jump from, one preferably better lit and over water, if possible. Now was no time to wait, however. The guards would be very alert after the escape of the two Americans.

Out into the darkness, the scream of the locomotive's steam whistle around him, the shouts of the soldiers behind him, and he howling with triumph, he flew. Then he struck the ground so hard that he was knocked out.

XI

When he regained his senses, he was lying on his right side. Darkness and silence sheathed him. But it seemed to him that, inside himself, pain was making its own light. It was flashing in his head, his neck, his face, his left shoulder, his left ribs, and his right knee.

Gritting his teeth and wincing, he sat up. The train had been going too fast to slow down immediately. It would take some time for it to stop and then back up. If it did so. It might still be heading unchecked toward the next station. There it would notify the locally based army officers, and they would send out a search party.

However, if it were backing up, it would soon be here. He had to get going.

He started as an owl hooted somewhere nearby, asking the owls' never-answered question about identity. "Who? Who? Who?"

He called out, speaking in English, "Anyone there? Hey, I'm Lieutenant Clark Savage, Junior! I just escaped, too! Anyone there?"

"Who? Who? Who?"

That was the only reply.

He did not think that the two Americans would suspect a trap. If they had heard him, they would have responded. They must be gone. Or, possibly, they were still unconscious or even dead. Jumping out of a coach going at fifty miles an hour was inviting Old Man Death to come early.

He had to get away into the forest as quickly as possible. But he needed the bundle to help him survive. Wincing and groaning, he got onto his hands and knees and began searching for it. Since he could see nothing in the blackness except the slightly darker mass of the forest along the tracks, he had to explore with his hands. They felt the wooden creosote-soaked ties forming the raised trackbed. A few seconds later, he determined that he was between iron rails. He did not know which of the two sets of tracks it was.

He began circling then. The initial circle would be tight. As he progressed, he would widen the spiral. However, he could not be sure it would cover all the ground that needed covering. He might go in a more or less straight line.

He hoped that he could find the bundle soon. He could not hear the train, but it might have stopped and then reversed its course. Also, he hoped that, if he found the bundle, he would not discover that it was actually something else. That is, the corpse of one of the Americans who had escaped through the window.

His right hand was on top of a rail. He was about to remove it when he felt a faint vibration through the iron. Either another train was coming on the inner tracks or the train from which he had escaped was backing up on the outer tracks. He could not stay here long to find out. He could not even hide in the edge of the woods to determine which train it would be. If it was the one he had jumped from, it would stop somewhere in this area near him. Then soldiers with electric torches would be beating the woods, hoping to flush him out. He should get as far away from here as possible, but he did not want to do that until he knew which direction was north.

He crawled over to the other set of tracks and put his ear against the cold iron of a rail. No vibration in it. But he did not know if this was the outer or inner set. In this darkness, it was impossible to determine that.

Frantically, forcing his pained body to move swiftly, he went on all-fours down the slope. He meant to keep searching until the lights of a train appeared. And then he said, "Ah! Thank God!"

His fingers had touched something soft. It was the bundle he sought. His hand gripped the rope around it, and he stood up. That caused him to groan more deeply and to draw his breath in harsh pain. His right second rib, in medical terms one of the "peculiar" ribs, could be broken.

Limping, he went down the grade slowly and into the woods. Like it or not, he had to stay fairly close to the tracks until he saw a train come by. Otherwise, he would not know which way he had to go to get to the Semois River. When or if he got to it, he would know that he was in Belgium. He was now in the Ardennes region, a thinly populated and forested plateau with many hills. Even if he knew the right direction to go, he might circle when in the lightless woods. There were no stars to guide him through the trees to his destination.

Presently, the headlight of a locomotive shone to his right. He waited until it got stronger. Then a shrill but mournful whistle sounded. He smiled. It did not seem likely that the train from which he had escaped would announce its presence by blowing a steam whistle. But he waited a moment before leaving. He smiled again when he saw that the locomotive was pulling the train. If it had been pushing the cars, it would have been the train from which he had escaped. However, that train might be backing up now and could soon be here, even though it would be moving slowly. The soldiers on it would not know just where he had jumped off, but they could make a rough estimate.

He turned and made his way through the woods. He

went too slowly to suit him, since he kept bumping into tree trunks and bushes and also had to make sure that he would not drop into holes. Moreover, he splashed now and then through bogs, in some of which he sank up to his knees. When he came to his first high hill, he made even slower progress. Sometimes, the climbing got too rough, and he would grope around for an easier place. Now and then, he rested for a few minutes. Then he went down the hill and came to another after wading through a swamp. This was too steep in many places for him to go in a straight line. Hours passed while his resting periods grew longer.

Good sense dictated that he should lie down and try to sleep until dawn. Then he could get a bearing. It was foolish to keep on when he might have gone astray and be walking southward. Nevertheless, he did not stop. He felt sure that he was headed toward the Semois River. Some inner sense told him that he was on the right course. But that inner sense had betrayed him in the past.

He made a longer halt than those before to put on his flying suit. It would make his walking and climbing slower, but the night air had become colder. While he was painfully donning the clothes, he was surrounded by mist. It touched him with cold, wet fingers and barred his seeing his own boots.

Still, he went forward until he came to a shelf of rock, beneath which was a hollow. He crawled into it and spent the remaining hours of darkness in a fitful sleep.

He awoke as rain poured over the stony ledge above the shallow hollow. He was fatigued and very hungry and thoroughly miserable, but he at least would not lack for drinking water. An hour and a half later, he came into sight of the Semois River as he reached the top of a tall hill. Though the sky was still clouded and there were mists blanketing the low ground, he could make out a village far to his left.

To his right, on the crest of the next hill, was a large château. Even from this distance, he could see that many windows were broken. He went down the hill and up the slope until he came to the top. From behind a tree in a grove, he watched for signs of life. No smoke came from any of the ten chimneys. No lights showed. No voice was raised. The small cottages behind the château—servants' quarters, probably—also had broken windows, and their chimneys were smokeless. The place seemed long-deserted.

Despite this, he approached the château cautiously, hiding behind a cottage, observing and listening intently. Then he walked out swiftly toward the central house. But, as he got halfway to it, he heard a growl behind him.

He whirled, the excruciating pain in his ribs making him gasp. Even as he did so, he heard several howls and much snarling. Seven big dogs were running toward him. Their coats were matted and dirty, and they were gaunt. They may have belonged to the now-absent master of the château, but they had been on their own for some time. They were hungry and had probably attacked other human beings. If they had not, they had by now overcome any shyness they might once have possessed.

All this flashed through his mind as he continued his whirl until he was facing toward the château. Then he was running as swiftly as he could, every jarring of a foot on the ground hurting his leg and the broken or cracked ribs. He got to the shattered French windows of a room just as the lead dog clamped its teeth onto his left calf. He sprawled through the opening and slid facedown on broken glass on a parquet floor, the dog hanging on. Fortunately, the heavy leather pants kept the teeth from doing more than breaking the skin of his calf. At least, he thought so. He had no time to assess the injury.

Like most of the pack, the dog was an Alsatian, commonly known in the States as the German shepherd. This one was over two feet high and weighed about eighty-five pounds. It was snarling and slavering while it kept its jaw-grip on the calf of the man it hoped to eat. The others had not caught up with it yet, but they were only ten feet behind the lead dog.

Savage twisted around and brought the edge of his palm hard against the dog's neck. Its grip relaxed as it lay half-stunned. Savage scrambled up, such sharp pain shooting through him that he felt as if he were going to faint.

But he staggered across to the nearest door of the drawing room and slammed it shut behind him as he plunged into the next room. Then he whirled again, at great cost in pain, and opened the door a few inches. Snarling, saliva dripping on the floor, big teeth gleaming, a dog's head came through the opening. Savage slammed his fist between the Alsatian's eyes. He yelled with agony from the pain in his fist, but the dog's eyes glazed. Savage grabbed its nearest ear and dragged it through. At the same time, he kept his shoulder against the door to keep the other dogs from bursting through. Then he shut it.

The pack howled and barked and yelped, and their bodies struck the door again and again. The lieutenant knelt down just as the dog got to its feet, its head hanging low. He closed his hands around its throat, wrestled it to the ground as it tried to bite him, and kept up the pressure until it had quit breathing. Its tongue stuck far out, part of it lying on the floor. Its overly doggy odor spread throughout the room.

There were three other entrances. Unfortunately, two of the doors were missing. Someone had broken off the hinges and carted them off. He did not know why all of the doors had not been removed. Perhaps the looters or scavengers had been interrupted. It did not matter. The fact that one door had been left was his salvation. A temporary rescue, however. Pale spaces on the walls showed where paintings had hung for a very long time. All the drapes, furniture, and carpets were missing. There were many holes in the walls, some gouged out, some made by bullets. Malicious destruction. The room Savage had first entered, the assumed drawing room, had also been stripped of everything, except for the remains of a grand piano. And in the room beyond the one in which he stood were several dried piles of human excrement.

The lieutenant was sorry about looters having gone through this place. That lowered his chances of finding any food. But he would explore the château anyway. That is, he would after he had made sure that the pack would not be coming into this room. The dogs must have been in here since the open French doors had become an invitation. They would know the layout.

Suddenly, the bangings of hurled bodies against the closed door ceased. He put his ear to the wood. The silence did not mean that the dogs had given up the chase. He went into the room to his left and through several doorways that were also missing their doors. Then he heard snarling and growling and the clicking of claws on a bare floor. He ran back, his pain never ceasing, grabbed a hind leg of the carcass, and hauled it through the entrance which still had a door. He closed that. Pulling the dead dog behind him, he went through a series of rooms until he came to the kitchen. This was huge and had several gas stoves and an enormous fireplace with a big iron spit in its gaping mouth.

A few kitchen utensils had been left by the looters. But the open drawers and shelves were stripped of supplies. He wanted a knife. He doubted that any had been overlooked. His head down, clamping his teeth from the pain, he hauled the carcass up the narrow and winding iron staircase to the second story. As he expected, this led to a hall. The doorless entrances showed him small rooms which must have been for servants.

Below, there was a yelping and barking as the dogs followed the scents up the staircase. Down the hall he went, looking for a door to close. Finding none and knowing that he did not have much time, he returned to a room in which parts of a bed had been left. The mattress and sheets and pillows were gone, but the posts and pieces of the frame were on the floor. He grabbed a post and stationed himself by the doorway.

When the first dog lunged in, it was slammed on the head. Its skull shattered, it crumpled, and Savage rammed the end of the post into the open mouth of the second dog as it leaped toward him. Pushing hard despite his pain, Savage propelled the dog out with the end of the post. He pulled it loose from the animal's throat, kicked the third dog under its jaw, breaking it, and banged the fourth on its head. It fell dead.

For a minute, he was not under attack. The dogs

were still eager to get at him, but the losses suffered were making them hesitate. He put down the post, stooped, heaved up an unconscious beast while he grunted with the agony, and hurled it into the hall. Instantly, the dogs were on the inert and defenseless body. Their snarlings, growlings, and snappings made a din while they tore it apart.

While they were fighting over the carcass, Savage dragged the dog he had first killed to the window opening. The glass had been broken, but jagged edges still stuck out from the frame. He punched out the shards with gloved hands and raised the heavy body and put in through the opening. Although the roof was very steep here, he had no choice but to retreat to it. He followed the carcass onto the roof. He had to grab its tail because it was starting to slide down the slick slates.

Sitting down, his knees raised in order to move his feet, he struggled along the roof until he came to a conjunction of two roofs. He got to the top and sat on the ridge for a while.

Faintly, he could hear the ravening dogs.

While he rested, he looked out over the gravel road leading from the front of the château and winding down through the forest. Not a living creature in sight, except for a hawk gliding toward the river. Here and there, he could see the dirt road along the Semois. To the left, it led to the village. Where it went to the right, he did not know.

By then, having gotten some of his strength back, though the pain was not less, he placed the carcass so it sprawled out on both sides of the ridge. He made his slippery way back down to the window through which he had come. He could see one dog out in the hall, tearing off pieces of flesh from a dead comrade, and two doing likewise in the room. Though one of them saw Savage's face, it did not stop eating. Evidently, the pack had killed the dog with the broken jaw and were now getting their fill. He hoped their bellies would be stuffed.

Within thirty minutes, the three survivors had gotten most of the flesh and organs inside them and were gnawing pieces off bones. Though they paid Savage no attention except to eye him now and then and to expose bloodied teeth in snarls directed his way, they would be a menace later. He could leave the house, but he doubted that he could take the dead dog on the roof with him. That move might make them go after him. They would not like to see him departing with a big meal.

He had plans to eat his kill.

That meant that he had to get rid of the still living dogs. He picked up a piece of broken glass, which was narrow and long enough to make a dagger. He crawled through the window opening while the two dogs in the room rose. Snarling, stiff-legged, they guarded their food. Then, as the man got nearer, one leaped at him. Savage thrust the end of the shard into its throat. The impact of the big dog sent him staggering back against the wall. The dog ran off howling, the glass sticking deeply in its throat. It was headed for the doorway but ran directly into the other dog. Thinking it was being attacked, that dog tangled with the wounded one. The lieutenant picked up a broken piece of board from the bed frame and began hitting both animals with it. Yelping and whining, they scrambled into the hall.

Shouting, waving the board, Savage ran all the dogs out of the house. They disappeared into the woods. But they would be back as soon as they got hungry again. After he had rested, he went out onto the roof and brought the carcass back. Then he searched through the many rooms of the château from top to bottom. He found some towels overlooked by the looters, stripped off his clothes, tore the towels into strips, and bound them around his ribs. This was not easy for one man to do, and he suffered much while doing so. Then, having put on all his clothes except the flying suit, he continued his prowling.

He noted the number of rooms, their dimensions, the exits, and the windows. If he had to get out fast, he would be familiar with the layout. It was while he was on the third floor that he noticed a discrepancy. The huge library room was a mess because of the strewn volumes on the floor and the missing shelves and shattered windows and broken statuettes. The big bronze plaque bearing the name and baronial arms of the old family that owned this château—de Musard—had been ripped from the wall. What struck him, however, was the unaccounted-for area between the back wall of the huge library room and the room beyond it.

He puzzled over that for a while before checking out the back wall. His probing fingers finally located a protuberance, a bell-shaped knob, in a fancy eighteenth-century decorative scroll at his eye level. A thin depression ringed the protuberance. The matching knobs lacked this.

He pressed it. It sank in for a quarter of an inch. A section of the wall began swinging out on an unseen center bar. He backed away. When the section was at right angles to the rest of the wall, it stopped turning.

Out of the darkness came a stench of mustiness and dead air and something rotten.

XII

The light from the big windows in the library illuminated dimly only part of the hidden room. He struck one of his few remaining matches and ventured slowly into the cavernous interior. He grunted with amazement at what he saw.

The flame went out. Though very curious to see more, he did not want to use all his matches. But he thought that he had seen several very large candles on the table near the far wall to his left. He groped through the darkness, his eyes gradually adjusting to it, came to the table, and felt a candle in a big metal holder. Using another match, he ignited the wick.

There were human and dog skeletons nailed to the blood-red wallpaper, many coupled in obscene positions or grouped in bizarre arrangements. In the spaces among the skeletons the crimson paper had been painted with figures: black cats, witches' cauldrons, demons, and half-human beasts.

A male skeleton, its bones wired together, hung from the center of the ceiling by a noose attached to its neck vertebrae. Red paint coated its breastbone. A huge wooden phallus was wired to the bones and projected upward. Goat horns stuck out from the top of the grinning head.

Chairs which looked like they were made during the reign of King Louis XIV of France were arranged in three rows of three chairs each in the back of the room.

Before Savage was the table, ten feet long and four feet high and made of some glossy and blood-colored wood. Around its bowed legs serpents coiled, their heads half-snake, half-woman. At each corner of the table was a black wax candle in a bronze holder. The holders had been cast into the form of devils, with their heads far back, holding between their teeth the bottoms of the candles. In the middle of the table was a long basin carved out of a single piece of black marble.

Five feet from the table was the wall. Attached to the wall was a slab of bronze with a figure in alto relief of a goat-legged, ram-horned, bull-phallused, and fork-bearded man, grinning, a tiny writhing nude woman clamped between its pointed teeth.

Savage leaned over the stone basin to see better what was inside it. Old dried bloodstains splotched its cavity. The bones of an infant, perhaps six months old, lay in the center. Beside them was a large sharp knife.

Savage was horrified.

What horrified him even more, while also mystifying him, was a long whitish worm moving slowly over the spine bones.

He thought that he had a thorough grounding in the invertebrate phyla. But he could not classify this creature. It was, as far as he was aware, a worm unknown to science. But then he did not know everything.

He took the candle out into the library and blew out the flame. He sat down. He was shaken. The concealed room was where Black Masses were held, or so it seemed to him. The infant and probably the people whose skeletons were nailed to the wall had been sacrificed during the insane rites practiced here. They could not have taken place without the knowledge and help of the owner of the château. Probably, Baron de Musard or whoever lived here was the chief priest of this ghastly religion, the roots of which went back to the Old Stone Age. But in this latter-day form, devil worship, it was a perversion of that ancient religion. It had been influenced and distorted by the Christian faith which was its worst enemy, had become the left-handed mirror image of the religion that was trying to stamp it out.

This glimpse into hideousness reminded Clark of what his father had told him when they were in the interior of Australia. Clark was fourteen years old then—was it only two years ago?—and had gone to the backcountry to learn tracking from the greatest experts in the world, the aborigines. A North American Indian or a Congo pygmy was a novice in tracking compared to the tribesmen of Down Under. So, Doctor Savage had put his son under the tutelage of Writjitandel of the Wantella people. Young Clark lived with the tribe, wore their simple clothes, ate the food they ate, hunted the animals they killed, and learned how to survive in one of the most desolate and harsh climates in the world.

At the same time, he studied his lessons from the books he had brought with him. This greatly amused Writjitandel, who could see nothing but a waste of time in studying printed matter.

Doctor Savage was then prospecting for gold fifty miles from the aboriginal camp. Every fourteen days or so, Clark ran fifty miles, stopping only briefly, to visit his father. It was during one of these visits that his father had spoken about the evil in this world and the need to fight it.

Clark knew that his father was obsessed with this, but he was not certain about its cause. Now and then, Doctor Savage had spoken of it. He was, however, rather vague in that he did not specify names or places or acts. All Clark knew was that his father had, as a young man, done something criminal and serious. But his father had regretted whatever he had done—repented, to use a religious term. Because of his evil deed or deeds, he had sworn to combat crime. Which meant that he had to battle against criminals.

Clark remembered sitting outside the shack near the diggings while a glorious desert sunset unfolded peacocklike at the end of the world.

"When I say evil," Doctor Savage said, "I am speaking in the abstract, of course. Philosophically and practically, there is no such thing as evil. It is not a person or an animal or a tree. It's a concept which humans, being human, have personified. Humanized. There is, I repeat, no such force or element or thing as evil with a capital E.

"But there are humans who do evil things. And we—I speak for Homo sapiens, of which I am, often regretfully, sometimes gladly, a member—also regard certain other humans as evil, just as we do certain destructive and killing natural forces, like storms, floods, volcanic eruptions, and diseases, and various animals, such as man-eating tigers, malaria-carrying mosquitoes, and so forth.

"But these are evil only because humans call them evil. They do so because they are bad for those humans affected adversely by them. You have ingested by now the essence of meaning of my little lecture, its core and direction, correct?"

"More than somewhat," Clark said.

His father spoke with an English pronunciation and pitch. Standard Oxford English, though now and then he uttered, with humorous intent, phrases in a dialect which his son, ever-curious and untiringly assiduous in research, discovered to be Yorkshire.

But his father never offered to disclose his origins or the story of how he came to flee England and to take up American citizenship, and Clark never asked. He respected his father's reticence and was grateful for the few hints he did get about the doctor's past. But after his father died, Clark intended to do some detective work. Meanwhile, the present and the future were all that mattered.

"It's difficult to define the criminal mind," the doctor said. "Why? Because everybody has the potentiality to be a criminal. But you know that. What I hope is that you will concern yourself with combating only the big criminals. Pickpockets and robbers and muggers are not in your venue. Unless, of course, you run into them during your battle."

His father spoke of fighting crime as if it were a war between nations, a struggle between empires. The borders were well marked, the boundaries long established, the causes of the war and the issues clearly defined. One side was black. One side was white. The doctor would not admit this in a philosophical sense, but he spoke of it as if there were no shadows, no gray zones.

Clark was not so sure.

"Crime?" he said. "Criminals? What about the wealthy and powerful who operate within the bounds of the law, and yet, as the journalists say, rob the widows and the orphans of their life savings? Deprive the poor and the powerless of their homes, of food, of a means of livelihood? Or exploit them mercilessly? What about lawyers who work on the narrow edge of legality, or cross it? Doctors who are quacks and crooks? And so forth?"

His father had thrown up his hands.

"Millions of them!" he had cried. "You can't change society all by yourself, though you can try. You can't change the nature of man. But you can do your little bit, my son. And if you defeat the big criminal, your little bit becomes larger."

There was the question of just how, if he became a surgeon, he would find time to be a fighter against so many criminals. His father, of course, hoped that the medical profession would be only one among several of his specialties.

They were rather vague goals that Doctor Savage had picked out for him. His father's experiences had, perhaps, twisted him a little. Certainly, he was not normal—whatever that meant—and he was a zealot.

On the other hand, his father had not insisted that he adopt his goals if he did not wish to do so. He had to give his father credit for that. He had given his son a choice. But had the son gone along with his father only to please him?

He did not really know. He suspected, however, that

he was like his father in many ways. The life plan that his father wanted him to follow did please him. He was not at all reluctant to accept it.

Whether or not there was such a thing as abstract evil, humans acted and thought as if there were. Clark knew that he was different in some things from other humans, but he was essentially the same in nature.

Nevertheless, he could never have done what de Musard and his band had done. That was a hideousness beyond him, as it was beyond most people. It was psychopathic, and perhaps de Musard had no control over his actions. But if he, Clark Savage, ever got a chance to put the murderers—and perhaps torturers—behind bars, he would do so.

There really was not much chance for that, though.

For a moment, he felt helpless before the forces of evil. There was that vast evil wreaking its deviltry just now, World War I. And there was the small but not insignificant evil wrought by de Musard and people like him. What could he, a single man, do about such things?

As his father had once said, he would probably get plenty of opportunities. Evil people would find him blocking their plans and would try to get him out of their way. And he would stumble into evil workings.

For the time being, he had to forget all that. He had to survive and to make his way, somehow, into neutral Holland.

XIII

He did some more exploring. It seemed to him that there might be another secret entrance to the hidden room. After an hour of experimentation, he found that he was right. The great bronze plaque of the horned god swung out when its left eye was pressed.

He closed the door leading to the library. Someone could enter through it and take him by surprise, though that was not likely. After putting the knife in his belt, he lit the candle again and went by its flickering light down a very narrow staircase in a brick shaft. Though he walked down three stories and the basement, he kept on going to another level, a subbasement. It was a very large room, stone-walled, damp, and musty. An air shaft led upward from a hole in the ceiling.

The room was not only a hideaway; the baron had stocked its many shelves with staples and delicacies. Barrels of water, a portable chemical toilet, and soap and shaving equipment were in one corner. Near another corner was a gun case with ammunition in a drawer beneath it. Clark chose a Smith & Wesson hammerless revolver and loaded a coat pocket with the .38-caliber ammunition.

Then, salivating, he opened cans of ham, biscuits, butter, lemon juice, and artichokes. He would not have to cook and eat that dog after all.

While he ate, he wondered again what had happened to the baron and the other people here. Obviously, the baron had been taken by surprise. Otherwise, he would have found refuge in this room. Either German soldiers or outlaws had surprised him. Or, possibly, the villagers in this area had suspected the baron of abducting and doing away with people. They might have taken justice into their own hands.

Whatever had happened, the place had been looted.

Savage suspected that he would never know. But this was his lucky day. He had discovered a wonderful hideout, and he could eat well while his wounds healed. When he left this château, and he would as soon as he was recovered, he would pack plenty to eat for the trip. Thus, he could avoid the need to steal food. That had caused many POWs to be caught.

Four days later, two hours after sunset, he went down the hill on the gravel road to the muddy road that ran along the Semois River. The sky was overcast. He carried an electrical torch from the baron's storeroom, but he did not dare use it. An hour later, he had stolen a small boat tied up to a dock near a lone cottage. When he got to the other side, he tied the boat to a stump and went through a stretch of woods before coming to another road. He crossed this into the trees. Because he could not see well in the darkness and refused to use the torch unless he absolutely had to, he made slow progress.

At dawn, he climbed a tree to scout out the territory. A few miles away was a small village with a road running through it. He would avoid that and cut through the farms that surrounded the village. During the day, he would sleep inside a large brush pile nearby. A few minutes later he crawled into it with his bag of supplies. He went to sleep almost at once, snug and warm in his flying suit, and covered by the brush.

Voices and the barking of dogs yanked his eyelids open. He slithered on his belly to the entrance of the hole he had made and looked out. The sunlight was bright. He estimated that noon was near. Through the spaces among the trees, he saw a man running swiftly. His greatcoat flapped after him while his long thin legs pumped. About two hundred feet behind him, dogs bounded. Behind them were a dozen gray-clad soldiers wearing coal-scuttle helmets. Several had stopped and aimed their rifles. The weapons banged.

The refugee threw up his hands and fell hard on his face. He did not move after that.

Poor devil! Clark thought. Another escaped POW.

He went back into the hole. Ten minutes later, he heard voices very near. That was bad enough. What was worse was the sudden clamor of dogs. They had been whining, but they now broke into loud and frantic-sounding barks. They had found something exciting, and Clark was afraid that he was it.

He was very much *it*. The dogs could not get at him because they were pulled back on leashes. But a German soldier, peering cautiously around the side of the bush, yelled that whoever was in the hole should come out. Now. Otherwise, he would be shot out.

Heartsick, Savage replied that he was an American soldier. He would crawl out and surrender.

It was hard to have gone through so many dangers,

suffered so many injuries, struggled so much, escaped so many times, be so close to being free of the enemy, so near to his goal, and then be caught because of dogs.

Clark had always loved dogs. At this moment, he hated the entire canine species.

He came out and rose slowly while a dozen rifles were pointed at him. He was searched, and his knife, pistol, and ammunition were taken from him. A soldier went into the hole and came out with the bag of provisions. This group was the nastiest he had so far encountered. Their officer, a captain, made no protest when the captive was stripped of his flying suit. Savage never saw it again. Nor did the captain say anything when a private rammed the butt of his rifle into the American's shoulder. Nor open his mouth except to grin when several soldiers beat him with their fists, knocked him down, and started to kick him. The lieutenant curled into a ball. Fortunately, nobody put his boot into his ribs, though they probably would have if the captain had not decided that their prisoner had had enough. He barked an order, and the soldiers backed away.

Between then and when he got to Camp Loki was a long and miserable voyage. Though interrogated five times at different locations, he refused to answer any questions. He was handcuffed throughout, except when locked in a cell at different stations. His complaints to various officers about his treatment, including the theft of his flying suit and provisions, were met with statements that it would be investigated. He did not believe them.

Halfway through the trip, some POW swarming with "cooties," the body lice so familiar to troops in the trenches, boarded the coach. The parasitic insects spread swiftly to the others. Their hosts itched and scratched and swore and became very irritable. Savage was infested with them.

The bites were bad enough, but the diseases they carried, especially typhus, worried him. It did not help him at all to know that the feces of *Pediculus humanus* infected Homo sapiens through skin abrasions caused by the scratches. Nor did it allay his fears when the carrier abruptly began suffering from headache, appetite loss, and apathy. The fever would inevitably start soon after. The soldier would then be afflicted with a series of chills, marked weakness, and a rash over most of his body. If the soldier did not die, he would recover eventually, other circumstances aside. But the soldier, like all those on the coach, had a low resistance because of the meager and unhealthy diet.

The German officer in charge was horrified at the outbreak. He wanted to stop at the nearest station and give the full treatment to the captives: shaving of body hair, a hot water-and-soap shower, a pickle bath in a chemical solution deadly to lice, and fumigation of all the clothes of the afflicted. But his request was denied, and the coach traveled on. Thereafter, the captain and his men stayed as far away as possible from the POWs. However, the sick man was taken off the train at the city of Munich.

There, Clark saw several taxies, the wheels of which had iron double-rims instead of rubber tires. The British naval blockade of Germany had caused many shortages. The rations were somewhat better here, though. And the prisoners were finally treated for the cooties. The quality of life improved for them, though not by much.

At Munich, most of the POWs were taken off, and another group, much smaller, was brought aboard. These men, like Clark, were manacled, and four more guards were added. One of the newcomers caught Clark's eye. He towered to six feet seven inches and was so thin that daylight should have shone through him. Unlike the others, he was in civilian clothes. His face was bruised and scratched, and one arm was in a sling.

Clark did not learn the man's name until they got to the camp. Clark was still kept apart from the group and was not allowed to speak to anybody but his guards. He thought that the Germans must consider him to be especially dangerous. From the talk among the guards, he knew that all on the coach were scheduled to go to Loki.

Just why a civilian would be sent there, he could not guess.

The coach was uncoupled and attached to another line of cars. Then the locomotive went gradually southeastward. It was evident that it was headed for Germany's Oberbayern province, the eastern part of which formed a knife point in the belly of Austria, Germany's staunchest ally. It was relatively near the beautiful city of Salzburg, Mozart's birthplace. The prisoners were in mountainous country which would get rougher and higher. And then Clark passed through a village which he recognized. At the age of ten, he and his father and their German instructor had stayed there for a while.

On the last day of the journey, the train turned onto a single set of tracks that looked as if it had been recently built. The train stopped after going a quarter-mile. Another train, a locomotive and two coaches, was waiting for it. The guards were replaced by those who would go along with the prisoners to their next destination—probably Camp Loki, Clark thought. These were middle-aged men but, except for one, tough-looking. He was a private and was tall, thin, bald-headed, and as sad-looking as a bloodhound. His name was Hans Kordtz, and he was assigned to stick close to Savage and to watch him carefully.

This information he whispered to Savage after they had boarded and the train had started rolling. Clark was still isolated from the other prisoners, but not by much. One row of empty seats was between him and the POWs behind him.

Speaking a sort of Pidgin English distorted by the local German pronunciation, Kordtz said, "You should be getting packages from home eventually. Mostly food, if you're like the other prisoners. I love chocolate, and I like all kinds of food. Except vegetables. If you need anything I can get for you, any little favors I can do for you without sticking my neck out too far, I'm your man.

"Especially if you have chocolate."

He leaned back and was silent for a long time. Then, speaking softly out of the side of his mouth, he said, "My wife is crazy about chocolate, too."

"I'll keep all that in mind," the lieutenant whispered.

Minutes passed. Then Kordtz said, "Real coffee would be very welcome."

"I get the picture," Savage said. "Your *Feldwebel* is looking our way. He's getting suspicious."

Kordtz glanced at his sergeant, a bull-necked and square-faced man with a long and upcurling Kaiser Wilhelm mustache. The rest of the trip, Kordtz was silent.

The train was on tracks running through country with which the lieutenant was not familiar. But he had been through it with his father and his language teacher. When the train turned south and came to the mountainside east of and above a large and very blue lake, he knew where he was.

Not far from here to the north was the town of Berchtesgaden. It was in a deep valley surrounded on three sides by Austrian territory. He had spent three days there, during which he had climbed Obersalzberg Mountain above the town.

The lake was the Königssee, King's Lake, also called Bartholomaussee, St. Bartholomew's Lake. It was 1,975 feet above sea level and in a deep cut ringed by sheer-sided limestone mountains rising to 8,200 feet. Its length was about five miles, and its width varied from five hundred yards to more than a mile. It had been stocked with Alpine trout. The area around it was a nature reserve, though there were some villages near it.

The rail bed on the eastern side had been cut recently from the limestone. On the left were very steep cliffs. On the right, close to the tracks, was the edge of the cliffs dropping straight to the lake.

After a while, the locomotive, which had been puffing and panting up a steep grade, came to a level and picked up speed. But not for long. The cliffs on the left suddenly fell away, just after the train had passed a hollowed-out area in the cliff in which was a guardhouse. Six riflemen stood outside the house, and three big Alsatian dogs stood by them.

A double row of barbed wire ran from beside the tracks to the house. A barbed-wire gate had been swung away from over the tracks to allow the train to pass. When shut, it would extend to a post driven into the rock a foot from the edge of the cliff. Two long horizontal poles stuck

out from the outer gatepost. The space between was filled
with barbed wire to prevent anyone from passing around
the gate on the narrow ledge.

The train began slowing down. The open area, carved
out of the rock, widened.

The lieutenant took in every detail. If he escaped
again, he needed to know everything about the terrain and
the man-made obstacles.

Hissing, bell clanging, the locomotive stopped.

"All out!" the sergeant shouted. "Prisoners, single file!
Keep quiet, or I'll shut your mouths for you, sure as my
name is Schleifstein!"

The captives picked up their belongings. Savage had
nothing to carry. He had purchased from a German soldier
a greasy and frayed stocking cap and a greatcoat with
several bullet holes and tears. He kept the cap on most of
the time to cover his shaven head. Though he would not
have admitted it to anyone, he was somewhat vain about
his reddish-bronze hair.

He stepped out on the right side of the train. The
prisoners were hustled into a formation facing the camp
while the train backed out. He swept the area with his
eyes. If it had been literally possible, his heart would have
sunk.

"I'll be superamalgamated!" the man beside him said
softly. He was the fellow in civilian clothes, the one whom
Savage had heard a prisoner describe as "the advance
agent for a famine, a stork-legged drinking straw, two men
tall and half a man wide, a shadow made flesh."

The civilian added, "If any offspring of our anthropoid
ancestors, Adam and Eve, can escape from this petrous
trap, I'll kiss his glutei maximi. His minimi, too. May the
sauerbraten-masticator who thought this place up be inflicted
with Tantalean and Sisyphean torments to the end of
Ragnarok and Götterdämmerung. And to the end of real
time, pseudo-time, and the entropic universe. And thereafter. Amen."

Savage continued surveying the area while several
corporals unlocked the handcuffs on the prisoners. The
ground was rock. There would be no digging of tunnels

here. Even if one could be carved out of the limestone, where would the tunnelers then go? There were sheer and smooth cliffs on three sides of the camp. The open side, which was behind him, led to the edge of the cliff, which rose from the lake to a thousand feet above it. That side was not fenced with barbed wire. No one in his right mind, however, would try to climb down that sheerness. The wind that blew up from the lake was enough to sweep off the rock face any climber who had no scaling equipment, no ropes or pitons.

The only way out was the way they had come in.

While roll call was being made, he sketched the layout of the camp in his mind. It covered much more area than he had first thought. In fact, it seemed to be not one camp but two. A tall double row of barbed wire divided it. This ran from the east cliff to near the open edge of the cliff along the lake. But it had a gate like the one opened for the train when it entered. The tracks ran into the second part for a hundred feet, then stopped. Beyond was a stretch of rock floor which ended at the cliff. Here the wall came to the edge of the mountain.

It was hard to take in everything. There were guard towers with two floors, manned by soldiers and supplied with machine guns and searchlights. There were many buildings whose purpose he did not yet know. He could see in the distance what seemed to be an opening in the mountain. A set of narrow-gauge tracks ran from it to the railroad tracks. A number of mining carts were on it. These tracks stopped by the railroad tracks, where a steam-powered crane stood idly.

He could not see everything to his right, because he was supposed to look straight ahead. But he could see that the camp beyond the wire wall was much like the one in which he stood, including an entrance to a mine. However, it was much wider and there were many more men in it. Even at this distance, he determined that they wore the uniforms of Russian soldiers.

He would have been surprised that Russian POWs had not been sent home if he had not known how slowly repatriation was accomplished. The Bolsheviks who had

taken over Russia after the revolution in 1917 had with-
drawn March 3 of this year from what they called the
"capitalist-imperialist" war. The Treaty of Brest Litovsk
had confirmed that Germany and Russia were no longer at
war.

Camp Loki was not only a prison for incorrigible
escapees; it was a camp for Russian POWs.

Sergeant Schleifstein reported to a lieutenant, who
reported to a captain, who reported to a major. The latter
was a gorilla-paunched, bushy-mustached, and very red-
faced man named Heinrich Schiesstaube. He was the
camp adjutant representing the camp commandant, Colonel von Hessel, who represented the Kaiser of Imperial
Deutschland. He roared out a long harangue while he
strode back and forth whacking his thigh with a riding
crop. Then he thundered out the camp regulations and
disciplines, his voice like God's on Mount Sinai. After this
he spoke about working in the salt mines.

Savage was not surprised that the two openings in the
east cliff led to salt mines. This area was famous for them.

No Allied man, Schiesstaube said, would be forced to
labor in the mine. However, those who did it would be
awarded extra rations and privileges.

Savage was to find out later that most of the POWs
had volunteered because of this, and also because it gave
them something with which to fill in the time. Another
reason was that they might somehow secretly dig an
escape tunnel.

By this rationalization, the volunteers appeased their
consciences for helping the enemies' war efforts. The camp
adjutant for the prisoners, Colonel Angus Duntreath, a
Scotsman, approved of their volunteering, also with escape in mind.

The Russians had no choice. If they were not officers,
they worked, and they did not get extra rations and
privileges.

The Allied prisoners were commanded not to commu-
nicate with the Russians. If they went within thirty feet of
the barbed wire separating the two camps, they would be
severely punished, perhaps shot.

Schiesstaube having finished his demands, promises, and threats, the new prisoners were marched off to their barrack. Savage was assigned a bed in a large room he would share with thirty others. He was no longer kept from his fellows. All were regarded as incorrigibles.

That evening, they were marched off to the big building which housed both the kitchen and the mess room for the POWs. The food was the usual teeth-breaking black bread, watery turnip or potato soup, sugared beet water, hard half-cooked potatoes, and cups of thin chickory. Savage ate all of it, looking around as he did so and talking to his seatmates. But he was mainly attracted to two officers who sat facing him, one table from his.

They were the two with whom he had fled from that French farmhouse. The man who looked like a Neanderthal and the man who had been shot while crossing the creek. The squeaky voice and the baritone, the one the apish man had called Ham. They had been recaptured and sent here. The handsome hawk-faced baritone must not have been wounded badly. He looked and acted as if he were healthy, though he may have lost a few pounds.

His dark eyes, ever probing, fastened on Savage. He nudged his companion and pointed at the young flier. Monk's little eyes widened, and he grinned. His teeth seemed big enough to bite through bone.

After the POWs had marched out of the mess hall, they were free for a while to do anything their keepers did not forbid. Savage went up to the two, who smoked while they watched some Britishers arguing about the possibility of playing soccer on a field of solid stone. He introduced himself.

"Lieutenant-Colonel Theodore Marley Brooks, French Foreign Legion, as of now," the baritone said. "Hope to transfer to the American forces, if I ever get out of here and back to the front again. This anthropoidal individual is Lieutenant-Colonel Andrew Blodgett Mayfair, U.S. Infantry. His presence here is accounted for by an experiment being conducted by the American government. It's sprung a bunch of chimpanzees from the zoo and enlisted them in the army. They're supposed to be good officer material.

But the government's going broke buying bananas for them. You can see why he's nicknamed Monk."

Mayfair—"Monk"—grinned. He said, "Ham's a lawyer, so you can't believe a word he says. Go ahead. Ask him why he's called Ham."

"You're just a lieutenant," Brooks said a little stiffly. He was no longer smiling. "So I advise you not to address me as Ham. I don't like it at all, mainly because it reminds me of a very distressing situation in which this eternal child, a jungle Peter Pan, put me in. A totally undeserved and eminently unfair predicament, I assure you. My loathsome colleague here will someday get what's coming to him, you can bet your fortune on that. Meanwhile, do not utter that disgusting epithet within my hearing."

Mayfair looked gleeful. "Don't worry, kid. I'll give you the straight poop later on."

"He's a chemist," Brooks said. "His brain, which wasn't much to begin with, has been rotted by breathing in all those toxic fumes. He confuses reality with fantasy. Don't believe a word he says."

"Look who's talking about lying," Mayfair said, and he snorted. "A lawyer, spelled s-h-y-s-t-e-r."

The lieutenant was surprised that two high-ranking officers would talk in such a manner in front of him. They were certainly odd. Also, democratic. Instead of that putting him at ease, however, it embarrassed him. Some time would have to pass before he accepted their never-ending squabbling and insult-exchanging as normal. Normal for them, that is.

Lieutenant-Colonel Brooks turned to Savage. "We've heard about you," he said. "Overheard two guards discussing your exploits the day before you arrived. Apparently, your reputation galloped in ahead of you."

"I escaped a few times," Savage said. "That's why I'm here."

Monk Mayfair snorted again. "Don't be so modest, kid!" he said loudly but squeakily. "We know about how you stole a Gotha bomber from a kraut air base right under their noses! The rest of it, too! In fact, I understand

that the camp commandant, von Hessel himself, had you
locked up and you escaped anyway!"

Clark Savage did not like talking about himself, espe-
cially when it might sound as if he were boasting. He said,
"The baron was accompanied by a beautiful Russian blonde,
Countess Idivzhopu. Is she here?"

"Is she?" Monk Mayfair cried. "You can bet your
sweet patootie she is! What a doll! Scrumptious! She got
here yesterday: you shoulda heard the whistles and wolf
howls! The krauts hustled us into the barracks and wouldn't
let us come out all day! But it was worth it, seeing a
woman like that after starving to death for sight of a real
Cleopatra! A real vamp, that one! Talk about your French
babes! Give me a Russky any old day!"

"Don't let your lack of enthusiasm get you down,
Monk," Brooks said. "Why von Hessel would bring his
mistress to this godforsaken place, I don't know. But..."

"You don't know?" Monk said. "Let me tell you about
the birds and the bees, the stork and the cabbage patch!"

"He's skirt-crazy," Ham Brooks said. "Which is too
bad. With a face like that, he scares women and babies,
and dogs growl at him."

"Yeah?" Monk said. "Who won out with Fifi the
barmaid in that town that sounds like a sneeze? A-choo?"

"The mangler of French means Acheux," Brooks said.

At that moment, the very tall and thin civilian strolled
up. He introduced himself as Doctor William Harper
Littlejohn. "Call me Johnny," he said, smiling. "I'm not an
M.D. The degree is in geology. I was also working on a
Ph.D. in archaeology when the war broke out. I was
helping dig up an ancient Germanic site near Munich
when America declared war. I should have known better
than to hang around so long, but... Anyway, I was interned
in a civilian camp. That I'm here tells you I was a fly in
their ointment, anything but balm in Gilead for them. I
was, as your optics assure you, finally caught by our
Teutonic antagonists."

"This is a military-prisoner camp," Brooks said. "I
don't think it's legal to put you here."

"Present your motion to dismiss him tomorrow," Monk

said, and he laughed. "I'm sure von Hessel will be sympathetic. If he doesn't have you shot."

Johnny looked around, then spoke softly. "The biggest collection of escape artists in the world is here. I don't care how daunting this place is. We can get out."

Brooks said, "You're a civilian, and you haven't been here long. So maybe you don't know the rules. Ours, I mean. All escape plans have to go through Colonel Duntreath and be approved by him. Escape is a group project here. Everybody works on it, even if it's only for the benefit of a few. I suggest you take your plan, if you have one, to the colonel."

Dr. Littlejohn looked embarrassed. "I have no plan to redelineate the probability of our futurity so far. But I'll mentate one and present it to our Caledonian Imperator."

"Use simple words when you explain," Monk Mayfair said. "Some of us ain't got much education. Nohow."

Savage said, "It seems to me that we can't make any plans until we know every physical detail about this place. That includes the mine. And correct me if I'm wrong, but none of us has been here long enough to learn all about the routine of the Germans here. We have to adapt any plan to that."

"Teach your grandmother to suck eggs," Monk said. But he smiled.

"Good thinking, Lieutenant," Brooks said. "I respect your opinion, because of your track record."

"Meanwhile," Monk said, "how about that countess?"

The two launched into a ridiculous discussion of a campaign designed to get the Russian blonde to themselves, when they could then pit their charms against each other, and let the better man win.

That seemed a waste of time, so Savage drifted off with the geologist, Johnny. But he looked back when he heard singing. The two had their arms around each other and were blasting out a song popular in the States, one that seemed appropriate for them:

"The Wild Wild Women Are Making a Wild Man of Me."

Later, they strolled, still singing, into the barracks.

This time, they were belting out "Sinbad Was in Bad All the Time." That, as it turned out, was also appropriate for them.

Being around them was like attending a Mad Tea Party, Savage thought. They were the March Hare and the Mad Hatter, though which was which he did not know.

The physical pattern of Camp Loki (named after the Old Norse evil trickster-god) surprised Savage. He had been told that it was basically a small fortress built over the entrance to a series of small caves dug in the salt dome. The POWs were kept in these caves. The setup was designed to make it one hundred percent escape-proof. Also, it was meant to lower the prisoners' morale, because they would seldom see the sun and sky.

Someone or something had caused the original plan to be changed. Now, the only remnants of the fortress were two stone towers, one on each side of the mine entrance for the Allied POWs. These were watchtowers. He would not find out until much later why the first plan had been shelved.

A flier, looking down on the camp, would see a pattern like a cross inside a horseshoe. The latter was formed by the semicircle of the cliff surrounding the stone floor. The cross was composed of barbed-wire fences. These divided the camp into four sections. The two parts near the edge of the cliff above the lake were the German portions. The northeast quadrant was tenanted by the Allied POWs; the southeast, by the Russian POWs. Each of the inner sections had its own entrance to the salt mines, and the Allied and the Russian men were separated there, too.

XIV

Savage spent the next few days studying and memorizing the layout of the place and the procedures followed by the Germans. He also cultivated Private Hans Kordtz, though that could only be done when no guards or officers were watching them. Kordtz was looking forward to doing whatever kind thing he could for Savage, in return for a share of the food and goodies Savage would someday get. Kordtz said that the German authorities had reported the prisoners' names and military post office addresses to the Allied authorities and the International Red Cross. The U.S. government would pass on this information to relatives at home. Packages of food and supplies sent by these to the prisoners would, theoretically, get to the intended recipients. Though not swiftly.

"If any letters to you get through," Kordtz said, "ask for chocolate when you write back."

The Bavarian lived in the village of Königssee, where he had been born and raised. He got home every two weeks for a three-day pass, if his sergeant was in a good mood. Things there, as he confided, were not always pleasant. Though he did not go into lurid detail, he gave the impression that his domestic situation was much like Rip van Winkle's. But chocolate, like music, had a charm to soothe the savage breast.

Clark did not see the commandant, von Hessel, during this time. He did see Lili Bugov, Countess Idivzhopu, once. She stepped out from the front door of the commandant's house during the morning *appel*, or roll call. She was in a low-cut, peach-colored morning dress; her ash-blond hair was piled up on top of her head in a most fetching arrangement. Behind her came Zad, her enormous bodyguard, whom Savage had thrown into the cast-iron bathtub in the monastery.

Despite Schiesstaube's ragings and bellowed commands to be silent, the prisoners saluted "the ravishing Russian," as they called her, in their various fashions. The British were the most restrained, confining themselves to low murmurs of appreciation. The French rolled their eyes and swore and blew kisses at her. The Americans gave vent to loud whistles and shouts of, "Oh, you beautiful babe!" or similar sentiments.

Clark Savage was silent, but he did look hard.

The countess did not seem offended. She smiled

radiantly and waved her hand at them and blew a kiss back.

"You're all barbarians!" Schiesstaube roared. "But you Yankees are the worst of all! Scum! Mongrels! Scourings of sewage ditches! Illegitimate offspring of hyena dung! Shut up, or you'll all be in solitary confinement!"

"Not near enough room for that!" someone shouted. "Besides, it's illegal!"

That would be Ham Brooks.

Schiesstaube whacked his riding crop against his thigh so hard that he yelped with pain and danced around for a few steps. That evoked laughter. When he had recovered, his face so red it looked as if it had been boiled, he shook the crop at the prisoners. He screamed, "I'll give you all a taste of this!"

Someone brayed like a jackass. That, Clark knew, would be Monk. Then his squeaky voice came clearly. "You got a riding crop! Get a horse, Hun!"

Johnny's voice followed his. For once he did not use big words. "The front half of one, anyway! You already make the hind half!"

That did it. The prisoners were confined to the barracks, were not given supper, and had to go to bed immediately after dusk.

"He must think we're little kids," Monk said.

"I hope we get breakfast," Johnny said. He not only looked half-starved all the time; he was.

The lieutenant had managed to learn what each building in the camp was for. The one especially intriguing him was von Hessel's laboratory. It was next to his house, connected to it by a roofed walk. The lieutenant's efforts to get the guards to talk about its contents and purpose came to nothing. Hans Kordtz, his most talkative informant, just shrugged and said that there was a lot of equipment and chemicals in there and a number of rats and monkeys in cages. Von Hessel spent much time in there. Too much time, most people thought. He seldom appeared in public except to stroll around the grounds, sometimes with the countess leaning on his arm. He let that *arschloch*, Schiesstaube, run the camp.

"Sometimes, though," Hans said, "the baron goes over to the Russian camp to visit their hospital. An awfully large number of them are sick, and there are some dying every day. They seemed healthy enough when they first came here, long before the Allied prisoners came—in fact, the camp wasn't completely built. Of course, they're mostly peasants; not very clean, to say the least."

Savage said, "Hmm!" and looked thoughtful. Then he said, "I meant to ask before this: Where do they bury the dead?"

Hans pointed at the mine entrance.

"There's a big room deep down there. They dig graves in it and cover the corpses with salt. Except for some whom the commandant dissects. I was told he also has a collection of tissue samples there."

Hans shuddered. "Pretty gruesome, if you ask me."

The American was more puzzled than enlightened by the discussion. Von Hessel seemed to be involved in many fields. It was likely that he was connected with or working directly for German Intelligence. At the same time, he was doing some kind of experimental biological research. And he was also commandant of a prison camp. Here was a fellow with many irons in the fire, several fingers in several pies.

Meanwhile, despite his burning curiosity about von Hessel, he had to focus primarily on breaking out of Camp Loki. So far, he had not figured out a way to smuggle himself out. The high-security measures here seemed to make that impossible. Moreover, unlike other camps, this one had a setup which would prevent the POWs from making fake German uniforms and fake travel and ID documents. Some guards might be bribed to bring in articles to their charges. But these items would have to be innocuous. The guards were strip-searched before they went on their infrequent leaves and after they came back.

The only possible expeditious instruments of quasi-instantaneous egress, as Johnny might say, were the iron pipes that brought up water from the lake. There were four, two for the Russian part and two for the Allied. Their diameters were approximately two feet. A strong man could climb down to the lake by gripping them, but he could not wrap his arms around them. Savage had stuck his head over the cliff edge to observe them. The daytime wind had struck his face. Squinting against its force, he saw that grooves had been cut in the rock and the pipes had been set in them. Then iron bands had been put over them and secured to the limestone.

Even if he could descend down a pipe, he would end in the cold water. He would have to swim for several miles along the cliff before he came to a beach.

If he went to the other side, he would find a similar situation.

The guards had not ordered him to get away from the edge while he was looking at the pipes. If he wanted to jump, good luck to him. If they saw him trying to climb down, they would have fun target-shooting.

The only barbed wire on the cliff edge was that around the pipes as they came to the rock floor of the camp. These double fences were circular, and the pipes were in their centers. Moreover, some twenty feet before the pipes came to the top, they curved into the rock, coming up onto the surface inside the barbed-wire enclosures.

To get to a pipe, a man would have to drop from the edge of the cliff and hope he could grab the pipe and then hang on. That maneuver would be born of desperation.

Each set of pipes led to a pumping station. If POWs could one night get past the roving searchlights and the dogs and sentries and could break into the pumping station and overpower its personnel, they should be able to enter the pipes. First, though, the pumps would have to be turned off to drain the water out of the pipes. But it seemed certain to him that a grating would be welded over the intake end of the pipe. He had asked Hans about it, but Hans had only smiled when the lieutenant questioned him. He was well aware of what Savage had in mind. But he was not going to tip off his superiors. He loathed Schiesstaube and had little liking for von Hessel. Besides, if he stool-pigeoned on the American, he would cut himself off from any chance of getting chocolate.

Savage did not abandon the idea of using the pipes. He would have to study other ways and means, though. The salt mine had not yet been considered.

He told Ham, Monk, and Johnny about his ideas for escaping. "We should all volunteer to dig salt," he said.

"Work?" Ham and Monk said at the same time. Both looked as if they had just tasted something bad.

"It means we'll get extra rations and some small privileges," the lieutenant said. "I've talked to some of those who work in the mine, and they say they're not pushed hard. Besides, the mine may be our only chance to get out of here."

"Well, I don't know," Ham Brooks said. "I'd get my uniform all mussed up, maybe torn, and my hands . . . they'd get callused . . . my nails'd be broken."

Monk laughed uproariously, then shouted, "Listen to the dandy! Beau Brummell hisself! The Park Avenue fashion plate! He never did a lick of honest work in his life, and he ain't going to if he has to stay here forever! Just what I'd expect from a Harvard graduate!"

Ham's face reddened, and his lips tightened.

"I wasn't born and raised in redneck country like a certain low-mind whose name I won't mention. And I can at least speak correct English. I didn't say I wouldn't work in the mine, and I assure you I can keep up any day with a trained ape. As for honest labor, when did you ever do any? Unless you call chasing cheap women that?"

Clark waited more or less patiently until they were done with their insults. Perhaps he was wrong in joining up with these two. Though he was sure that they were brave and capable enough, he did not know if their compulsive squabbling would interfere with their efficiency. However, despite this, he liked them very much, and he felt that he could trust them in any dangerous situation. Though how two such supposedly intelligent men could act so much like Tom Sawyer and Huckleberry Finn, he could not fathom.

"You keep demeaning me," Monk said, "I'll tell Clark and Johnny and how you got the moniker of Ham."

Johnny sighed and said, "I'll volunteer, if only to absquatulate from the Duo of Discord."

Monk said, "Huh?"

The four went to Colonel Duntreath and told him they were willing to chop salt. The colonel informed Schiesstaube that he had additional workers ready for tomorrow. That evening, while Savage was talking to Johnny outside their barracks, he saw the train pull in. Presently, four POWs got off a freight car. He recognized two of them. They were the big man with the huge fists and the small pale man who had gone headlong out of the coach window, thus diverting the guards enough for Clark to dive through a window. Though they had not planned to help him, he was grateful to them.

The two were taken into Schiesstaube's office. After an hour, they were escorted to the delousing shack. A half-hour after this, reeking of fumigation, they were led into Savage's barrack by a sergeant. Captain Johnson, the POW camp adjutant, took them into a tiny cubicle given Duntreath for an office. When the two left it, they were surrounded by the other POWs. Savage was among them.

Suddenly, Monk's shrill and grating voice soared above the others. He pushed his way through, crying, "Hey! John Renwick! Remember me, Renny? The Acme Chemical Corporation plant we worked on in Brazil! You were the chief engineer, and I was the chemical consultant! Andrew Blodgett Mayfair! Monk!"

He wrapped his long arms around Renwick and tried to dance him around. The Goliath moved no more than if he had been a boulder. His face did not change. But Savage was to find out that the more Renwick was pleased, the more somber was his expression.

Monk gave up trying to whirl him around and stood at arm's length looking up at him. "Boy, that was a hell of a job! Heat and rain and mud! But we had fun, didn't we? Remember that brawl in the tavern? We took them to the cleaners, right? Mopped up the place and then ran like hell from the police! Oh, them women, real black-eyed cuties, they were! And the whiskey we put away!"

Renwick's voice was like thunder over the hills.

"I gave it up."

"What?" Monk said. "The women or the whiskey?"

"The booze. I've lost a fortune paying fines for all the walls I put my fists through."

"Well, if I had to choose which one to give up, it'd be the booze. Thank God, I don't have to. Hey, let me introduce you around. Men, this is Major John Renwick, Renny to his friends. One of God's finest engineers, afraid of nothing or nobody. He's built more dams and bridges and railroads than there are warts on a hog!"

Renwick then introduced his pale companion as Captain Thomas J. Roberts of the Signal Corps. Roberts was short, skinny, and had very large ears that stuck out like the wings of a bird getting ready to fly. They were the thinnest Savage had ever seen. With a strong light behind them, they shone as if they were silk sails in a sunset. His hair was yellow; his eyes, very pale blue.

His forehead bulged as if an excess of brains was trying to break through the bone. That impression was not false. As Renwick said in his introduction, his pal was a wizard of the juice. Which meant that he was a very talented sorcerer of the electron. He had worked for and studied under more famous wizards of electricity. These were Thomas Alva Edison, who held patents for a thousand inventions, including the incandescent electric lamp, the phonograph, and the motion-picture projector, and Charles Proteus Steinmetz, who had provided a firm mathematical basis for alternating current.

But, as Savage discovered, though Roberts was very valuable to the Signal Corps, he wanted to fly fighter planes. If he ever got back to his outfit, he would apply for a transfer to the Air Service.

"I call him Long Tom," Renwick said. "Here's why. The Germans broke through a sector up near a village we called Merdeville for reasons I won't go into. Roberts here, he was caught in the village while he was repairing phone lines. He took over a bunch of Signal Corps men, cooks, truck drivers, whatnot, and organized a stiff resistance. He loaded a seventeenth-century cannon in the village square with scrap iron and blew up a house occupied by enemy troops.

"The cannon was the type called a Long Tom. So, he's been stuck with that nickname since."

"You use the materials at hand," Roberts said sourly.

Clark Savage wanted bold men with appropriate skills to carry out his escape plan. As soon as he had one, that is. The newcomers looked like very good men to recruit. One was a very experienced construction engineer; the other, a superb electrician. These, with Johnny, Ham, and Monk, could form an audacious nuclear team dedicated to getting out of the camp. However, he would have to study these two to make sure his evaluation of them was correct.

The next day, early in the morning, he, Monk, Johnny, and Ham went to work in the salt mine. They were given work clothes and miners' helmets bearing electrical torches, but were not given work shoes. Savage decided that he would write another letter to Dr. Jerome Coffern in New York. This man had been Clark's tutor in chemistry and was also a good friend of his father. Doctor Savage had appointed Coffern to be the guardian of his son while the father was in South America. Clark had not yet received an answer to his first letter, nor the food and supplies he had asked Coffern to send him. But he would wear out his shoes from the mine labor and would need replacements. Whether he would get them was another matter. The U-boats, German submarines, were sinking Allied merchant ships right and left. There were also many obstacles preventing land mail from getting through: wartime disruption of normal service, inefficiency, bureaucratic red tape, and, inevitably, thieves.

The tunnel which the four men entered had been cut out of limestone. After two hundred or so feet, it led to the salt dome. The core of this, as Johnny informed the lieutenant, contained halite, sylvite, and other potash minerals. He told Savage a lot about salt domes, all of which Savage already knew. But he did not say so. He would let the archaeologist-geologist display his knowledge and so get the satisfaction a teacher has in instructing the ignorant.

Later, he was glad that he had not taken a chance on offending Johnny and perhaps shutting him up. Johnny told him something he did not know and which was known by very few of Johnny's profession. He had a magnificent memory.

That item was that the Germans were also digging into the dome on the other side of this mountain.

"The operation on this side, where the camp is, is small-scale," Johnny said. "It helps the German war effort a little, but I think it's mostly set up to keep the prisoners busy and out of mischief."

Beanpole Johnny did not use sesquipedalian words when he was talking only to Savage. He had quickly found out that the young lieutenant was not mystified by them. That took all the fun out of it.

"Do you know if the shafts on the other side have met any on our side?" Savage said.

"Not the last I heard. But by now there could be a relatively thin wall between the two operations."

"How thin?"

"Oh, perhaps several hundred feet. Perhaps more. But the Germans will make sure they don't run into each other."

Johnny smiled, and he said, "You're contemplating the possibility of digging through to the other operation."

"Not unless I knew that the end of our tunnel was near enough to the end of theirs to justify digging," Clark said. "We can't just tunnel blindly in the desperate hope we'll run into one of their tunnels."

"If we could get the materials to make a seismograph and something to initiate a shock wave, say, dynamite, we could locate the nearest open area to ours. If, also, and that's an even bigger if, we could do it unobserved by the guards. That won't be easy. As for dynamite or any explosive, even if we can get some, how do we use it without attracting the guards' attention? Et cetera and et cetera, forever and amen."

"Some things are impossible to do," Clark said. "But this isn't one of them."

They proceeded with some other POWs and several

soldiers through tunnels illuminated brightly by overhead light bulbs strung together. They walked along a single set of narrow-gauge tracks on which four-wheeled carts were pushed. Presently, they reached their work station. This was an enormous room which had been hollowed out of solid salt. Unlike a coal mine, no support posts on the sides or overhead beams were used. Pillars of salt had been carved out to support the ceiling. The room looked like the interior of a whitish cathedral or a great chamber in a medieval castle. Tunnels were being dug from this room, assumably to areas where other big hollows would be made. Or, perhaps, they led to spaces already dug out of the solid salt. But Savage and his companions were set to breaking off chunks of salt with pickaxes and spades in this space.

Once, as Hans Kordtz would tell Clark, there had been wheelbarrows to be filled and to be pushed to the carts, into which the barrow loads would be dumped. But these had been requisitioned to send to the mills for melting. The desperate need for steel and other metals had caused them to be taken away. In fact, the kitchens of the citizens everywhere in Germany had been stripped almost bare of pots and pans. Their owners had donated them to the war effort.

Savage had passed big blowers in the tunnels which moved the air out. There were more noisy fans in the huge room. He saw the openings of shafts overhead. These must have been cut through the caprock enclosing the salt dome and then through that to allow fresh air in. He had not seen any openings in the mountain above the mine entrance. When he came out, he would look for them.

The mouths of the shafts where the fans were installed were wide enough for a man to crawl through. But how would an escapee get to them? They were forty feet from the floor. And there might be one or more fans in the air shafts to help suck the air down. They would be impossible to get through.

Maybe.

The miner-prisoners worked steadily, filling burlap

sacks with the broken-up salt, then lugging these on their shoulders to the carts and emptying the sacks in them. When they got thirsty—and just being surrounded by the salt made them thirstier than they should have been—they were allowed to drink as much as they wanted from canteens and bottles. The guards, meanwhile, tended to hang together, smoke, and talk. They only shouted at their charges to get back to work if they were too obviously goldbricking. Lunch was served at one o'clock. It was a fist-sized chunk of the dense black bread, a thin potato soup with meat fragments, and beet mash.

"I could eat four times this just for breakfast," Johnny said. "How long is it going to take packages from home to get here?"

A guard who understood English and overhead him said, "There's talk that you'll soon be getting only two meals a day. Shut up, and be thankful for what you do get."

Clark eavesdropped on the guards as much as possible. He was especially interested when two of them began talking about the high death rate in the Russian part of the camp. Corporal Zinzenmaier had gotten his information from a guard, Stern, who accompanied von Hessel whenever he visited the hospital for the Slavic POWs.

"Five yesterday," Zinzenmaier said to his buddy, Corporal Rothstein. "Six the day before. Three they expect to die tomorrow, if not before. Twenty-five newly sick. If this keeps up, there won't be any left within six months. There's only four hundred alive out of the one thousand that came here. It may not be long before all the Ivans are buried in the salt chamber."

"That doesn't worry me," Rothstein said. "What does is that we might catch whatever's killing them off. Which is what, by the way?"

"God knows!" Zinzenmaier said. "Whatever it is, our *Bazillensammler* (bacilli-collector, referring to von Hessel) doesn't take any chances. He and the others wear surgical masks while they're there. Just before they leave, they take showers with hot water and strong soap and then wash their hands in carbolic acid and their clothes are fumigated. Stern says it's a hell of a nuisance, but better than coming down with what the Russians got."

Savage wanted to ask Zinzemaier about the physical symptoms of the disease. He was afraid that he not only would not get an answer but the guards would go to where he could not overhear them.

"That's scary. What's to keep the sickness from spreading to our camp?" Rothstein said.

"That particular one? I don't know. Except maybe it's the inoculations we got when we first came here. But that isn't all, you know. The Russians have had cholera and typhus and God only knows what other filthy diseases, but they died out when the sick were quarantined."

Savage felt uneasy, not because of the last remark but because he and his fellow prisoners had not gotten the shots Zinzenmaier had mentioned. Also, there was the mystery of why von Hessel, a bacteriologist famous, or infamous, for his unconventional experiments, would be assigned as commandant of a POW camp. And there was his laboratory.

Clark suddenly shivered. The chill running over his skin and seeming to make his hairs bristle was not caused by anything physical. The coldness and, yes, the horror, sprang from the revelation that von Hessel was using his Russian POWs as subjects for his scientific, or pseudo-scientific, tests.

That was not only extremely immoral and unethical and barbaric; it was dangerous for everybody in this area, including von Hessel. Controlling a disease, especially an unknown or new one, is not easy.

He considered Zinzenmaier's remark that all the German soldiers had been inoculated on coming to the camp. Unspoken but implied was the fact that the soldiers stationed in the Russian camp had not been infected with the malady striking down so many of the Slavs. Despite this, von Hessel always took sanitary precautions before returning to this part of the camp.

Yet, the baron knew as well as anyone that warfare involving bacteria was as perilous for the disseminator as for the enemy. It was a weapon which, inevitably, would slay both the victim and the wielder. The Germans had discovered that when they started using chlorine gas against the Allies. The wind would suddenly change its direction and envelop the Germans in their own poison. But disease would kill far more than toxic gases could. It did not need a passport to travel from one country to another.

Von Hessel was keenly aware of this.

Thus, if he had such a weapon, he would not submit it to the Imperial German highest authorities for consideration until he had an inoculation to keep the Central Powers population safe from infection.

Savage doubted that the conservative German general staff and the Kaiser, all of whom thought of themselves as highly moral, would approve of this. Poison gas was one thing; deadly bacteria, another. However, if the situation of the Central Powers became very desperate, they, like Samson, might pull down the temple pillars on their own heads along with those of their foes.

Why had not the French, British, and American prisoners been inoculated?

Because, Clark thought, every biological experiment had to have its control group. He and the others had been left wide open to the disease because they were the controls.

As far as he knew, none of them had been infected by the unknown plague, if indeed there was such. The hospital on this side had its sick POWs, but they were suffering from easily diagnosed illnesses. Some of the Russians might also be controls. Not everybody in their camp had come down with the disease. Not so far, anyway. But it was possible that von Hessel was working in his laboratory on a more virulent form.

Did the countess know that her lover was doing this to her own countrymen?

Would she care?

In the midst of Clark's fear and loathing, he saw the hidden room and its grisly furniture and bones in that mansion in Belgium. It was for him the ultimate evil, and also the symbol for the evil that dwelt everywhere in the world. He would never forget it.

But was the evil worked by Baron de Musard a very small and insignificant evil compared to that which von Hessel intended to do? Yes, it was, just as the world war was a great evil.

He thought, Cool down, Clark. Be objective. Your passions and imagination may be outracing reality. You have no real evidence that von Hessel is doing what you think he is doing. Investigate. Get the facts. Be sure.

Nevertheless, he was upset and could not stop thinking about it. And, now, he could appreciate even more his father's fierce, perhaps fanatical, desire to fight against Evil and to make sure that his son carried on the fight. But Clark did not image Evil in his mind as an abstraction. His father's Evil existed no more than did a Satan, a fallen angel horned, hoofed, and tailed and carrying a pitchfork. The concrete lowercase evil did exist, in that it referred to human beings who did evil deeds. And even that "evil" could not be clearly defined logically in many cases; that sometimes depended upon who was defining the word.

In this situation, however, Savage had no doubt about the evilness of the man whom he thought was doing the deed. There was no gray area of philosophy, semantics, or morality here—if, indeed, he was perpetrating the deed.

There might be another explanation for what he suspected was taking place.

Too much thought led to inaction. He was no Hamlet or, at least, did not want to be one.

On the way out of the mine after the cease-work whistle was blown, Clark wondered what had happened to Monk Mayfair and Ham Brooks. He had seen Renwick and Roberts laboring on the other side of the enormous room, but the wild couple was supposed to have been in the gang as well.

Not until he had gotten back to the barracks did he find out about them. Hans Kordtz told him. They had been tardy showing up for the shift because Brooks had accused Mayfair of putting a cockroach under his bed blankets. In the quarrel that followed—Monk had denied being the culprit—a window was broken. The sergeant in charge of them summoned Schiesstaube. The adjutant was upset because of the presence of the insect, which indicated unsanitary conditions for which the commandant might blame him. He was also enraged because of the broken window.

While the two were standing in the adjutant's office, they broke into song: "We're Going to Hang the Kaiser Under the Linden Tree."

Schiesstaube screamed at them to stop singing or he would clap them into solitary confinement, which he was thinking about doing, anyway, because of their previous breaches of discipline. Monk and Ham dropped that song, but a minute later launched into another: "We're Going to Take the Germ out of Germany."

Off they went to spend five days in lightless cells with no communication with anyone.

The solitary-confinement rooms were in a small and isolated house in the northeastern corner of the camp. Though the two had been ordered not to speak to anyone, they bellowed insults at each other. Anyone within fifty feet of the thin-walled house could hear them. After a while, they began singing together, even though they were at opposite ends of the house.

"Alexander's Got a Jazz Band Now" and "Barnyard Blues" were only two of the popular American songs they rendered with gusto, though not with much harmony. As a result, Schiesstaube added the punishment of bread and water as their only diet.

Clark Savage shook his head in disgust. Those two clowns were not going to be dependable in carrying out an escape plan if they kept on behaving like this. He hoped they would realize this while they were locked up. Though he was only a lieutenant and much younger than they, he was going to have to talk to them like a Dutch uncle. Or get Colonel Duntreath to dress them down. That was a better idea.

During supper, he was somewhat down in the mouth. His father had told him that the greatest obstacle in carrying out a plan was the people involved in performing it. One of his numerous tutors, a Persian Sufi, Hajji Abdu el-Yezdi, son of Abdu, son of Abdu, had stressed the same difficulty. But Clark had to experience it before fully realizing it.

He rose from the meager meal with his belly and, therefore, his whole body and being dissatisfied. Two minutes later, Sergeant Schiesstaube entered the barracks with two guards. He went up to Savage.

"You are invited to dinner at nine o'clock by Colonel von Hessel," he said. "That's what I was told to tell you. But, actually, it's a command. I wouldn't turn down the invitation if I were you. The commandant doesn't like to be disappointed, and he told me to tell you that. I'll be here at a quarter to nine to conduct you to his quarters."

Johnny, standing nearby, said, "Oh, oh!"

The lieutenant's first response had been surprise. His next was a rush of joy. His belly—that portion of the anatomy which usually takes precedence in most human beings—glowed with anticipation of the excellent and bountiful supply of food he was sure to get. His third reaction was alarm over Johnny's exclamation. And over the suspicious expressions of those around him.

They were thinking, Why should he, a mere lieutenant and so very young, be a guest at von Hessel's dinner table? Thoughts about treason were bouncing around in their heads. He would have wondered about that if someone else had been invited.

He hastened to the POW adjutant, Colonel Duntreath. The Scot knew about his experiences with von Hessel.

"This puts me in a bad light, sir," Savage said. "Do you think I should reject the invitation?"

Speaking with the thick burr of a Perthshireman, the colonel said, smiling, "Put your mind at ease, son. You could stand a big meal. Couldn't we all? And, if von Hessel means to pry information out of you, which he does, of course—I have faith in you. Your record speaks for you."

Momentarily, the colonel frowned. "If what you've said is true, of course."

He smiled again under his thick cinnamon-colored mustache.

"I'll be checking on that, if I can do it. Meanwhile, go

and have a good time, but be on guard. I'll inform the men that you're not suspected of being a traitor and that you seem to have the strong character required to resist the Hun's temptations. When you get back, give me a full report of what transpired.

"You have my permission to dine with the baron, and also my blessing. Not to mention my envy. I'm not just referring to the feast. That Russian countess... well, I don't mind telling you, son, I'm fifty-five years old, but when I see her, which is too seldom, the cockles of more than my heart warm up."

The lieutenant blushed. Seeing this, the colonel laughed loudly and dismissed him.

That evening, accompanied by the sergeant and four armed guards, Clark Savage walked to the baron's house. On the way, he saw by the arc lights near the cliff edge that the train had pulled into camp. Before he got to the commandant's, he observed three POWs get out of a freight car. Suddenly, one of them attacked a guard. He was pulled off and beaten with the butts of rifles before he was dragged off. Later, Savage would find out that the obstreperous, and, in his opinion, foolish one, had been put in solitary confinement. The blows from the rifles were bad enough, Savage thought. Having to listen to Monk's and Ham's banter and disputing and, especially, their singing was inhumane punishment.

XV

Lieutenant Savage was escorted back to the barracks at four in the morning. He was very tired and wrestling with his conscience. Like Jacob with the angel at the foot of the ladder, the story from the Old Testament, he thought. Or like the *Arabian Nights* tale about the Old Man of the Sea straddling Sinbad the Sailor's back and with an iron grip around the Arabian mariner's neck. His conscience was the angel and the Old Man of the Sea, and he was Jacob and Sinbad.

Sinbad was sin bad. Or bad sin. Was there such a thing as a good sin?

Actually, he was only bothered a little about what he had done. Fortunately, or unfortunately, depending upon a person's viewpoint, he had not been subjected as a child to indoctrination in any particular religion. His father was an ex-Anglican who had become a deist—that is, one who believes that there is a God but that He, She, or It went out for lunch after creating the universe. And hasn't come back yet. Clark had been exposed to many faiths during his travels around the world with his father and during his tutelage by various men in cities and in jungles, deserts, and mountains. The result had been to make him widely acquainted with everything from Greek Orthodoxy to voodooism.

He had escaped much of the puritanial sexual morality of the United States of America of the early twentieth century.

On the other hand, he had a personal morality, a sort of eclectic code peculiar to him. That is, he had picked and chosen those parts of all the moralities he had encountered, and he had put them together to shape what he considered was good. But had he harmed the countess in any way? Had he done the baron an injury? Had he hurt himself?

Ham Brooks and Monk Mayfair would not have been disturbed by any such thoughts. Not those Gold Dust twins of lust, as Long Tom called them.

But he was not they. Though he had had some experience with women on five continents, the fair sex was not his department. Except for some nannies of various races when he was an infant and some of his father's mistresses, he had had relatively little intimacy or even prolonged close contact with women. Variety, yes, but no genuine friendship or deep warmth.

Women were a mystery to him. But then every man he knew—and many had been surrounded by females all their lives—had said the same thing. The Eternal Feminine was incomprehensible and unpredictable. More the latter than the former.

His father had finally realized that the strange upbringing of his son had failed to enrich him in one very important field. It had made him, in a deep sense, a deprived child.

Too late. Unless Clark himself did something about it.

Perhaps, he thought as he entered the barracks, I'm overly concerned. What I did I enjoyed as much as anything I've ever done, despite some slight worries about whether or not it was right. And about getting caught.

As he had said when he was struggling, not very strongly, over accepting or rejecting her invitation, "Oh, well! Why not?"

Sergeant Schleifstein left him at the barracks door and stomped away. The sergeant was very tired and disgruntled. He had been forced to stand outside the door of the baron's house and wait until the countess summoned him to conduct the American flier back to the barracks. He did not say anything to Savage, but he was obviously unhappy and deeply suspicious. He knew that the baron had passed out and been carried to bed. He had expected the party to be over then. But, no, he had had to wait for four hours until the lieutenant had come from downstairs.

Savage went into a dark building and groped his way to the big room on the second floor. He had to light a match to make sure he was near his own bed. He saw that the covers and sheets had been torn off and tossed on the floor, and his mattress had been turned over. On top if it was a piece of notepaper. He lit another match to read the handwriting on it.

Littlejohn, in the bed next to his, said, sleepily, "Your bed's a mess because Schiesstaube came storming in here at midnight on a surprise inspection raid. He and his progeny of female dogs turned everything upside down looking for artifacts we might've hidden to help us escape. Like spades and pickaxes to tunnel out of here, haw! Or, airplane parts we could put together and Icarus ourselves to freedom. He says he's going to keep doing this at random intervals. I think he's just a petty, lilliputiansouled, winxing, hufty-tufty trundle-tail who wants to keep us from getting sleep."

Johnny sat up in bed as Clark lit another match.

"What made you so late, anyway?"

Savage did not reply. He read the note, which was from Colonel Duntreath. It said that it was now too late for the lieutenant to report to him. He should do it in the morning before going to the mine.

Savage sighed. He was going to get very little sleep before roll call came.

"That prisoner that just arrived," Johnny said. "The one who attacked a guard after he got off the train. He's in solitary confinement. I heard he's Captain Benedict Murdstone, English, infantry, a regular wildcat. Escaped three times. Sounds like my kind of guy."

Savage made his bed in the dark and crawled in.

Johnny said, "Do my nostrils detect the odor of alcohol in various prepared forms? For God's sake, Clark, you haven't been drinking with the Teutonics, have you?"

"Some."

"They treated you swell, huh? The baron didn't try to seduce you, did he?"

Savage smiled in the dark and said, "No, the baron didn't."

He went to sleep at once. It seemed that he had just closed his eyes when the wake-up siren wailed over the camp, followed by the German bugle call. While he was trying to get rid of the terrible taste in his mouth with a brush he had purchased at the prisoners' canteen, Duntreath's aide came into the washroom. He was Captain Deauville of the French artillery. He told Savage that he should report to Duntreath after work. The colonel was too busy to talk to him right now.

Shortly after Savage came out of the mine, he saw Baron von Hessel and Countess Idivzhopu promenading along the cliff edge. The countess saw him even though he was far off. She waved a gloved hand at him. He did not respond. She must have said something to von Hessel, because he turned to look at Savage. His teeth shone in a wide smile.

Clark shook his head. He supposed that the baron knew very well what had happened after he had been carried off drunk to bed. Savage did not understand the man's apparent lack of jealousy or why he had been so cooperative.

The baron's character was complex and streaked with dark aspects. But then, whose wasn't?

After washing up, Clark reported to Colonel Duntreath. If the Scot had heard about last night—the whole camp was buzzing with gossip and Savage had had to endure a number of questions and jokes—he gave no indication of it. He told the lieutenant to report everything that he had observed and heard at von Hessel's. But when Savage launched into his story with a minute description of everything, including the food items and the manner in which the tableware was laid out, he was stopped.

"Good God, man!" the colonel said. "Are you a human camera? I don't want everything verbatim."

"I do have almost perfect recall," Savage said. "It's part natal, part training. I'll just give you what I think is important."

His mental fingers were crossed when he said this.

"I'll decide what's important," Duntreath said. "I may ask you to expand on certain points."

Savage told him that those at the table were the baron and the countess; himself, of course; Major Schickfuss, the adjutant of the Russian camp; Schiesstaube's chief aide, Captain Haken, whose right hand had been blown off at the Russian front and now sported a curved steel piece; and a civilian, Herr Professor Kornfunken. All Savage had been able to find out about him was that he was a bacteriologist from the University of Berlin and was leaving in the morning.

"Schiesstaube wasn't there. He was on duty, but I think von Hessel would no more eat with him than he would with a hog. The baron loathes his adjutant, if some remarks he made about him truly indicate his feelings."

"Who doesn't loathe that detestable scoundrel?" Duntreath said.

Also present were the Russian servants. Zad, the

hairy and smelly giant, had blown a kiss at Savage. But Savage did not report that.

Nor did he say anything about his reaction when he saw Lili Bugov, Countess Idivzhopu. Her all-white gown was the most low-cut he had ever seen. Savage was not the only man whose eyes kept straying back to the superb cleavage. She reminded him of the novelist H. Rider Haggard's seductresses. The two that burned in his mind and elsewhere were Ayesha, also called She-Who-Must-Be-Obeyed, the goddess-heroine of *She,* and Helen of Troy of *The World's Desire,* the femme fatale whose face launched a thousand ships. There Lili sat, looking like them, and also like the ancient Egyptian deity of Love, Hathor.

The table did not exactly groan under its weight of food, since it was solid teakwood. But it bore a burden even more opulent and saliva-releasing than that at the monastery: two roast suckling pigs, a side of roasted beef, fried chicken, huge yams, fruit and vegetables of many varieties. He told himself to hold back on stuffing himself with the meat. He needed the fruit, especially the lemons, to combat the scurvy threatening him because of the lack of citrus in the camp diet.

During the course of the banquet, he slipped several pieces of chocolate into his pocket. These would be for Hanz Kordtz, the guard.

Von Hessel had observed this—those blue eyes seemed to miss nothing—but he only smiled with one side of his mouth.

Clark skimmed over the discussions between him and the baron on various philosophers. Duntreath, hearing the names of Kant, Nietzsche, and Schopenhauer, raised his bushy gray-shot eyebrows and said, "Who?"

Clark also only mentioned the paintings on the wall. What relevancy did the names of Duchamp, Arp, Tzara, Picasso, and Braque, artists important to the dadaism and cubism movements, have to this intelligence report? Nor did he think it necessary to describe the baron's comments on such works as "Nude Descending a Staircase," "Shaven Horse Leaping Off a Cliff," and other flat and fragmented paintings and photocollages which Duntreath would not understand and he did not either.

That von Hessel loved and collected these objects because he thought they foreshadowed the breaking down of nineteenth-century man and the formation of the new man, the twentieth-century mechanical, dehumanized, and soulless man, would not interest the colonel.

"This war heralds a new era, a new type of Homo sapiens—a different kind of Western Man, anyway," the baron had said. "Fragmented, empty and lacking wholeness, poverty-stricken in spirit, unable to face the black void of his own death and of the death of the universe, of, as Nietzsche said, the death of God Himself. The war has shattered the old mold. The new mold is not yet completed."

Meanwhile, he drank glass after glass of French wine, and the countess was not too far behind him. Savage felt that he should drink a little wine, mainly because the baron had insisted. By the time von Hessel had melted into a muttering and half-conscious heap, Savage had had more alcohol that evening than in his entire life. He hated his loss of control at the same time that he enjoyed it. His training had been directed toward complete mastery of foolish impulses and an always-objective attitude.

"Did the baron interrogate you about military matters?" Duntreath said. "Or anything that he should not know, such matters as Allied home-front morale, the economic situation, and so forth?"

"Not once."

"Did he reveal during the course of his intoxication anything about the situation of the Central Powers, anything specific or general that might help us if we can get the information to our Intelligence?"

"Nothing. He did say that England was Germany's greatest enemy, that the Germans thought of themselves as representing the new order whereas England represented the old order, that the English were nineteenth-century man and could not pass away quickly enough."

"Hmph!" Colonel Duntreath said. "That rubbish is not exactly a secret to us. Sheer rot! We'll see who triumphs!"

"He said that even if the English won this war, they would lose the next a generation hence."

Savage added a comment touched with malice because of Duntreath's ill-hidden contempt for colonials and especially for Americans. Duntreath was not a bad guy, though somewhat priggish and stuffy. He did try to be fair in his dealings with the French, Australians, and Americans under his command. And his war record showed that no one had more courage. But he was a snob, an arch-conservative.

"The man talks as if he had a loo in his mouth!" the colonel, his face now red, growled. "Is he some sort of Bolshevik? However, there is something extremely important that I would like to know. I've heard reports . . . never mind the source . . . that the baron is conducting some kind of beastly experiments in the Russian camp. His subjects may be peasants, but, by God, they're human beings! Or so I've been told. What is von Hessel doing with them?"

"He never said anything about that, though I tried to steer the conversation toward it," Savage said.

Duntreath, his expression curious and unreadable, cocked his head. "Did the countess say anything about that?"

"No."

The lieutenant could feel the warmth in his face.

"Von Hessel's character is relevant," Savage said, eager to get off the subject of the countess. "Any weaknesses of character could be used against him. He hates his father. He said he was the typical Prussian aristocrat—brutal, a mighty hunter of animals, a womanizer, a terrible boozer, very self-centered, selfish, and ignorant of anything outside of his very narrow circle of learning. Only worse than most of them. He may be exaggerating the Junkers' faults, generalizing on the basis of certain individuals.

"Von Hessel loved his mother but resented her because she did not stand up for her children against her husband's indifference and often sadistic treatment of them. She died some years ago. Von Hessel's father had given her several venereal diseases . . ."

"The filthy beast!" Duntreath said. He seemed to be embarrassed.

"He was pretty drunk when he told me all this," the lieutenant said. "It seems to me that von Hessel has tried to be everything his father wasn't, be just the opposite. But it's evident he fears that he is too much like his father. There's a certain strong tension in the man..."

Duntreath interrupted. "What has all this psychologizing, like that Austrian Jew, what's his name..."

"Sigmund Freud."

"...a pervert, I understand, got to do with us?"

Savage refrained from telling the colonel that he, with his father, had attended a few lectures by Freud. Doctor Savage had much the same opinion of Freud as the colonel did. Clark thought that there might be some substance in the theories of the founder of psychoanalysis. The proof was in the pudding—that is, time would show their validity or invalidity.

"I deal in facts, not in fantasizing," Duntreath said. "In truth, you didn't find out much of value, did you?"

Maybe not to you, but certainly much to me, Savage thought.

The next two weeks passed slowly and drearily. Von Hessel and the countess took the train for an unknown destination and did not return for six days. The Russians continued to die at an abnormal rate. The hospital on the Allied side was filled with men suffering from dysentery and pneumonia. Hans Kordtz was pathetically grateful for the few pieces of chocolate that Savage gave him. He promised to keep on telling the lieutenant everything he heard or saw around the camp. And Savage kept trying to conceive of means and ways to escape.

Mayfair and Brooks, noticeably thinner but their exuberance undiminished, came out of solitary confinement.

The only big excitement was when the Red Cross parcels finally arrived. Savage's contained three chocolate bars. He ate one and gave the other two to Kordtz. He also divided the cigarettes with Kordtz, Ham, and Monk. Renny refused those that Savage offered him. He had quit smoking because tobacco was too difficult to get. Johnny and Long Tom had never gotten the habit.

An intense camaraderie had grown among the six Yankee prisoners. Though the lieutenant was younger than the others, the lowest in rank, and everyone in the group was a born leader, they slowly came to regard Savage as their chief. He made no effort to gain that status; it came about naturally. Monk was the last to give in, and he did so only after the famous arm-wrestling match.

Mark had challenged everyone in camp whom he thought was strong enough to give him any sort of contest, the guards included. Only Savage had refused to try him. But, after Monk had taunted him a number of times, Savage consented to a match.

Everybody in the barracks, many in the other barracks, and many guards gathered around the table. The bets rained among them. Most were eager to see Monk beaten, but the odds favored him ten-to-one. Ham put his tobacco and money on the lieutenant as a matter of principle, though he said that no human being could outmatch an ape. If Monk wasn't an unknown species of gorilla, Ham said, he would eat his hat. Without salt and pepper. Now, if it were a contest of wits . . .

The contestants, facing each other, sat down at a table and planted their elbows in the positions designated by the referee. They clasped their right hands together. Clark, looking at Monk's unusually thick muscles and the unusually thick bones to which they were attached, wondered if he had not erred in accepting the challenge. The hand gripping his was one that could bend pennies with its fingers. It was said that Monk could tie the barrel of a rifle into a knot.

"Don't feel bad when you lose, kid," Monk said. "I'm the world champ."

Savage smiled slightly.

The referee said, "Ready! Okay, I'll count to three. On three, go! Either of you cheat, I'll thump your heads with this stick!"

Monk was exceedingly strong, no question of that. He was a pocket Hercules, a compressed Samson. As the struggle developed, the veins rose on his forehead as if they were snakes breaking through earth from underground. His face got very red. He sweated. He strained. He clamped his big blocklike teeth together. He grunted.

Clark Savage was having no easy time, either. Five minutes passed, and neither yielded an inch. Their arms were as unwavering as those of two statues. But like Monk, Clark was sweating profusely.

The referee called a ten-minute time-out. Monk gasped, "You ain't no kid, kid! No one's ever lasted more'n thirty seconds with me!"

The onlookers yelled and cheered. They increased the amounts of the bets or made new ones. Those who had hung back from the gambling joined in. But the odds had gone down to one-to-one. Ham lost his head and bet his tobacco and chocolate for the next three months on the lieutenant.

Slowly at first, then acceleratingly, Monk's right arm went from the vertical toward the horizontal. Suddenly, the back of his fist was on the table.

"Savage wins!" the referee shouted, but only those near him heard. The din of voices and of the stomping on the floor was loud enough to make the windows tremble. Even the Germans who had won were yelling and dancing around with each other.

"Aw, I was weakened by having only bread and water when I was in solitary," Monk said. But he was grinning, and he slapped Savage's bare shoulder. "You're a better man than I am, Gunga Din!"

"Yeah, and he's only sixteen!" Ham Brooks yelped. "Wait until he gets his full growth!"

"I'm still waiting for yours," Monk said. "Your mental maturity, I mean."

Despite his defeat, Monk was congenial and talkative. He decided that it was time to tell Doc how Theodore Marley Brooks had gotten his nickname of "Ham." The two had met at the front and become buddies, despite their differences in education, intelligence, and temperament, Monk said. Though he did not say so, he implied in his tone that Brooks was definitely his inferior in those respects.

"He played a rotten, low-down trick on me," Monk said. "I didn't know much French then. So, before a ceremony in which we were to be decorated by a French general, this gutter-life shyster coached me in a few complimentary phrases I was to tell the general. They— haw! haw!—were words you wouldn't spiel at a cab driver, let alone a general. So—haw! haw!—I got clapped into the slammer for a while until I straightened the miserable business out!

"Then, a week later, someone snitched to the general that Brooks here had stolen a whole truckload of hams. He proved himself innocent, though I ain't too sure about that. Ever since, he's been stuck with the moniker of Ham. What I don't like, though, what really hurts me, is that he's blamed me for that! Can you believe it? Haw! Haw!"

Ten minutes later, the party broke up when Schiesstaube made one of his infamous surprise inspections. His search party found nothing, as always. He raged around, striking his riding crop against the pillars and the furniture and shaking it in the faces of the prisoners standing at attention.

At four A.M. next morning, he stormed in again and awakened everyone. But someone—Clark suspected it was Monk—had left a pail of water above the door attached to a rope, the other end of which was tied to the knob. Schiesstaube, always the first to enter in a raid, had gotten drenched. He made everybody pay for his humiliation by keeping them up for two hours while he demanded to know who the culprit was. No one offered to betray the guilty man, of course. Actually, no one except that man knew who had done it. Unless, as Savage thought, Ham had helped Monk.

He could not help grinning, along with many others. But he knew that the two were going to get all of them in very bad trouble someday with their pranks. They were older than he, but he was much more mature. However, they had a lot more fun than he did. He had missed out on much of that as a child because he had had very few playmates. The serious streak in his nature was broad, too broad.

Schiesstaube finally decreed that everyone in the barracks would be put on half-rations until the perpetrator was revealed. Colonel Duntreath protested to von Hessel. The baron, who must have enjoyed his adjutant's soaking as much as anybody, canceled the punishment. His reason was that the order was illegal. Ham doubted that, but Schiesstaube knew better than to argue with his superior.

News about the latest developments at the Western Front was brought on the train. Jubilant, the guards told the POWs about it. The Kaiser's troops had struck a smashing blow south of Ypres. They had stormed Messines Ridge and taken Armentières. The British front had a wide gap in it. But the news a few weeks later was that the Germans had not had enough reserves to keep complete control of the situation.

Britain and France were also suffering lack of reserve power. But they had high hopes that the American troops, fresh and unscathed by war-weariness and backed by the industrial might of the States, would eventually bring victory—if the British and French could hang on long enough for the Americans to bring in their full might.

Captain Benedict Murdstone, the English infantry officer whom Savage had seen attacking a guard after getting off the train, was released from solitary confinement. Duntreath interrogated him, then assigned him a bed in Savage's barracks. The fellow was tall, blond, blue-eyed, and would have been handsome if it had not been for two defects. One was his nose, and the other was his nose; one personal calamity piled on another. He had an enormous proboscis. It could have been, with a great deal of charity, considered noble and impressive. But it was spoiled by a scar at its end. The tip had been cut off by a shell fragment in the early days of the great March offensive by the Germans. Monk got off on the wrong foot with Murdstone by addressing him as Schnozzola.

Clark got along with Murdstone fine, despite his evident snobbishness. The fellow was very well educated, spoke with an Oxford accent, and had escaped three times in five days. And he was very eager to try for a fourth. Perhaps, Clark thought, he might be a valuable addition to the escape party. But Clark was cautious and made no mention of this. He wanted to study Murdstone.

Meanwhile, after the arm-wrestling match, Monk began calling Clark "Doc." Many a man who was still in medical school when he went into the services was nicknamed this. Clark protested that he had no M.D. degree. It did no good. The use of the title spread. After a while, all the POWs, except for Duntreath, addressed him as Doc.

Then Savage cast the title in bronze, as it were, by resetting Murdstone's nose after it had been broken. That came about because Monk had resented Murdstone for correcting his grammar and also for making a slighting remark about Ham Brooks. Monk thought that he had a monopoly on insulting his buddy. Captain Murdstone had foolishly invited Monk to engage in fisticuffs with him. Two blows, one to the Englishman's belly and one to his nose, started and ended the conflict. Neither of them wanted the Germans to find out about the physical violence because they probably would have been put in solitary or, at least, heavily fined. So Doc had fixed the nose, and Murdstone told the guards that he had walked into a support beam during the night.

After that, many prisoners, and even some of the guards, came to Doc to treat their minor ailments. They did not care to go to the hospital if they could avoid it. It was filled, the German doctors and orderlies were overworked, and the waiting time for treatment was long. Most of all, the POWs regarded the hospital as a breeding ground for serious diseases, which it was.

Meanwhile, Doc Savage worked in the mine and spent a lot of time and thought on plans for breaking loose from Camp Loki. Spring had come to the lowlands, but it had not yet worked its green way up to the mountains. It was raining hard almost every day. He had observed that the level of the camp floor was slightly tilted to allow rain runoff. To aid this, channels from the base of the cliffs around the camp to the edge of the cliff rising from the lake had been cut into the limestone. These were deep enough to conceal a man if he lay flat in them. But, every forty feet, iron grillwork had been set in them. Any prisoner who tried to use the channels to get to the edge of the camp would have to crawl over the barriers. He would be exposed for a few seconds.

But a man doing this at night could wait until the ever-probing searchlights had passed him by.

Even if he succeeded in getting to the cliff edge, however, what could he do after that?

Then there was the daunting route to freedom from the camp. It was set in the southeastern corner of Germany. The shortest course was to travel south through a small section of Germany, cut through Austria, and then go through that part of Italy now held by the army of Germany's ally, the Imperial Austro-Hungarian Empire. Once the escapees got through the war theater and, somehow, through the Austrian front line to the Italian front line, they would be safe.

However, between Camp Loki and their destination was range after range of high and rugged Alpine mountains.

Going on the curving and up-and-down path they had to traverse, they would walk at least 260 miles. This would be high up. Hence, the weather would be cold and stormy. They would have to avoid the scattered villages. Any food they ate would have to be taken along with them from the camp. Unless, that is, they could manage to steal it. And that would increase the danger of being caught.

A man could get discouraged just from thinking about the obstacles.

Then there was Murdstone. He was an entomologist, and since Savage was the only other person in camp who knew anything about the study of insects, the captain liked to talk to him. But he could not conceal his surprise that an American, especially one so young, would be so well acquainted with the subject. His reaction was similar to that of the white American who discovers that the Alabama Negro he is talking to graduated from college. His attitude was not common among English scientists. Savage knew that because of his experience with some of their savants.

Murdstone did not know that the Yankee lieutenant was listening more carefully to his pronunciation and intonation than to the meaning of his speech.

Savage had discovered something from it, but he was keeping it to himself for the time being.

He did note that Murdstone was getting on an intimate footing with Colonel Duntreath. They played bridge in the commander's office with two other cronies. And the colonel seemed to have great confidence in the captain.

One day, while they were chopping out salt in the mine, Johnny came to Savage. He said, "Doc, you know about our little problem in getting a seismograph? So we can measure the thickness of the wall between us and the rooms the Germans are working in on the other side? Find a chamber or a tunnel?"

Savage nodded.

"Well, we can't steal one, because there's none to steal. But we can improvise one from materials available in camp. A Milne horizontal pendulum seismograph. We can make a boom, pivot, plates, and a recording drum. We can snatch an oil lamp, any one of those used in the barracks. I got a pocket mirror. The light-sensitive graph paper'll have to be stolen from the German supply shed or the baron's lab. That's a problem. A silk thread is not."

"Great! Tell me more about it!" Doc said. He did not tell the geologist that he had already figured out how to make the machine. He had been waiting for the right moment to suggest its manufacture. But he would let Johnny feel good about conceiving his proposal.

When the rail-thin fellow was done explaining the entirety of the project, Savage said, "I don't think it's just the time for that. I suspect, however, it will be soon. You see, I have another project in mind that should be done first. Let's get Monk, Ham, Renny, and Long Tom together tonight. I'll explain then."

"I like those two clowns, and I respect their expertise in their chosen professions," Johnny said. "And there's no doubt about their courage or quick thinking or loyalty. But do you really think we can trust them not to screw everything up with their shenanigans?"

"Monk and Ham know when to stick to business," Savage said. "Besides, they'll try anything, no matter how dangerous."

"They lack good sense?"

"They live life to its fullest," Doc Savage said. "But that means they're willing to risk their lives. They know that those who dodge the demands of life just to hang on to their lives don't have lives worth living."

"A lot of alliteration in that statement," Johnny said.

At seven that night, the six talked in low tones by Savage's bed. The rain beat hard against the windows but could not be heard above the loud voices of the many men talking or shouting as they played dice or card games. Smoke from cigarettes and pipes coiled bluely through the huge room.

When Doc had finished outlining his plan, he was questioned by some of the group. Most of these were doubts that tonight was a good time for his plan.

Savage said, "Yes, the wind and the rain will make climbing more difficult. But it'll also obscure the guards' vision. And they won't be alert. They'll think that anyone who would go out in this weather would not be in his right mind."

"Which he wouldn't," Long Tom, the eternal pessimist, said.

Doc ignored that. "I'll probably not see you men after I slip back in. Here's what I'd like you to do tomorrow, Tom. The Germans are shorthanded. Their chief engineer is sick and not likely to live. Moreover, one of the men who works in the generator plant is showing signs of aberrant behavior, and he'll probably be taken away from his job, maybe sent home. I want you to volunteer to work in the plant. You'll get a good idea of its layout and also how to sabotage it if you get a chance to do so."

"That'll have to go through Colonel Duntreath," Long Tom said. "What reason will I give for offering to help the krauts' war effort?"

"Whatever you tell him, don't tell him we have a plan and we need you in the electrical plant."

Long Tom made a face as if he had bitten down on a very hot pepper.

"You don't trust the colonel?"

"I trust him completely. But he might say something to Murdstone."

"Holy cow!" Renny said. "You mean . . . ?"

"I have a reason for not trusting Murdstone," Doc said. "But I could be wrong. Meanwhile, we make no accusations that might be invalid."

"So Bugs could be a traitor?" Monk Mayfair said.

He had quit calling Murdstone "Schnozzola" because Doc had told him that it was wrong and cruel to give a nickname based on a physical peculiarity. Mayfair had protested that everybody called him "Monk." But Ham had pointed out that his situation was different. He reveled in the name.

So, Monk now addressed Murdstone as "Bugs" because he was an entomologist.

"Not a traitor," Doc said. "Maybe, and I stress the *maybe*, a German spy."

"Haw! Haw!" Monk said. "Duntreath's buddy!"

"Pipe down!" Ham Brooks said. "You want the whole camp to know what we're talking about?"

"Okay," Monk said, very mildly for him. "But, Doc, you're taking an awful chance. What if Schiesstaube makes one of his surprise inspections? He did twice last night, once at one o'clock and two hours later. I ain't getting any shut-eye. See these bags under my eyes? You could put baby kangaroos in them."

"He hasn't, so far, anyway, made a roll call during the raids," Doc said. "If he notices I'm gone, start a diversion, get his mind off me."

"Ham and I've put in enough time in solitary," Monk said. "Long Tom here has to volunteer for the generator plant. That leaves Renny and Johnny."

Renwick and Littlejohn said that they would do it since Monk and Ham were not up to it. That started an argument which threatened to get out of hand and cause all four to be confined. Doc told them to shut up. That they immediately obeyed, looking sheepish, evidenced their high regard for him. Unconsciously, they had elected him as their leader. He had accepted that trust as if he were born to it. In a sense, he had been. His training, however, had greatly buttressed that innate sense of command.

"I'll sneak out a back window, since there isn't any back door, after everybody's gone to sleep," he said. "Wish me good luck. I'm going to need it."

XVI

Wind and rain lashed at him as if they were outraged at his defiance of them. Perhaps a hundred feet above the camp, he clung with his gloved fingers and his booted feet. The fingers were gripping cracks in the rock, and the toes of his boots were on very narrow outcroppings. They could easily slip off. Four times, he had lost his hold, though each time he had been able to hang on with one hand while he regained his former position.

Below, the searchlights in the watchtowers of the twin camps roved around on the buildings, on the spaces between, and on the edge of the cliff above the lake. The arc lights set along the perimeters of the area and near the barbed wire bisecting it were dark. Two nights before, they had been shut off to save fuel for the generators. But, at random intervals, they were turned on for a few minutes. So far, they had not caught any prisoner out where he should not be.

Savage hoped that they would not catch him in their photonic net when he returned. That is, if he did return. Now that he was ascending the cliff behind the camp, he was not sure that he should be here. His "youthful impetuosity," as Renny called it—a phrase he had picked up from Johnny—was really juvenile folly. But here he was.

He was not going to go back until he had done what he had set out to do. Or had died trying.

Ever since he had gotten to Camp Loki, he had studied the cliffs surrounding it. At first, they had looked as if they had been machined smooth. Closer inspections had revealed that many cracks and tiny ledges made them rough. The difference was like seeing a shaved face with the naked eye and then through a magnifying glass. Climbing it without equipment—ropes, snap links, pitons, a small pick, and a hammer—would be no breeze. Even with these, he would have had a hard time.

Savage had scaled mountains in Switzerland, Peru, Colorado, and Nepal—the Alps, the Andes, the Rockies, and the Himalayas. He had started when he was eleven years old. His last instructor was a Tibetan of Nepalese ancestry, Dekka Lan Shan, a specialist not only in mountain-climbing but a teacher of yoga and self-defense. He had a grandson born in San Francisco and completely Americanized. Dekka had asked Savage to look up his grandson, who bore the same name, if he ever got to California. But Savage had not had the chance to do so.

At the moment, it seemed that he would never be able to honor Dekka's request.

Up he went, groping, gripping, and straining. Had it not been for the rain, his clothes would have been sweat-soaked. At an altitude above the camp floor of about seventy feet, his hand closed on the edge of a thin shell of vertical rock. When he had pulled himself up alongside and past it, he was on the floor of a hollowed-out area. The thin rock was a shield which concealed the space behind it. Four feet or so from this was the opening of a shaft he felt with his hands after taking his gloves off. A large fan had been secured in the hole by steel pins driven through the rim and the stone beneath it.

It might be worthwhile, he thought, to bring up wedges, chisels, a sledgehammer, and a crowbar to try to pry the fan out. But these tools would have to be stolen from the camp storage building. No easy task. And what then? Escapees might be able to slide down the ventilation shaft into the mine and descend on a rope to the floor of the immense chamber. Then, however, they would have to break through the wall separating this mine from that on the other side of the mountain.

There had to be other ventilation-shaft openings, especially above the Russian side of the camp. But finding this shaft was a secondary goal. He had a long way to go to get to the primary one.

He started working upward and toward his left. After an hour of torturous effort, he was several hundred feet higher and perhaps six hundred feet closer to his destination. The rain had stopped fifteen minutes ago. Then he had reached the top of a ridge, a saw-toothed projection. When he got to the other side, he was in almost total blackness. The light from the camp was a very dim glow.

He felt safe enough now to use the electric torch. There were none for sale in the canteen, a store not quite as bare as Mother Hubbard's cupboard. But Hans Kordtz had made arrangements with another guard to bring one when he came back from leave. That had cost a cow-choking wad, as Monk would say.

Doc had not even been sure that the guard was going to be allowed to bring it in. There was no camp regulation against prisoners buying torches, but Doc had worried that Schiesstaube might decide to forbid this item. He was both unpredictable and arbitrary.

It had been inventoried, of course; nothing went in and out of Loki that was not recorded. But at least it had gotten in.

Unfortunately, the batteries would soon need replacing, or so Kordtz said. He doubted he could get more for the lieutenant. "The war, you know."

Turning the torch on now and then, Savage worked down a cliff. This was much rougher than that behind the camp but was not as precipitous. Then he went up another one that was somewhat more difficult. On the other side, he came to a chimney, a deep and narrow fissure in the cliff. Bracing his feet against one wall and his back against the other, he went down slowly. By the time he had reached the twisted boulder- and rock-strewn floor, he was frequently surrounded by light. Lightning had decided to take a hand in things. It filled the chimney fitfully as if it were pouring electricity into a pitcher. Thunder boomed, its echoes ricocheting from wall to wall like cannon shells.

He was not sure of just where he was. It seemed to him that he had one more barrier before him. Then, unless he was off in his calculations, he would be on top of the cliff that faced the lake. The lightning showed him that the fissure curved around the wall at one end. Since the flashes also revealed that no abysses lay ahead of him, he turned the torch off. Using the intermittent streaks of whiteness, he guided himself around the corner.

There was another fissure there, at right angles to the one he had just left. It was more narrow but still wide enough to squeeze himself up through it. His knees kept bumping into his chin. The back of his jacket was wearing out from the friction. He might have to explain that to the Germans when he got back. If he got back.

A hundred or so feet up, he was blocked by a boulder that had fallen and become wedged in the stone throat of the chimney. He slid sideways until he saw, by a lightning flash, a narrow hole above him formed by the rough, curving side of the boulder and the fissure wall.

He had to go through the opening as if he were a worm scraping itself through a hole punched in a can top by a knife. He could not bend himself in and use his knees, except at a very slight angle. Even so, the friction was enough to tear the cloth at the knees. And he had to grip for the slightest handholds.

On the other hand, he would not slide back down fast.

A very fat man would never get through this hole. Monk was not fat, but he had an enormous barrel chest. If he made it at all, he would scrape off his clothes and the thick curly mat of hair beneath them.

After he had hauled himself onto the top of the boulder, he rested. He was cheered by the break in the cliff just in front of him. It was shaped like the head of an arrow. After he had gotten his strength back—some of it, anyway—he walked spraddle-legged on the sides of the notch. Up he went over a thirty-foot-high, almost vertical slope, then over a relatively flat area. By the streaks, twists, and zigzags of lightning, he saw the lake below.

Beneath him was the railroad track hugging the band between the cliff above and the cliff below. Telephone wires were strung on very short poles alongside the track and next to the upper cliff.

He climbed down that, not with the celerity of a mountain goat or a monkey but with the cautious slowness of a snake. After descending fifty or so feet, he found a ledge.

It ran for ten feet, tapering off at both ends, and was eight feet above the railroad tracks. It was just wide enough to stand on with the toes of his boots sticking over its edge and his back against the cliff face.

He stood there for a while, his hands held out and turned inward to grasp the slight projections of rock. The wind blew colder here than it did farther in. It was coming up from the lake, but it was not nearly as strong as it would be during the daytime.

For a moment, he was tempted to try to get back to the camp by walking on the railroad tracks. The thought of returning via the same route by which he had come made him shoulder-slumping weary.

He turned around slowly and began the perilous ascent. By the time he was coming down the cliff behind the barracks, he had to whip himself not to go faster. His strength seemed to be oozing out of his fingers and toes. The lack of food and the stress of climbing in the dark on the wet rock made him weaker than he would otherwise have been.

Below, now that the rain had stopped, the dogs had been taken from their cages below the watchtowers. They were straining at their leashes as they led the guards behind them. But none were near the barracks—as of now.

He hung on while he watched four blanketed bodies being carried by guards in the Russian camp. The living prisoners were sleeping. This was a good time to remove the dead to the salt carts on the narrow-gauge rails and thence into the burial chamber in the mine.

When he got to the bottom of the cliff, he ran to the barracks building. Quickly sliding the window up—he was grateful that no one had locked it—he crawled up and inside the big sleeping room. Then, cautiously, he passed through the snoring and muttering and groaning sleepers to the stairway to the second floor. The steps tended to creak. The whole place had been built under such urgency that the usually top-notch German workmanship had been sacrificed.

He got to the top of the stairs, went down the short hall, and turned in to the huge sleeping chamber on his right. He stood at the doorway for a minute and scanned the many recumbent forms. No lights were on. But the very first pearliness of dawn—the false dawn—showed him that no one was awake. He did hear a man coughing and swearing in the latrine at the far end of the room. Probably some poor soul with "camp cough" and suffering from dysentery.

Though he was exhausted and had to get his clothes dry—if he had time for that—he had to smile. By two walls in this latrine were long, gently sloping troughs. Water ran down these to the pipes leading to the sewage chamber in the mine, a gigantic room enclosed in salt. The POWs had to stand or sit above the troughs to get rid of their body wastes.

A few days ago, Monk had caught Ham while he was squatting there and had emptied a cigarette lighter of its fluid. As it was carried along by the water, it had been lit by Monk. It blazed up and scorched Ham's posterior before he could leap away. A dozen other men had just escaped being burned.

Shouting with laughter, Monk had run out of the room before he could be caught.

Ham's revenge had been mild, though he would have liked to do better and probably would someday. He had stuffed Monk's sheets and blankets into the open end of the drainpipe. That had caused an awful mess. Fortunately, the men had pulled the bedding out before the guards discovered the backup. And they had forced Ham to mop up the floor.

Ham had complained that some hairs had been singed off during the cigarette-lighter episode and that he had jumped away so fast that he had reopened his old wound again. He was referring to his arm, which had been struck by a bullet when he and Monk had been in the stream near the French farmhouse from which he, Monk, and Doc had fled. Monk said that was nonsense, that Ham had suffered only a flesh wound which had healed up long ago.

Savage went slowly through the room and eased himself down on the bed. While he was removing his boots, he heard a stir in the bed next to his. Johnny sat up on one elbow. He whispered, "How'd it go, Doc?"

"Tell you after I get some sleep," Savage said. "I am soaked, but I'd better try to get rid of the water with my body heat. If a guard comes in now, he'll wonder why I've hung out my uniform to dry.

"By the way, did Schiesstaube make a raid?"

"For a change, no. I think he's worn his little self out. If he makes us lose sleep, he loses it, too."

"He seldom makes a surprise check when it's raining hard out," Doc said.

"So that's why you picked tonight?"

"It helped me decide. But I didn't want to put it off any longer. Good night, Johnny."

XVII

"Monotony, boredom, and desperation," Long Tom said. "Add those to the diseases that infest prison camps. They're the worst. Diseases kill the body. The others kill the mind."

"Our little ray of sunshine, our electrical spark of happiness," Renny boomed. "But you're right on the nose."

Today was Sunday, the POWs' only day off from the mines. The Five and a Half Musketeers, as Ham called them, meaning that Monk was the Half, were standing around the open area watching the British playing soccer in one corner and the Americans playing baseball in another.

Months ago, Von Hessel had given them permission to make nets, inflatable balls, bats, and gloves, and cowhide balls. They had had to supply much money to get the guards to scrounge up the materials needed for these, and they had had to make them themselves.

"It could be worse," Long Tom said, taking a perverse pleasure in making his pessimism even blacker. "At least, we still have a chance to escape, slim though it is. But if this camp had stayed as it was originally constructed, we'd be done for. When it was first built, there was no camp such as you see here. There was a small fortress built over the two entrances to the mine. Which then was a series of relatively small chambers hollowed out of the salt. The prisoners were to be kept there.

"But some high-muck-a-muck, a relative of the Kaiser and also of the British king, raised hell when he came here for an inspection. He said the conditions for the prisoners were inhumane. So the fortress was torn down, and the camp was constructed like it is now.

"Anyway, the fortress and the salt rooms wouldn't have been big enough. There were too many troublemakers dumped here. The original setup couldn't have handled them."

Doc nodded. Hans Kordtz had told him the same thing.

It was mid-June. Spring had turned to summer. The mountain country was green, and crops were growing down in the valleys. There were rowboats and sailboats on the lake now, though no tourists were aboard them. The fishermen were not interested in the beauties of nature. They were catching all the Alpine trout they could. And these were not for import but for local consumption. The rationing through all Germany was even more severe than before. The potato-crop failure of 1917 had resulted in turnips as a substitute. The citizens and the POWs had to restrain the urge to vomit when they smelled turnip.

Hans Kordtz had told Doc that the church bells in his

village—in fact, all over Germany—were being taken down and melted for their metal. Last year, the streets of Berlin had been dug up to get at the copper telephone mains, which would be used in the making of cannon shells. Few brass doorknobs were left on private houses—anything of brass, in fact.

Yet, the German officers in the camp were still boasting that the Central Powers would win, that one supreme effort was all that would be needed to conquer their enemies. From May 27 to June 6, the Third Battle of the Aisne had carried the Imperial Army to within thirty-seven miles of Paris. But the American 2nd Division, fighting alongside the French at Château-Thierry, had stopped the Germans there.

The Americans were finally beginning to realize their vast potentiality not only as suppliers of materiel and food but as a fighting force.

Field Marshal Ludendorff was astounded at his success. He withdrew troops from Flanders to launch a massive attack at Compiègne. But, after six miles, the Germans were halted. Hans Kordtz had relayed the news to the six men.

"Every time I think the war is going to end, it gets up and starts all over again," he said. "It'll stop when we've all starved to death or are reduced to throwing stones at each other."

Though he was not supposed to fraternize with the POWs, he, like most of the guards, ignored the order. If, that is, Schiesstaube was not in sight.

Like most military regulations, this was disobeyed if the soldier felt he could get away with it. As Monk said, "It's more honored in the britches than in the observation."

The POWs had received parcels from abroad through the International Red Cross and the Young Men's Christian Association. Doc had told Dr. Coffern in his first letter to ship them via Denmark, a neutral nation. This was the quickest route.

As a result of the parcels, most of the Allied prisoners were eating better than the camp Germans. Not only that, but they were receiving half-pay from the German government owing to an agreement between the antagonist governments. The prisoners now had more means with which to purchase canteen supplies and to bribe the guards.

Schiesstaube would look for supplies the inmates might be accumulating to take with them on an escape attempt. He really did not expect to find any, since it would have been very difficult to conceal them. But Doc had taken them at night up the cliff from time to time and placed them in a hollow sixty feet high. Several times, he took Monk along with him because the fellow could climb like an ape. Once, he took Long Tom along; the electrical engineer had had some experience in climbing while training in the Signal Corps. The six men kept this a secret from the other prisoners. They were supposed to report any plan, or any part of it, to Colonel Duntreath. But Captain Murdstone was now on the escape-organization committee appointed by Duntreath.

"How come you're so certain Bugs is a German plant?" Monk said.

Doc decided to tell them. "I can't be certain. That's why I'm not accusing him to the colonel. I don't want to put Murdstone in an unfair situation, one in which he would suffer though innocent. The reason I suspect him is linguistic. I have a keen ear, if I do say so myself. I've had some training in language, though I'm no genuine expert. But it seems to me, just listening carefully to Murdstone, that there's a faint underlying German pronunciation under that almost-perfect Oxford accent. I thought maybe he had spent a lot of time in Germany and it had affected his speech, however faintly. But he says he was never in this country except on one summer holiday."

"If we prove he's a kraut," Monk said, "what do we do with him? I'd like to cut him up and eat him for supper! That way, we could get rid of the evidence! No corpus delicti or habeas carborundum!"

Ham snorted with derision.

"We have to improvise," Doc said. "I see no reason to kill him. He's just doing his patriotic duty. We spy on them; they spy on us. I'd rather keep him around until we have to get rid of him. If we exposed him now, the

Germans would just send in another plant. For all we know, there might be two of them here now. Or more."

Monk sucked in smoke from his Camel cigarette. After blowing it out, he said, "I really got ants in my pants, Doc. We can't put this off very long. I say, to hell with dillydallying around. Let's make the break soon!"

Ham puffed on his Lucky Strike, then said, "This can't be hurried, any more than one of those chemical tests you do in your lab. Everything has to be just right when we do it. You want to starve in the wilderness or get caught by a patrol because you charged off like a bull in a china shop?"

"I ain't built to be a POW," Monk growled.

"No, you're built to be an ape."

"Men," Savage said, "I'm inexpressibly weary of this life and eager to get going. But there's a lot to be done yet to get ready, and we don't have any assurance we can do everything that needs doing. For instance, we now have the materials needed to make a Milne seismometer. But we're in the same position as the mouse who had to bell the cat. How do we do it?"

If it were done, it would have to be at night. No sentry was then posted at the mine entrance. Why would a prisoner enter it? There were many rooms and tunnels, but the searchers would not take long to run him down. As for sabotage, what was there to wreck that could not be quickly repaired?

"I'm not sure it's worth the risk," Doc said. "We do have a possible escape route up and over the cliff. But it's very dangerous, very chancy. We really should have ropes, pitons, and all that. We can't get them in our section. We have to steal them from the German side. We don't even know if there are any in their storage shed. There might be ropes and hammers there, but pitons, snap links, and so forth? Is it worth taking a chance to determine if there are any there? Even if we could get over or through the barbed wire and elude the guards and dogs and unlock the shed, we probably will find that we risked everything for nothing."

"There's too many ifs, ands, and buts," Monk said.

"We're getting to be too much like the centipede that got to wondering just how he managed to work his hundred legs together. He ended up being confused, not knowing how to coordinate any of them."

"Maybe you're right," Doc said. "In any event, we don't have a stockpile of supplies big enough to take us far. We have to wait."

Savage was concerned with more than he had told them. There was the mystery of just what von Hessel was doing to those Russian prisoners. The answer seemed obvious. But that was a generalization. He did not know the specifics. Lacking that information, he could not tell the Allied authorities what terrible disease might be loosed on the Central Powers' enemies. Or what the vaccine was that the Germans would use to protect themselves.

Finding that out was far more important than escaping at the first opportunity. It was the most vital information that the Allies could ever have, far more necessary than any military data he could give them.

Of course, it was highly probable that von Hessel had not succeeded in perfecting the vaccine. The number of corpses taken out of the Russian POW hospital seemed to indicate that. On the other hand, they were also dying of the common camp diseases: typhus, dysentery, and a host of others. Without correct information, he could not know just who was being killed by von Hessel's experiments and just who was not.

Baron von Hessel. He was an enigma who made enigmas. A very complex and unanalyzable man. Advanced and very liberal, in that he recognized the inherent equality of the races and of the sexes. He did not hesitate to admit that the great majority of people were oppressed and exploited by the few. But he had no desire to change the situation and seemed to have little sympathy for the unfortunates enmired in it. He was intent only on getting all the power he could for himself. To hell with the rest of the human species.

It was doubtful that he was very patriotic. If he was preparing a biological weapon that would make his native country win the war and perhaps rule the rest of the world, or what would be left of it, he was doing it to gain power—POWER political, economic, and personal. He would be the savior of his nation, a great hero.

He was very well educated and abreast of knowledge in many fields. He could discuss Plato, Aquinas, Gibbon, Homer, Hafiz, and Confucius. He could quote the poets, dramatists, philosophers, and scientists, both ancient and modern. Yet, that evening, just before he had passed out at the dinner table, he had muttered, "As Blaise Pascal so truly said, philosophy is not worth an hour's study. That goes for literature and history, too."

During the evening, he had said that he was fascinated by the elder Savage's desire to make his son into a superman who would battle Evil. And by the son's attainments in reaching the limits of man's physical and mental abilities. But von Hessel thought that it was a waste of time and, more specifically, of Clark's life. He would be in a battle which would never end and which he could not win.

"You'll perhaps be victor in a few campaigns," he had said. "But the population of earth is going to increase, to swell geometrically, no matter how many war and starvation kill. As fast as you cut down one army of Evil, two more will replace it."

Von Hessel had practically given the countess to his young guest. Was it because he wanted to use her to get secret information from Savage? Or was he a pervert who got a dark joy from her description of the lovemaking? Or did he just not care?

Savage doubted that he would ever know.

One of the things the baron had said was that, when the world ended, the greatest mystery would still be the human soul. Chemistry might analyze all substances. Astronomers might see to the boundaries of the universe. Physicists might detect the tiniest particle of matter. But man would remain the unfathomable secret.

Savage thought that von Hessel was the ultimate nihilist. And that, despite his great knowledge and abilities, despite his surface complexity, he was a labyrinth that led to emptiness. There was no Minotaur in the heart of the maze; there was a black void.

But, he realized, he could be wrong.

Late one night, Doc was going through his two-hour exercises in a corner of the dormitory. By now, the others who shared the huge room no longer considered his workout a novelty. To them, it was just one of the numerous eccentricities which many POWs displayed. Especially now, when the stress, strain, and desperation were making some of them behave more than just peculiarly.

Just that morning, an English flier had screamed out that he was a gyrocompass and was heading for home. He began whirling, his arms held out, and humming loudly. When it became a screech, he spun into a window and crashed through the glass. Unconscious and bloody, he was carried off to the prisoners' hospital. The window was not repaired. Sergeant Schleifstein announced that there would be no more glass for the barracks, that glass was in short supply. The prisoners could fix the window up however they wished. Or they could just let the wind and rain blow in.

Just now, Doc was not doing mental situps. He was considering various escape plans and weighing the chances of success of each against the others. He had half an hour to go before finishing his exercises when he was interrupted. So were the other POWs. Schiesstaube and a dozen guards burst into the barracks and stormed upstairs. The adjutant, however, was preceded by the sergeant when he came through the downstairs door. Ever since the bucket of water had drenched him, Schiesstaube was the second man through the entrance.

Red-faced, yelling, and thwacking his riding crop against the side of the doorway, Schiesstaube strode into Savage's room. Four armed soldiers fanned out behind him.

"Attention!" Monk shouted in German. "Here comes the pimple on the Kaiser's ass!"

Whatever the adjutant's original intention, it was forgotten for the moment. His heel drummed on the wooden floor as he walked swiftly up to Mayfair. He halted before him and roared, "What did you say, you ape-swine!"

The adjutant was not the only one who seemed to be uptight. Monk glared at him, his face almost as red as the adjutant's, his neck quivering.

"I'm fed up with you krauts and especially you!" he squeaked. "I've taken your crap long enough!"

Ham Brooks, standing to one side, was frantically making signs to Mayfair to be silent. Doc said, softly, "Take it easy, Monk. You don't want to be in solitary again."

He thought, There's too much at stake just now.

"You will tell me what you said!" Schiesstaube screamed. "Or I will shut your filthy, imbecilic monkey-mouth for a long, long time."

Monk squealed like a pig and then said, "Oink! Oink!"

The adjutant said, "Oink? Oink? What does that mean? Explain your barbarous tongue, pig-dog!"

"Hey, you're zoologically mixed up, ignoramus!" Monk said. "I can't be a pig-dog and a monkey at the same time, though I know one Hun that can be! Oink! Oink! You want to know what means? It's what a pig says! It sounds like German to me! Oink! Oink!"

"For God's sake!" Ham said, and he groaned.

"Oink? Oink? I am your superior officer!" Schiesstaube shrieked.

Sergeant Schleifstein came into the room, doubtless attracted by the commotion. He shook his head at Mayfair to warn him to be quiet. He did not like the adjutant, and he loved to hear Monk's stories about his amorous exploits in Brazil while working for the chemical company.

Monk pressed his lips together and gave the adjutant the raspberry.

Schiesstaube brought his riding crop hard cross Monk's face.

Monk roared and grabbed the adjutant by the neck with one hand. The other, now a fist, slammed into Schiesstaube's solar plexus. The adjutant dropped his riding crop and doubled over. Sergeant Schleifstein yelled a protest and lifted his rifle. The other soldiers cocked theirs.

The POWs froze.

Schiesstaube spun around and straightened up, though he kept his hands pressed to his solar plexus. His mouth was open; his face was twisted. If Monk had not been so filled with a white-hot fury, he would never have hit a man who had his back turned to him. But now, his right fist slammed into Schiesstaube's spine at a point midway between the shoulder blades. The crack of breaking vertebrae was like the snapping of a whip. The adjutant fell facedown on the floor.

Schiesstaube did not move after that. He never would.

The sergeant slammed his rifle butt against the side of Monk's head, knocking him down and, momentarily, out. Then Schleifstein knelt and examined the officer. Monk groaned, opened his eyes, and started to get up.

Schleifstein shouted, "Stay down, Mayfair! Or I will shoot you!"

"Better do what he says," Doc told Monk.

Looking up at the ceiling, Monk spoke in his normal squeaky voice. His face was now almost as white as the sergeant's.

"I really did it this time, didn't I?"

"You damn crazy fool, you sure did!" Ham Brooks cried.

Doc weighed the chances of overpowering the guards. He decided quickly that it was not the time for action.

XVIII

Too often, the clouds blanketed the camp or hung heavy not far above it, the rain drizzling down on the buildings and on the spirits of both keepers and kept. But, today, the sun shone brightly and warmly. At late afternoon, it was still a pleasant June day, one to fill men with the joy of being alive.

Ham Brooks, walking back from the German section, did not look as if he would ever enjoy anything again. His head was lowered, and his shoulders were slumped. He stopped while the guards swung open the barbed-wire gate. His face did turn up toward the barracks building then. Doc, standing in the window, saw grief cut into his face.

He spoke to Renny and Long Tom, who were by his side.

"Bad news."

"I expected it," Roberts said.

"What else could it be?" Renwick said, his words seeming to stay in his chest.

"I understand that Brooks is a hell of a lawyer," Long Tom said. "But the devil couldn't win this case."

"Open and shut!" Renny said. He lifted his giant right fist as if to slam it against the window frame. But he lowered it.

They went outside to greet Brooks. The gate had closed behind him, and he was trudging toward them. They hastened to meet him, as did many others.

Doc, stopping near him, said, "No go?"

Tears were sliding down Ham's cheeks. He shook his head.

"It was hopeless from the beginning. I did my best, and they did hear me out. Nothing unfair, everything legal, just as a court-martial should be. But there could be no other verdict. Colonel Duntreath was there. He'll be along soon, I expect. He'll agree with me."

"Well?" Long Tom said.

"He'll be shot at dawn! We'll all have to stand there and watch it, I expect. Damn him, why'd he do it?"

"How's Monk taking it?" Renny said.

"Defiant, as always. He told the Germans how Schiesstaube had struck him, but it didn't cut any ice. Too many witnesses testified that Monk had provoked Schiesstaube."

"But Schiesstaube hit Monk first," Long Tom said.

"That's no excuse. Not in their eyes."

"Where's Monk going to be kept tonight?" Doc said.

"In the solitary in this section or in a building in the German part?"

"In the German part," Ham said tonelessly. "He was taken out the back door and to the armory next door. Von Hessel ordered him to be put in irons."

Savage gestured to his four compatriots that they should withdraw some distance from the other POWs. When they had done so, he spoke softly to them.

"Now that we know exactly where Monk is, we won't have to look around for him first. We can go directly to the building when we rescue him."

Renny said, "What?"

Ham smiled. His eyes, so dull before, were bright. "Now you're talking!"

"I'm all for it," Long Tom said, frowning. "But how in hell are we going to do it?"

Doc did not tell them that he had hoped the escape would be well planned and well organized. Monk had, no pun intended, thrown a monkey wrench into the works. But he was not going to be tied to a post and shot if his friends could possibly prevent it. Of course, his friends might be killed trying to free him. The odds were very much against them. But if that was how it was going to be, so be it.

Doc gestured at the many prisoners in the yard. They were in large groups and talking and waving their hands. Some of the voices were loud and angry.

"They're upset by this. They hated Schiesstaube, and a lot of them think Monk's great, even if he is obnoxious sometimes. Also, they're the cream of the cream of escapees. Incorrigibles. They're very frustrated because this place seems breakout-proof. They'll be ready to try something desperate."

Doc was silent for a moment. His face was impassive, but his thoughts were like a boiling storm cloud. Much better organized, though.

He looked past the barbed-wire fence. Colonel Duntreath was walking away from the building in which the court-martial had been held. With him was the Frenchman, Captain Deauville, his assistant. Duntreath looked very sad. Even his bushy mustache drooped, as if with sorrow. But Deauville was scowling, and his teeth shone in a ferocious grimace.

"You and I, Ham," Doc said, "will get the colonel and the captain aside. We'll talk to them about trying something tonight. Maybe, if all of us act together, we can make a mass escape."

"Duntreath's pretty conservative," Ham said. "He might put the kibosh on the whole thing."

"Deauville'll help us talk Duntreath into it. But, first, we have to consider Murdstone."

"There's not much time to find out if he's a spy or not," Long Tom said.

"Go invite him to come with us to confer with Duntreath," Doc said.

Renny looked astounded. "Holy cow! That might be like inviting the fox to speak to the chicken parliament!"

"Think about it," Savage said. "Go ahead, Long Tom."

Doc looked at his wristwatch. And then, faint and distant, came the whistle of a locomotive. It would be pulling in exactly on schedule, just like all German trains were supposed to do. It came here every other Sunday.

The gate closed behind Long Tom. Men crowded around him, barring him from Doc's view. Roberts saw Murdstone standing outside a barracks door. He was smoking a cigarette and smiling slightly. He certainly did not seem concerned about Mayfair's fate. However, Savage thought, that did not mean he was a spy. He and Monk had gotten along with each other like a cobra and a mongoose.

Doc looked past the barbed wire again. Now the locomotive was past the edge of the cliff. Its whistle shrilling, its bell clanging, hissing, puffing black smoke, the engine slowed to a halt. It stopped so that the first freight car behind it would be alongside the unloading platform. Soldiers slid the doors open, and they began hauling out boxes and packages. Ordinarily, some POWs would have been requisitioned to do the heavy work, but the Germans were playing it safe today. They were going to keep the prisoners behind their fences until after Mayfair had been shot.

Doc looked at the Russian section. Hundreds of the gaunt and ragged men were gathered as near to the fence as they were allowed. Had they heard about tomorrow's execution and were curious? Or were they just waiting for the train to come into their camp and bring food and supplies?

Doc wished that he could enlist the Russians in some kind of uprising. Too late to do so now.

Among the freight brought in today should be parcels for the POWs. They had all been painstakingly inspected by the Imperial post office workers before being sent on. The packages would have been taken apart and poked and probed for hidden compasses, maps, wire cutters, files, saws, and other contraband materials. Heels of shoes and boots would be inspected for concealed tools. The lining of clothing would be fingered, and, if something was detected inside them, ripped open.

But von Hessel was not satisfied with this. He had ordered his soldiers to make another close inspection. Then the parcels were delivered to the other side of the ten-foot-high barbed-wire fence.

Here came the baron now, tall and handsome, the closely cropped mustache and hawk nose looking impressive beneath his officer's cap. He was headed for his laboratory. He was smiling as if he had not just helped sentence a man to death.

And here came Countess Idivzhopu, Lili Bugov, taking an afternoon promenade in a beautiful pink dress and wide-brimmed sky-blue hat and holding a pink parasol. Her giant Santa Claus-bearded servant was behind her. She smiled, though this time the POWs were not whistling at her.

She turned around near the loading platform. Her eyes seemed to meet Savage's. She smiled even more widely, and she waved a pink-gloved hand. He did not know if she was greeting him or someone else. She would have to be very callous to ignore his feelings about Monk.

Then he knew that she had waved her hand at him.

Zad, his yellow teeth shining wetly, was waving at him. No doubt of that.

Savage turned away from them.

Long Tom had gotten Duntreath, Deauville, and Murdstone away from the others. They were standing by the door, Long Tom jabbing a finger at Savage. After which, he waved him and the others toward him. A minute later, they were all crowded into the colonel's small office. They argued more than they conferred. Deauville, whose fieriness reminded Doc of his flight commander, de Slade, was all for busting loose as soon as possible. Murdstone, if he was a spy, was also an agent provocateur. He was very much for taking action. And he was also helpful in suggesting just how to achieve their goal.

His intent facial expressions, his vigorous gestures, and the huge scarred nose bobbing up and down like a buoy in a violent storm made him seem genuinely enthusiastic. Maybe he was. However, he was speaking with a slightly stronger German pronunciation now. His excitement was betraying his origins. The others were not aware of it. But they did not have Doc's sensitive ears, nor his training.

Still, this was not hard proof that Murdstone, or whatever his real name might be, was a plant.

An hour had passed. Duntreath had been willing to listen to the arguments and pleas. Nevertheless, he was not going to give in. A mass attempt at a breakout would only result in the slaughter of the prisoners. It was his duty to watch over their safety. He was the keeper of his flock. By Gad, he would not permit all his sheep to be destroyed for the sake of one! He would, of course, authorize a plan if it seemed to have some chance of success. But he had heard nothing to convince him that now was the time for it.

"Believe me, gentlemen, it galls me as much as it does you to just stand by and witness the execution of Mayfair. But what else can we do?"

Duntreath was right. He could not order his men to

commit suicide or bless any venture that would put all of them in grave danger. Not if the project seemed doomed.

For a moment, Savage considered a mutiny. That indicated his desperation. To arrest and confine the colonel and to take matters into his own hands would be illegal. It would also result in Savage and his cronies being court-martialed if they did get back to their units. They would end up like Monk, shot at sunrise, but the firing squad would be composed of their own people. Not only death but dishonor would be their lot. At least Monk would die with honor.

Even if they did not touch the colonel but went ahead on their own, they would go to an Allied military prison for life. Or be shot.

After the meeting was over, Doc met with his enraged colleagues. He explained the situation, though they were well aware of it.

"It's not good sense," he said, "and it's not soldierly, either. But, whatever else anyone else does, I'm not sitting with folded hands."

"It won't have to be a one-man war, Doc," Ham said.

Renny, Johnny, and Long Tom did not hesitate to assure him that they were in it all the way.

"I got three others at least that'll join us," Renny said. "Beeton, an Aussie. O'Brien, Irish, of course. And Cohen from Brooklyn, the French Foreign Legionnaire, the Fighting Yid. Wild men all."

"Bring them here," Savage said.

He spoke to Long Tom. "Do you think you'll still be scheduled to work in the generator plant?"

"I don't know," Roberts said. "I'll go to the fence and ask if I'm supposed to report for the second shift."

Presently, Roberts came back. "Schleifstein says every prisoner scheduled for work in the German section, except the boxcar unloaders, is to report as usual."

"Good," Doc said. "I'll tell you what to do before you leave."

He looked out the window at the train. Though no new POWs had been brought in, one passenger coach was attached to the freight cars. That probably meant only one thing.

He said, "Long Tom, keep an eye on Murdstone. Johnny can relieve you before you go to work so you can get your instructions."

Roberts rubbed his hands. For once, his sour expression was gone. He smiled and said, "Great! Finally! A chance to short-circuit the Boche!"

Shortly before evening roll call, Doc looked out a window again. He was pleased when he saw that dark clouds had built up in the west. He hoped that they would bring rain tonight. The earlier, the better.

He also saw the baron and an escort of six soldiers waiting at the gate to the Russian section. He watched them go to the hospital there.

There was tension in the air in the mess hall. The men spoke in low tones, and many looked toward the table where Doc and his friends, including Beeton, O'Brien, and Cohen, sat. Duntreath was not at his table. Deauville usually sat with Duntreath, but he came to Savage's table for a while. He said, "I have heard, never matter from whom, that you and some others are planning something drastic. I am not asking you if this is true. But if it is, I'll do all I can to help. After it's started, of course. I cannot go against Colonel Duntreath's orders. But if things are put in God's hands, then who am I to oppose Him?"

"Thanks," Savage said. "*Man proposes; God disposes.*"

"The English poet Alexander Pope was a wise man when he wrote that."

After returning to the barracks, Doc lay down and rested for a while. He had not had time to do any of his exercises.

Johnny reported that Murdstone had so far done nothing suspicious. Duntreath seemed unaware that the barracks was seething with excitement. He was sitting in his office, the door of which was open, and puffing away on his brier pipe. He was staring straight ahead, though now and then he would sigh deeply.

"All the soldiers left after roll call," Johnny said. "There's not one in our compound. But there are plenty stationed along the barbed wire. The dogs are out earlier than usual, too. They must sense something. They're certainly whining and barking a lot. Maybe it's the storm coming, though."

Savage got up. He could see bright lightning streaks in the black clouds. And a thin mist was settling down over the camp. It would thicken, if past experience meant anything. And it usually did.

"At least we're getting a break with the weather," Johnny said. He shook his head. "I can't stop thinking of Monk in that cell waiting for dawn to come."

Doc looked at his wristwatch. He said, "Where's Murdstone?"

"In the colonel's room, playing bridge with him, Major Wells, and Deauville."

"If anybody notices I'm gone, especially Murdstone and Duntreath, distract them somehow."

Johnny grinned. "How about knocking them over the head?"

"Whatever it takes."

Johnny opened his mouth as if to say something, then closed it and walked away. Savage was not sure, but he thought that the skinny man's eyes had misted. Monk would probably be killed, and Johnny was grieving about it. It had not, however, paralyzed him.

The mist was pressing dark, wet hands against the windows. The arc lights had been turned on for the first time in many weeks. Evidently, von Hessel believed that the situation demanded every lumen that could be gotten; forget about economizing on coal tonight. The additional lights did not help much. Now, Savage could see neither the barbed wire nor the soldiers along it. Here and there were tiny glows and an occasional flash. These would be the oil-burning lamps placed by the line of troops and an electrical torch turned on now and then. The probing searchlights were also no longer visible, except when a beam swung near the fence. These formed glowworm ghosts which failed to outline anything.

He went to the back side of the house and raised the window slowly to avoid noise. He leaned out. No lights there, no figures moving around, no voices. The way was clear to the base of the cliff if he wished to take it.

If Monk had not been so hotheaded, he would be with the escapees tonight. No. There would be no break-out tonight. Conditions for such were not yet right. They would all still be waiting.

Doc closed the window. By the lights of the too-few lamps in the huge room, he went back to his bed. Renny, Johnny, Beeton, O'Brien, Cohen, and several others were waiting for him. One was a Belgian infantry captain, Cauchon. He played bridge with Duntreath when a regular was absent. Savage did not like him because he was a martinet, one who followed the book of the military and believed that the whipping post was fit punishment for the slightest neglect or misdemeanor by any but a commissioned officer.

The other two Belgians in the camp referred to Cauchon as "Cochon"—French for "pig."

Renny throttled down his thunderous voice and looked around. Then he said, "I got some more men for the job. They're just waiting for the word."

Doc nodded at them, then said, "I'll give you all plenty of time to get ready. Thanks for volunteering. If you know anybody else you can really trust, please bring them here for a briefing soon. A preliminary briefing, that is."

Some of them evidently had questions they would have liked to voice, but they were dismissed by Doc. The big engineer and the rail-thin man stayed. As soon as the others were out of earshot, Doc said, "Captain Cauchon? I wouldn't have thought he'd be the type to go against Duntreath's orders."

"I wouldn't either," Renny said. "But he somehow found out about what's afoot. He came to me and asked me about it. I didn't acknowledge anything at first; he's such a stickler for correct military behavior. But he does have a hell of an escape record, and he hates the Germans for what they've done to his country. He said it's the duty of every POW to escape. That, he said, superseded the authority of a higher officer."

Renwick raised his huge hands and shrugged. "So, what could I do? He already knew something was in the wind."

"He may be okay," Doc said. "But . . . I don't know. Tell you what. Watch him for a while."

He wanted to say that the damage, if there was any, had been done. But Renny's expression showed that he regretted having brought him along.

"If he does turn out to be a sour lemon," Renny said, "I'll kick myself from here to Berlin."

"We're probably too cautious," Doc said.

"Yeah, who wouldn't get crazy-suspicious here?" the engineer said. "I'm a man of action. This life is slowly driving me nuts—maybe not so slowly. If something doesn't break soon, I will. I'll put my fists through some doors, anyway. Not that these doors are any challenge."

He hurried off after the Belgian.

"Johnny," Savage said. "I asked Doctor Coffern to send me a new pair of boots. They may be in the shipment brought in by the train today—if there is any. But I can't wait until tomorrow for them. You have an extra pair which came with the last Red Cross shipment. Could I borrow them? Until we get back to the front, anyway?"

"Sure. Lucky we're the same size, huh?"

Johnny did not ask him why he wanted the boots. By now, he knew that Doc would not answer a question until he thought it was the right time to do so. It was an attitude, one of a dozen idiosyncrasies, which the five friends respected. It always turned out later that he had a good reason for keeping certain information to himself. But it sometimes irritated or frustrated them. Monk was especially upset by it.

Johnny delved into his duffel bag and handed Doc the boots, size 13. By then, Doc had his off. He tried Johnny's and found they were almost a perfect fit. Doc opened his shirt and the front of his longjohns. From under a cloth strip tied around his middle, he removed a small screwdriver and a small clawhammer. Hans Kordtz had sold him these. They had also cost Doc a good sum as bribe money for the guard who had frisked Kordtz when he came back from his leave.

Doc pried the heels of his boots loose and removed the nails.

Johnny said, "They must've been examined at the postal center and then here. They're not hollow?"

Doc said, "They are. But jam-packed solid. The contents look like rubber."

He took from his duffel bag a hand towel he had gotten in his last package. After wrapping this around himself under the strip, he buttoned up. He then took a cigarette lighter from his pants pocket. Johnny's eyes widened. Doc did not smoke, so why did he carry a lighter?

Savage slid a half-shell up from the device and snapped the flint. Fire leaped up. Seeming to be satisfied that it still worked, he put it back in the pocket. Johnny had never seen a lighter with a sliding wind guard.

"No harm in telling you now that we probably won't be able to use the route up the cliff and over the mountain," Doc said. "The situation has changed. Unfortunately, our cache is now on that ledge up there. We probably won't have time to go up and get it."

"I had my doubts about the feasibility of using that route," Johnny said. "There would have been casualties, maybe fifty percent or more. And jumping from that ledge onto the top of the train as it passed under us, oh, man!"

"Of course," Savage said, "we may have to do it yet."

"Oh, I didn't mean I wouldn't try it!" Johnny said.

"I never doubted you would."

All that planning, Doc thought, and all those gadgets hidden in my uniform, and now we have to improvise almost bare-handed. Oh, well, he told himself, maybe it's better this way.

He put the heels in a pocket and then took several items from his duffel bag. One was a toe clipper he had purchased in the canteen. It was heavy and sharp enough to cut the barbed wire. He knew. He had tried it out one rainy night.

Speaking of rain, the drizzle had stopped. Ham, who had been standing by an open window, called him to his side. "Doc," he said, "the train isn't supposed to leave until morning. But I hear steam hissing and wheels rumbling."

Savage listened carefully. Ham was right. Though the sounds were faint at this distance and muffled by the fog, they were unmistakable. Apparently, the boxcars had been unloaded at both this side and the Russian side. Now, the locomotive was moving. Then the engine bell rang as a warning. It was backing up.

But the sounds stopped a minute later. The train must have halted at the platform on this side. Doc strained his ears, if such a thing was possible, and finally could make out a shuffling noise, the panting of the engine. The train was standing by. For whom? Why? When would it start rolling again? Soon? Or in the morning?

Doc was about to summon Renny and the others when he heard the big engineer bellowing. He turned just as Renny burst through the doorway to the hall. Renny stopped and waved at Doc.

"Come quick! All hell's busted loose!"

XIX

Doc was up and off from his sitting position on the bed as if he had been shot from a bow. Renny had not waited for him but had turned and gone to his right down the hall. However, Savage had only a short way to go. Duntreath's office was at the end of the hall, a room between the walls of the two large barracks rooms. Some men were crowded around it and starting to shout. Doc could not see what they were doing, but he did smell smoke.

Other men were pouring from the two rooms into the hallway. Renny was shoving away those around the door. Doc plunged through the aisle created by Renny, but he had to elbow some men aside. A man had been trying to break the door down by kicking it. It was the only one in the building that could be locked. Smoke was seeping out around its edges.

Renny had yanked the man away from the door. He roared, "Stand back!" Just as Doc got to him, Renny drove his fist through a panel. As he reached inside, he said, "Cauchon, Murdstone, and Duntreath are in there!"

He coughed as smoke enveloped his head. Beyond the dense black clouds, flames lit the room. Hot air blasted through the doorway as Renny turned the lock on the inside and swung the door in. He stepped back.

"I heard yelling, and somebody hit the door hard, and then something broke, and there was a shot!"

Doc stepped past him, his arm held up to shield his face. The smoke made him cough, and it stung his eyes. One corner of the room was ablaze, but the smoke made it difficult for him to see clearly. And then he was hurled backward as a man sprang from the cloud. Both Doc and the man staggered back. Doc bumped into Renny. He saw now that Murdstone had hit him.

Again, Murdstone leaped at him. He was bleeding from a cut above his eyes and was possibly blinded by the blood. The front of his jacket was stained with a large red splotch. His pants were smoking, and one ear was blackened from fire.

He held a revolver in one hand and a long knife in the other.

Doc glimpsed the colonel lying faceup on the floor. He was burning as if on a funeral pyre. Near him, an outflung hand cooking in a flaming pool of liquid—the oil from a shattered lamp, Doc suddenly realized—lay Cauchon. He was face downward.

All this was taken in as he ducked, because Murdstone had raised the revolver. The man began screaming, then fired the gun twice.

A bullet whistled past his ear.

Somebody behind him cried out, "I'm hit!"

It did not sound like Renny, but he could not be sure.

Murdstone, his face bloody and twisted, lunged out into the hall. His knife thrust at Savage, and the revolver banged again, half-deafening Savage. Behind him, men yelled and swore as they tried to scramble out of the line of fire and rammed into each other.

Doc caught the wrist of the hand that held the gun and twisted. At the same time, though not without being slightly pierced in the chest, he grabbed the man's knife hand. This he bent inward with such force that the knife point drove into Murdstone's belly. The revolver clattered on the floor. Murdstone staggered backward and fell, his legs sticking out into the hall.

Doc bent over to grab the man's legs. As he did, he glimpsed through the flames and smoke the rickety old cabinet which the Germans had provided for Duntreath's office. Its doors, usually locked, were open. A shortwave radio set was inside the cabinet, its earphones lying by it.

He felt sick with doubt. Perhaps he had been mistaken and had done Murdstone an injustice. If so, he had terribly wronged the man.

When he had carried the man down to the end of the hall, smoke billowing after him, he placed him on the floor. Men crowded around him. He shouted at them to give him room. To his relief, he saw that Renny was not wounded. The engineer had borne the POW whom Murdstone had shot into the big room.

Murdstone's eyes were covered with blood. His mouth was open and moving. But his voice was very faint. So was his pulse. His huge nose, where it was not streaked with blood, was very pale.

Doc, now on his knees, bent over to place his ear close to Murdstone's lips.

He said, "Lieutenant Savage here, Captain. What happened?"

Murdstone muttered, "Duntreath . . . traitor . . . or German agent. Cauchon . . ."

Doc waited several seconds for him to continue. Then he said, "Cauchon?"

"Went to . . . reported . . . you . . . others."

Blood was welling from a corner of his mouth.

"Cauchon, was or wasn't he a traitor or agent?" Doc said.

"Don't know . . . never know. Cauchon and the colonel . . . arguing. I knocked on door. It was . . . locked.

Then heard scuffling, blows. Cauchon unlocked the door... stabbed in... colonel."

Doc had to demand that the onlookers quit talking. He waited a few seconds, then said, "Murdstone?"

"I went in... Cauchon... he fell... radio set... knew then... German spy..."

"Cauchon or Duntreath?" Doc said.

"The colonel... a plant. Cauchon... must've... colonel stabbed him... I... we struggled. Lamp fell, broke... fire... stabbed me... shot me... killed... colonel... couldn't see, thought he might still be alive... attacked... shot, stabbed, got me. Or somebody else?"

He spoke with more force now. Doc hoped that that was a good sign. But it was probably an onrush of strength, a gathering of vitality just before death came, a final protest of life against its being ended.

Doc did not answer the question. Extremely upset, he was afraid that, if he did confess that he had given Murdstone his fatal wound, he would weep.

He said, "I thought you were a German spy. Your accent was German, though very faint."

"No... British citizen... born Bremen... ten years old... raised Berk..."

The blood spurted from his mouth. It was the last thing that would come out of it.

By then, a bucket brigade had been formed. But there were too few buckets, and the effort to put out the flames would probably have been futile, anyway.

Doc stood up. He had been wrong, misled, and he had slain the wrong man. If only he had disarmed Murdstone... Murdstone would probably have survived. But he had been so sure. No. He should have seen that the man was blinded by blood and driven wild with fear that the colonel was still alive and would kill him.

There flashed into his mind the words of Hajji Abdu el-Yezdi, his Persian Sufi tutor. "Men are like tigers, striped with character traits. You have a very broad stripe of violence. You must narrow that. It is true, as you Feringi say, that the leopard cannot change its spots. But men are not leopards, not in many respects, anyway. For your own good and for that of others, change that stripe. If you do not, you will become as those you call evil."

There was no time to think about that now. Nor was there time to grieve or to reproach himself for having erred so greatly. The Germans would soon notice the fire, if they had not already done so, and they would be coming in.

There was also doubt about whether or not Duntreath had been able to use the radio to warn von Hessel of the planned breakout. Doc did not think that Duntreath, or whatever his real name was, had done so. But he could not bank on it.

He wished that he could reconstruct the events leading to the deaths of the three men. But he would never be able to do that.

Doc went to where Renny was ministering, as best he could, to the wounded man. Renny rose when he noticed Doc. He said, "The poor guy's done for, I'm afraid. That slime, Murdstone! If he's not dead yet, I'll kill him, the dirty spy!"

"No," Doc said. "Murdstone's innocent! I . . ."

He choked, then swallowed the confession. No time for that.

"Duntreath was a German agent. Duntreath. I don't know about Cauchon. It doesn't matter now. Duntreath had a radio hidden in his cabinet. Listen! I want you to go to the other barracks. Tell them about Duntreath. Try to whip them up, if they need any encouragement. Tell them we're going to try for a big breakout. Take Ham with you. Do it quickly! I'll be going after Monk!"

Renny said, "What! You can't mean . . . ?"

He snapped his jaws shut. Of course, Doc meant it.

"Get going," Savage said. He ran down the hall close to the line of men stumbling away through the smoke. They had given up trying to quench the fire. When he got to the area where the revolver had fallen, he got down on the floor and began searching. The smoke stung his nostrils and eyes, and he began coughing. He groped around until he found the revolver. Its metal was close to being too hot to handle. Flames licked at him. If he had been a foot closer to them, he would have been singed.

Stooping, he ran back down the hall. A glance into both of the barrack rooms showed him men hastily putting their belongings into bags or boxes. Some men were already clattering down the steps, where they would run into others leaving the doomed place. He joined these.

But when he got to the first floor, he battled against the mob headed toward the front door. Finally, he broke through into one of the big rooms. There were still some men there, but they had not yet collected all they wanted to take with them.

When he got to a back window, he checked the revolver. Though Duntreath was German, he had hidden a British weapon in his cabinet. It was a Webley & Scott .455-caliber Mark VI six-shooter. Two undischarged cartridges were in the cylinder. He unloaded the spent cartridges and put the weapon inside his belt. Then he raised the window and crawled out.

The flames had shattered the glass in the window of Duntreath's office and were eating up the wood above it. He could see a trifle better with its illumination. The dogs were whining and barking, making an undertone to the talking of the POWs outside. He assumed that the dogs and the guards were still on the other side of the fence.

Away from the fire, he was in darkness. The lamps the prisoners had carried outside were very dim glows. Then he was behind the other barracks and could see nothing. But, keeping one hand trailing along its wooden side, he got past the building. He moved slowly then until he came to a water-runoff channel cut into the stone, near the cliff on the north border of the camp.

He followed this until he ran headlong into the barbed wire. The pain from several barbs in his face reminded him that he had forgotten to check the extent of injury done by Murdstone's knife. He put his hand inside his longjohns and on his breast. The point had gone into the breastbone but not very far. There did not seem to be much bleeding, though it was difficult to determine. The knife had probably stopped when it hit the bone. It did not matter. He had neither light nor time to make sure.

From long and close observation, he knew that the cliff here was not climbable. He got down in the runoff channel and gingerly felt the extension of the fence which blocked the channel. To his left came the tumult of dogs and men. Some of the guards were shouting at the POWs, but he could not make out the words. He got out the toe clippers and went to work on the wire. Presently, he pushed away the cut ends and crawled through the opening beneath the main fence. Not without getting wet, though.

The guards, he supposed, would have been lined along the fence within sound, though not view, of those on either side. That would be the logical order to keep any POWs from climbing over the fence or trying to cut through it. There were not, as far as he could detect, any soldiers in his immediate area. Either they had been called away to enter the camp or the logical arrangement of them by the fence had not been ordered. Whatever the situation, the way ahead for him seemed to be clear.

The tumult in the camp had become an uproar. He strained to see lights but could not. He kept on crawling, stopping briefly now and then to listen. No one was near. If anybody was, he was certainly quiet.

After about forty feet, he got out of the channel. He figured he should be near the building closest to the fence. Moving slowly, his hand held out in front of him, the fog as thick as ever but luminous overhead from the arc lights, he at last touched the building. This was one of the German barracks. He groped along that, noting that there were no lights inside it. Then he was at the building where Monk's cell was said to be.

Now, he walked even more slowly and more carefully. He did not want any sentry to hear his footsteps.

The sentry was not capable of hearing. Doc stumbled over him and fell forward. He caught himself on his hands without making much noise. He groped over the body to the face, still warm. The helmet was gone. When he moved the head, it went far to one side. The man's neck was broken. And his rifle and bayonet were also gone.

Doc was not much given to swearing, but he did so now. Then he muttered, "How did he do it?"

He found the door and its knob. It moved inward at a touch, its hinges creaking slightly. There was no light in the room. Monk must have extinguished any lamps and, perhaps, taken one with him for later illumination. Doc decided that he had no time to investigate. If he found Monk, he would get the details of the escape from him. What mattered was that Monk had gotten loose and was prowling around out there. But he might still be manacled.

Savage went along the back of the building, around its side, and then along the front. He had to satisfy his curiosity about the guard out front. Had Monk taken care of him, too?

Yes, he had. There was none there, which meant that Monk had dragged him off someplace. Maybe inside the building.

But Monk would not have taken this sentry's rifle and bayonet. At least, he might not have done so; you never knew about Monk. Doc opened the front door and stepped inside. He felt around for a minute, then decided that a light would be no danger. Using his lighter, he quickly found the missing man. He was lying faceup near the wall. A gaping wound in the side of his neck showed where Monk had put the bayonet through it. His own bayonet and rifle were gone. Monk had taken them with him.

Doc went through this room to the next and found a third man. His neck was broken. Manacles and a set of keys on a metal ring were lying on the floor near him.

Somehow, Mayfair had gotten loose and overcome the one man left inside the building to guard him. Doc decided to get going. He could ask Monk what had happened when or if he came across him.

Just as he stepped outside, he heard shots. They seemed to come from the POW camp, though he could not determine direction in this darkness and in the muffling fog. He stood for a moment while he listened. A fight was raging to his left. The guards, though armed, were at a disadvantage because of the lack of visibility. Also, most of them were middle-aged or even elderly men who had never been in action. They were up against young men who had fought in battle and who also were incorrigible escapees.

The screaming, shouting, barking, and howling and the shots increased. By now, surely, the guards left in the barracks and those in the watchtowers also knew what was happening. But they could see nothing. Then he heard boots clip-clopping fast on the stone. There were many, which meant that these were Germans sent to reinforce the others. They seemed to be moving along relatively swiftly. He stopped and got down close to the stone. Soon, a line of dim and swaying glowings appeared ahead of him and going at a right angle to him. He supposed that the lead man was directing himself by the runoff groove which led to the POW camp.

He went forward, bending far over. The channel was a broad black line in the dark gray. Following it, he came to one of the many bridges across it, five planks nailed together in a square form. After crossing it, he had to run, still almost doubled over, until he caught up with the last man in the line. When Doc was right behind the soldier, so close that he had to be careful that he did not step on the heels of his boots, he could still only see him as he would see a phantom. The man was carrying a burning kerosene lantern in one hand and his rifle, fixed with a bayonet, in the other. He held the lantern before him, swinging it back and forth.

There was no way in which Doc could grab the man, his rifle, and the lantern at the same time. He would have to let the lantern, and possibly the weapon, clatter on the stone. They did so as Doc hooked his right arm around the man's neck and choked off any cry from him. Nobody called from the fog to ask what had made the noise. The lantern had fallen on its side and rolled into the mist. Doc kidney-punched the soldier, and he became limp. Doc eased him to the stone.

The very dim glow of the lantern suddenly became a flame. Its kerosene had spilled out and caught fire. The brightness enabled Doc to see the face of his victim when he bent close to it.

Hans Kordtz's long, narrow, and sorrowful features were under the helmet.

Doc swore softly. He had become rather fond of the old guy. He unbuttoned the man's clothing and stuck his hand under them. He detected a faint heartbeat. He was glad about this, though it gave him a problem which he had to solve at once. He should make sure that Kordtz was dead. But he could not kill him. He liked the German, and it just was not necessary.

He might regret sparing Kordtz if he got back into action. Better he should be temporarily crippled and in such pain that he would be out of combat. Doc snapped Kordtz's leg. After relieving him of his extra ammunition, he rolled him into the channel.

He picked up the rifle, checked that it was ready to fire, and ran as swiftly as he dared along the channel. When he caught up with the last man in line, he slammed him on the back of the neck with the rifle butt. The man's spine was probably broken. Doc stuffed more ammunition magazines into his pockets. After rolling the soldier into the channel, he picked up the rifle.

By now, the lanterns marking the line of newcomers to the fray had spread out. But they were still rather close to each other. The leader was barking commands which were an almost indistinguishable part of the general din. Doc went forward, the brightnesses beyond these men his goal. When he got close to the fence, he saw that all the barracks were burning. The POWs had set them on fire.

Before the barracks in which Doc had lived, illuminated like figures storming the gates of hell, was a swirling, shrieking, howling, and screaming mass. Evidently, the first contingents of Germans had been ordered into the compound to subdue the prisoners. The leader must have lost his head, since good sense should have told him to keep his men on this side of the fence.

The newcomers, however, did not join the struggle. They massed just outside the open gateway. Whoever was in charge of them seemed to be unable to make up his mind. He could not order them to fire at the POWs. At their distance, they could see the individual fighters, but they could not determine whether or not they were friend or foe. And the leader hesitated to throw his men into the hurly-burly. At least if they stayed outside the gate, they could shoot any POWs who came through it. The flames were bright enough for that.

Doc began firing at the men outside the gate. He shot twice, then ran to his left. The men he had fired at became less visible, but they still made outline targets. He shot twice more. So far, four hits.

Then he was down in the runoff channel. The soldiers were firing wildly. Only one bullet came near him. That screamed off the edge of the channel and into the cloud behind him. He aimed carefully and shot twice more and thought that he had not missed. After that, the soldiers lay down on the stone floor and began shooting.

He moved along the channel after each time he shot. He aimed toward the flashes but had no way of knowing if he was hitting any of them. Several more bullets came close; one clipped off stone splinters which stung his face.

After that, he directed his fire at easier targets, the lanterns. These exploded and spread flaming pools around the troops. Realizing that they were more clearly silhouetted, those on the ground stood up and ran into the mists. Doc loosed one shot after another as they broke, and got at least three of them.

Suddenly, there was a comparative quiet. Then he heard Renny's stentorian voice. "Doc! Doc! Are you out there, Doc?"

Savage called, "Here I am, Renny! Out here! You got things under control?"

"Yeah!" Renny boomed. "Those that aren't kaput have surrendered!"

"There may be others coming!" Doc shouted. "The guards at the Russian camp! Watch for them!"

Renny's voice came closer. "I want to talk to you, Doc!"

Using each other's voices as beacons, they came

together near the gate. Renny had a rifle, the bayonet of which was bloody.

"Monk's out there somewhere raising hell," Doc said. "He got loose and is on a tear."

"Damn! That's good news!" the engineer said.

"Organize the men and bring them to the locomotive," Doc said. "I'm going on ahead to try and stop it, if it isn't already gone. I think von Hessel was planning to leave tonight. He may have taken off by now. Anyway, the guards in the watchtowers have to be taken care of. First, though, I've got to tell Long Tom to stop the generators, maybe help him to do it. He was scheduled to knock out the generator plant personnel and then wreck the dynamos two hours from now. We sort of jumped ahead of schedule."

"You can't see it from here," Renny said, "but the arc lights were out fifteen minutes ago. I guess Long Tom figured things weren't on schedule. He went ahead on his own."

"Good man," Doc said. "Just so now we don't shoot each other in this cloud. Or Monk doesn't shoot us."

He attached another magazine to the rifle and plunged into the darkness. He followed the channel, which would lead him straight to the locomotive. However, first he had to do something which he had not mentioned to Renny. The telephone line had to be cut. It might be too late for that, though.

When he had gone about ten yards, he crossed the channel and headed toward the north side of the enclosing cliffs. There would be less chance he would run into reinforcements there. Also, by following the cliff, he would come to the telephone pole at the corner of the cliff and by the railroad tracks. When he got to the limestone barrier, he turned left and walked along it. But he stopped when he saw a big bright glare shining through the fog.

He went toward it, then saw that it was one of the German barracks. Monk must have set it on fire.

He went on and came to the next barracks building, which was also blazing. That Monk was a one-man army. The building after that was also bright with fire.

The next one was not only burning, it was exploding. It was von Hessel's laboratory, and the chemicals in it were blowing up and sending off pretty colors. Doc had no time to enjoy the aesthetic display. He hoped that all the deadly bacteria and viruses which he thought were in the devil's workshop would be destroyed.

He went on to the baron's quarters, a large two-story house. Monk had not gotten to this one. Perhaps he had been interrupted or had thought of better game. If Doc had not had very urgent business elsewhere, he would not have been able to resist his curiosity. He would have searched through the house. But it was dark, and no lamps were lit in it. Either the baron and the countess had fled with the servants or they were hiding in there.

He did not think that von Hessel was one to cower in the blackness.

He moved as swiftly as he dared. The dreadful thought that he might be too late spurred him on. However, when he came to the building which housed the telephone and the telegraph transmitting apparatus, he halted. The building had no lantern lights in it. That seemed strange. The operators would stay at their posts until ordered to leave.

Though he knew that he should keep on going, he entered the house. His lighter was burning, its glow leading him through the shadow-shrouded interior. He came to the next room. The light showed him a soldier slumped over the key of the telegraph transmitter. A man with earphones on lay on his back under the telephone switchboard. Another soldier was sprawled out, faceup, by the doorway. He had been shot in the forehead. The others had been pierced with a bayonet.

All the wires connecting the equipment to the wires along the tracks had been torn out. Doc would have liked to make absolutely sure that the wires could not be reconnected for a long time. But he could not stay to do that.

He did, however, pile papers in a corner and set them on fire. Then he left.

Stepping out of the house, he heard noises which had begun since he had entered it. There was an uproar of voices from the direction of the Russian camp. Mingled with it was the chatter of machine guns. The POWs there must have decided to take advantage of the darkness and of the battle in the Allied camp. They were attacking the watchtowers. The Germans there had no searchlights or arc lights by which to direct their fire. The Russians would be weaponless—unless they had taken them from dead guards—but they were out to kill their captors and then escape. They had little to lose except their lives, and these were so miserable and doom-laden that they were not worth much.

Very, very faintly, below the shout of battle, was a shush-shushing. Doc recognized it as the steam hissing from a resting locomotive. It had not pulled out. Not as yet. But it might at any second.

He angled swiftly through the mist, but slowed down when he thought he was nearing the runoff channel. Then he saw its dark band. Now trotting even faster, stooping to keep it in view, he came to where he could hear the panting quite distinctly. He slowed down, moving with his rifle held ready. Then he heard iron wheels turning on the tracks and the increasing rate of breathing of the machine. Throwing off caution as he would have cast off a useless burden, he began running as fast as he could.

Shots, as if muffled by cotton, came from the cloud ahead. Then, about thirty feet deeper into the cloud, he fell headlong and hard over something. His hand hit the stone so violently that it let loose of the rifle. He scrambled up and turned. His probing foot touched something. Whatever it was, it groaned. A man. Then a familiar squeaky voice said, "Die, die, you . . ."

Doc got down on his knees and flicked the lighter. Monk was lying there, eyes closed, blood welling from the inner part of his left thigh. At the same time, the puffing and shush-shushing became louder. He smelled acrid coal smoke. A glance upward showed him something red in the air and moving away from him to his right. It was the fire from the smokestack of the engine.

Savage checked the wound quickly, conscious that the train was getting away from him more swiftly every second. The bullet had rammed through the flesh very near to the thighbone. It may or may not have struck it. But the bleeding hole on the other side of the flesh showed that the bullet had left the leg.

Monk could die from loss of blood. However, if the train got away, its departure might doom Monk to death anyway—every POW left alive in the camp, in fact. Monk had tremendous vitality, and he might get help soon.

It was perhaps the hardest decision he had ever had to make. But the many lives in danger outweighed the one. Monk would approve of Doc's judgment. At least, he hoped he would.

He put away the lighter as he rose. He groped around in the fog and quickly found the rifle. Running, he came across the tracks at once and turned to speed along them. The headlight of the locomotive was dark. The engineer did not want to warn anybody in camp that it was leaving. In any event, the light would have been useful only to illuminate where the train had been. The engine was pointed in the opposite direction of its path of travel. But there were headlights attached to the last car in the train, the first in line now, so that the engineer could see the tracks ahead. These were on now, the end of the train being past the corner of the cliff.

It was a good thing that the light pointed his way was not on, he thought. If it had been, the guards in the nearby watchtower might have seen him. He doubted that they would have made out more than a moving form, but they might have figured out it was a POW. In which case, they would be shooting at him now.

Even as he pumped his legs to catch up with the engine, he had a fleeting thought. The heels he had pried off his boots were a mixture of rubber and an explosive. The towel tied around his stomach under his shirt was impregnated with incendiaries, including thermite. This powder of aluminum and iron oxide would, ignited, give off an enormous amount of heat. He had planned to tie a boot heel to each of two legs of the watchtower, wrap a strip of the towel around the heels, and blow up the legs.

Down would come the tower, and the guards therein would be shattered like Humpty-Dumpty.

The chuff-chuffing was louder; the red glow was nearer. He sprinted while hoping that he would not trip on the ties of the tracks. Then he was past the barbed-wire gate, its edge moving toward him as he approached it. A man must be swinging it back to close it. Savage barely escaped hitting it with his shoulder. A shout rose from behind him.

Shots came from behind him. A bullet came close enough to scream in his ear. It would be ironic, and just like the gods to decree such, if he was struck now.

But the gods had spared him. No more bullets came near.

Another irrelevant thought—or perhaps it was not so irrelevant. He did not believe in gods or the fates. But, in times of intense crisis and danger, he tended to revert to the emotional being in him, the Old Stone Age savage who worshiped malign and benevolent forces, dark enormous things. Part of the unconscious mind took over, and the unconscious was linked to the ancient ancestral memory.

Then he could see the front of the locomotive. It was outlined very dimly by the indirect but bright light of the firebox in the cab. Its door was open so that the coal-heaver could fill it. He sprang onto the cowcatcher—what was the German word for it?—and hung on with one hand to the ledge above it.

It took him a minute, maybe a little more, to sling the rifle over his shoulder and climb up to the top of the locomotive, then walk spraddle-legged and swaying to the roof of the cab. The heat coming from the boiler through the iron plates and through his boot soles did not invite tarrying.

He lay for ten or so seconds on top of the cab, listening intently. His rifle had been unslung and was ready to fire. But it would be awkward to handle when he dropped over the roof. He took the revolver out. It had two cartridges. However, there were probably more than just the engineer and coal-heaver down there. It seemed to him that soldiers stationed in the cab had been the ones who shot at Monk.

He could hear no voices, if there were any, because of the sounds of the engine and the wheels.

Ahead, past the cab and the coal-tender ahead of it and the roofs of two freight cars, were lights. He was sure they were streaming out of the windows of a coach. Von Hessel and his entourage should be in that car. If there were any soldiers on top of the cars, they were invisible in the dark fog.

He scrooched ahead a little. Lying flat, his chin against the cab roof, he could see the man who shoveled coal into the firebox. He waited until the fellow had scooped up a big shovelful and turned away to carry it a few steps before throwing the fuel into the open mouth of the firebox. Then he moved forward again and looked over the edge of the rooftop.

He was prepared to be seen. A soldier might glance upward. There were two soldiers below, one on each side of the cab and leaning out in the space between the cab and coal-tender. They were looking back along the tracks—a waste of time, since they could not have seen anything if it had been within three feet of them.

He pulled himself closer to the edge and leaned over, his revolver in his hand. One bullet went into the spine of one man, near the neck. The other bullet sliced through the neck of the second man. Both fell silently.

Doc did not have time to put the revolver back in his belt. He dropped it onto the floor of the cab. Then he rolled from the cab roof, holding the rifle high with one hand. He landed on his feet and started to bring the rifle up. At the same time, he yelled in German that the engineer and the coal-heaver should freeze.

He had expected them to be paralyzed with fright and surprise. But the coal-heaver, a sturdy young man with one eye, was made of stout stuff and quick reflexes. He threw the coal in his shovel in Doc's face. Momentarily blinded, Doc staggered back. Then he and the man were fighting on the pile of coal in the tender. Its acrid odor stung his nostrils.

If the young man had had the coolness to hit Savage over the head with the shovel, that might have ended the fight. But he had dropped the shovel and was trying to choke Doc. His grip was very strong. His sweat stench mingled with that of coal dust. His contorted face was very close to Doc's.

Savage bit down on the long nose and jerked his head. At the same time, he brought up his knee between the man's legs. The man fell away, writhing. Doc rolled away and got up as fast as he could. The engineer, a man of about fifty, had not been so quick to react as the young man. He must have been stunned by the two shots and then the dropping from above of a big man, his bronze hair shining from the firebox light, his tawny and gold-flecked eyes gleaming, his face as frightening as that of a snarling panther.

But, once he had recovered a little, encouraged by the coal-heaver's attack, he left his post. He seized the fallen shovel, lifted it up, and, yelling, started to bring it down against the American.

Metal rang as the shovel struck Doc's uplifted rifle. Doc stepped up close and brought the rifle butt around and up. It struck the engineer under the chin. He fell backward, his head so close to the firebox mouth that the hair began to smoke before Doc could drag him away.

Panting, Doc told the engineer to get up and stop the train.

It was only then that he became aware of something soft and wet in his mouth. He spit out the end of the nose.

XX

The engineer paid no attention to the command. He had not heard it and would hear nothing for some time.

Doc told the young man with half a nose to get up and move the controls to halt the locomotive. But the coal-heaver was still in too much pain to do anything but hold his crotch with one hand and his nose with the other while he moaned and cursed.

Doc felt sorry for him and astonished at himself. He had not meant to bite down so violently. His drive for survival had overwhelmed his reason.

Several years ago, he had had an hour's instruction in operating a steam locomotive. Now, watching the two men on the floor with one eye, he stopped the train. Its brakes and wheels squealed as it shuddered to a halt.

He stepped over the bodies and looked back down the tracks. The shining disk in the cloud would be the lights from the guard station which the train had passed when going to the camp. There was a gate to be opened by the guards—that could be crashed—and machine-gun and rifle fire to endure. That gauntlet would be run when the time came.

The lights in the coach showed several heads sticking out of windows. They were too blurred for him to see their faces. No doubt, somebody would be coming up to find out what had happened.

He eased in the long lever which started the engine back toward camp. After a few seconds of travel, the engineer showed signs of recovering consciousness. The coal-heaver was gingerly touching his mutilated nose, which was not bleeding very much. He was also glaring with hatred at Savage.

Savage looked back out through the window. Von Hessel must know that something was very wrong. He would send a soldier, maybe all the soldiers he had with him, to find out why the train was going back to camp. It would be impossible to fight them and keep an eye on the two men in this cab.

Doc told them to jump. "Do it now, no arguments!" he said. "We're still going slowly. You won't get hurt. I'll count to three. If you're not gone by three, I'll shoot you!"

He was sitting on the engineer's chair, the rifle, a bayonet attached to it, across his lap.

Reluctantly, holding the bleeding tip of his nose and promising to kill Savage when next they met, the young man climbed down the steps and leaped off into the fog. The engineer followed on his heels. Doc dumped the corpses of the two soldiers and then shoveled coal into the firebox. He turned on the big headlight, but it did not help him much in seeing the tracks ahead. The train did not have long to go before it got to camp. The question was whether it would get there before the troops from the coach got to him.

He went into the coal-tender car and climbed up on the coal pile. The freight car attached to the tender had no door at either end. It could be entered only through the sliding doors on its sides. Any attackers would have to approach him from on top of the freight car.

But he would not be able to see them until they had gotten very close to him. He had turned out the electrical lights in the cab and shut the firebox door, but a ray of firelight shone through a crack in the door. It was an indication of the wartime shortages that the door had not been replaced. That illumination would outline his head and give the attackers an advantage.

If they did come, that is.

They did. He saw the vague forms on top of the boxcar emerging from the mist at the same time that they saw him. He fired from a semiprone position, only his head showing. The flashes from his rifle would betray him but there was no helping that.

His three shots seemed to take effect. At least, the figures faded from sight. Bullets had struck close to him but had gone screaming off the iron edge of the coal-tender. However, if he did not soon shovel more coal into the firebox, the decreasing fire would cause the water in the boiler to slow its production of steam. And the train would slow down, then come to a halt.

He leaned over the side to stare ahead. He smiled grimly. Lights shone fuzzily through the cloud. The arc lights were on again. That meant that the POWs had the upper hand.

Suddenly, more rifle shots came from out of the dark, and four figures appeared. They were making a desperate charge, never mind the losses. One of them was much bigger than the others. Doc knew that it was Zad, the countess's gigantic servant, even as he put a bullet in his middle. Zad fell off to one side, probably off the car.

Bullets caromed off the metal before and behind him. One broke up coal nuggets by the side of his face; the fragments stung his skin and blinded his right eye for a moment.

But that temporary loss did not keep him from firing. A second man went down, then another. The fourth came flying across the space between the freight car and the tender, his rifle held before him, its bayonet gleaming dully in the firebox light. Doc had moved to one side after his last shot. Now, he thrust upward and skewered the soaring man in his left thigh.

The soldier kept on going, slid on the loose coal, and fell face forward in it. His impetus had removed his leg from the bayonet, but Doc was up on his feet—though he slipped and fell as soon as he was fully risen. However, as he fell, he drove his bayonet into the side of the man's neck and out the other side. He scrambled up and jerked the blade out, then whirled. No forms loomed out of the dark grayness; no fire from gun muzzles blazed.

He was about to take a chance and open the firebox door to throw in more coal when a voice came out of the fog. It spoke one sentence in English, then in French.

"I have a proposal, whoever you are."

It was von Hessel's voice. It did not sound desperate. Its tones were cool and underlined with wry amusement.

"Are you English or French?" he said.

Doc answered, making his deep voice somewhat higher in pitch, "Speak French." Any slight thing he could do to mislead the baron would be to his advantage.

"I have a proposal, whoever you are," the baron said again. "Take the train to Fischhorn and let me and the others off. Then you may do with it what you wish. I can make you very rich; you'll never have to worry about anything ever again."

Von Hessel chuckled and said, "Of course, I can't spare you from disease, death, or your own foolishness."

Doc said, "Baron! No deal! You're going to pay for your crimes! I know about your experiments on the Russians, about your efforts to create a new and devastating disease, and about your efforts to make a vaccine against it! You are evil, Baron von Hessel, and you will die for your crimes!"

There was silence for a few seconds. Then the voice spoke again, but in English. "You took me aback for a moment, Lieutenant Clark Savage, Junior, superman-to-be. But I should have guessed that it was you. Who else could have caused all this chaos and destruction and brought about this successful uprising? I underestimated you, my fine American friend."

"No friend of yours!" Savage shouted.

He looked from side to side quickly but mostly kept his gaze straight ahead. Just because the baron seemed to want to negotiate did not mean that he was not up to some trick.

"I can make you very wealthy, Lieutenant."

The baron reminded him of a tiger. But, Doc thought, there's more than one way to skin a cat, small or great, and the tiger is a great cat.

The train, which had been moving ever slower, by microdegrees came to a halt. It kept on shush-shushing, hissing, and panting like a tired monster that had run out of energy. Savage was surprised that the slight gradient did not pull it along, but the locomotive, as if it had a mind of its own, refused to move another inch. Nevertheless, Savage put the brake on.

He propped the rifle against the cab wall. Then he opened the firebox door and clanged it hard against the boiler. He seized the shovel and scraped it along the tender floor. The baron would think—Clark hoped—that his antagonist meant to throw in more coal. For a few seconds, the American would not be able to handle a weapon. If that did not bring the baron in, nothing would.

The sudden reddish light from the firebox showed Savage two things.

One was that there was a ledge on the face of the cliff six feet away. It had to be the same ledge that he had found when he had climbed up the mountain behind the camp and gone to the other side. It was at the same height above the ground and was as broad and as long. His dangerous climb that night had not been, as he had thought, for nothing.

The second disclosure was such that he forgot about the ledge at once. A pair of leather-gloved hands was moving along the top of the tender wall. While the baron had tried to distract him, a soldier (or maybe the baron himself) was sneaking along the tender wall, gripping its top, sliding his hands along it, his feet dangling, hoping to be quiet and unobserved enough to get to the cab while the American was concentrating on the baron's offers.

The soldier—or baron—must have realized that the firebox light, though not very bright now, had revealed his hands. He had the choice of dropping onto the rail bed and running like hell or trying to shoot his enemy. He was either brave or foolhardy and, in either event, very strong. With one arm he pulled himself up so that his head stuck above the top of the coal-tender wall. His other hand came up holding an automatic pistol. By then, the American had bounded out into the tender, his feet slipping on the loose coal, his hands snatching the rifle from the wall. Before the soldier could level his automatic, his head was jerked backward as the rifle butt struck him between the eyes. Without a cry, he fell back and down. His pistol clattered on the crushed stones; his helmet clanged slightly a fraction of a second later, muffling the thud of his body.

Savage whirled, now holding his rifle with one hand. With the other, he slammed the firebox door shut. Once more, he spun, then gazed into the fog. He could hear no sound of feet, see no dim figure popping out of the blackness. He went then to the other side of the cab and tried to make out shapes. He could see nothing.

Then, von Hessel's mocking voice spoke. It was soft, and the exact spot from which it came was hidden.

"A very good trick, my very young but very clever friend! You hoped to lure me into charging you, guns blazing, as the cowboys do in your Western cinemas. You failed, but, then, I failed with my little diversion. So far, the score is even."

The baron must be close enough to see the fallen soldier, however dimly he sees, Savage thought. To do that, he has to be on the side from which the soldier came—unless he is on top of the freight car just beyond the tender. Savage, crouching, went to the opposite side of the cab. He stayed behind the steel wall next to the entrance opening. But he partly stuck his head out.

"What do you say to my offer?" von Hessel said. His voice seemed to have shifted location.

"Nothing doing," Savage said.

"You refuse to sell your soul to the devil. Not for money, anyway. But what if I offer you something no amount of money can buy? Something no one else in the world but myself can give you? Something that Faust once bargained for, but with no catch in the contract for you. If you go to hell, you'll do so for some other reason, something you brought on yourself."

After a long silence, the baron spoke again. His voice was so soft that Savage could barely hear it. Were other soldiers creeping up on him while von Hessel kept him occupied? He strained his eyes looking at the place where the ledge had been visible when the firebox light penetrated the mists. Should he jump onto it now or later? Should he use it at all?

Von Hessel's voice was like a soft breeze.

"You were mistaken when you thought that I was offering you money. I knew that you would not be tempted by wealth. Why should you? You expect to make your fortune when you become a surgeon. Anyway, there's speculation in certain quarters that you have an independent and vast source of wealth. Or rather, that your father has it, and that you'll inherit it someday. Many people are curious about that, and, in the future, that curiosity is going to cause you much trouble.

"However, let's drop that subject. Let's speak, not of cabbages and kings and whether pigs have wings and is the sea boiling hot, but of my experiments with the Russian prisoners. You were twenty thousand leagues off the mark when you surmised that I was trying to create a disease which would be even worse than the black death of the medieval ages. I wouldn't try to do that even if I thought it could be done. Plagues backfire on the people who use them as a weapon. Moreover, my kinsman, stupid Kaiser Wilhelm, would not permit it to be used.

"My bacteria were being used in conjunction with certain chemicals to achieve a quite different goal. One you'd think impossible to achieve."

The baron paused, and then, somewhat louder, he said, "But it's a goal that can be achieved! I know! I know because I achieved it once! And I can do it again!"

"What are you getting at?" Savage said. The baron had his interest. That was what the baron wanted, Doc feared—keep the enemy intent on his words while soldiers crept toward him.

Savage went to the opposite side of the cab and looked and listened hard ahead of and behind him. There seemed to be nothing out there. Then he put the rifle down, gripped the top of the cab, and pulled himself halfway through the window to scan both ways. If any soldiers were on top of the freight cars, they were hidden and noiseless.

He returned, rifle in hand, to his crouching place by the opposite entrance.

"Explain!" he called out.

"I look as if I'm thirty years old, as if I were born in 1888! But I was born in 1858!"

Savage did not reply. But he felt a coldness not caused by the misty air. It poured over his skin as if it were rubbing alcohol, and it seemed to soak through and find a path to his heart. His mind had leaped ahead of von Hessel's words. He knew what the man was going to say next.

Nevertheless, despite believing the baron—though why he should have he did not know—he said, "Come on! What kind of a trick are you trying to pull now?"

"No trick! I truly have a gift that no man could refuse! I'm willing to give it to you because I am, I don't mind confessing, in a very bad situation. I need you, and if you help me, become my partner—we'll work out the details on the contract later—you'll share a secret that's worth far more than all the gold and diamonds in the world! It's what every man and woman has dreamed of since Homo sapiens started dreaming!"

The baron paused. Savage thought that the man must be alone out there. Surely, he would not voice his offer where others could hear him. Unless, Clark thought, he's making all this up. But Clark doubted that the baron was lying.

"I can give you . . . let's call it an elixir, that will considerably slow down the aging process! It's not the fabled drink of immortality, but it will keep you young for a reasonably long time. And it's possible that, eventually, before we get too old to care if we live or die, we could create a true elixir of immortality! Never age and never die, barring homicide or suicide or accident. We won't even get sick! I've not had any bodily affliction, not even a cold, since I took the elixir. I've been places where those around me were dying with deadly diseases, and I was untouched!"

Again, the baron paused.

Savage decided that he had stayed in one place too long. Von Hessel must know that he was in the cab. And von Hessel was not going to give him the elixir—if it existed—unless he was forced to do so. He was not finished with trying to kill him. And, if he did not succeed now, he would attempt to murder his "partner" sooner or later.

Yet, Clark Savage was nearly overwhelmed with temptation. Why not agree to share the secret of the elixir? Get it, then escape from this man? Give the secret to the world? Let everybody have it. No old age, no death from disease? But was that really desirable? Wouldn't it end in causing many other problems? Such as overcrowding of the now-spacious world, starvation, wars to make room?

No time to consider such matters.

Savage shook his head and laughed soundlessly at himself. What was the matter with him? He was actually believing that the baron could do what he claimed to be able to do. And he was tempted to accept the offer! He, who had thought himself above temptations! First, the countess, and now the baron. No. He was not going to fall from his own high self-estimation again. The first time had been caused by a weakness of the flesh, a weakness common to humanity and quite forgivable—in human terms. But this time . . . the baron's temptation smacked of the devil, smelled like Satan himself. In fact, the baron talked as smoothly and as convincingly as Old Nick.

"I must be nuts!" Savage murmured. "And I'm sure as hell not the hero I've been thinking I was, even though I tried not to feel I was the High-and-Mighty! Most humbling, and God knows I need it!"

He rose and flexed his muscles. Then, going by his memory of the location of the ledge, he leaped from the cab. He landed a few inches short of where he had planned to, though the front half of his boots did make contact. He almost slipped. But he leaned forward and then moved his feet forward. He was facing the cliff, his forehead grinding into the rock. He turned slowly around, careful not to lose his balance. He had held out the rifle so that its barrel would not bang into the cliff and alert the baron.

Now, using his voice-throwing technique, learned during many tedious lessons, he called out.

"You're offering the secret to me? But if you have it and it does work, why were you experimenting on the POWs, and killing them while you were doing so?"

He could not know how effective the "throwing" of his voice was. The water-heavy atmosphere might cancel his technique. On the other hand, it might increase the effect. He had to chance it, though he disliked depending upon luck.

"I was born in 1858, and I can prove it," the voice in the fog said. "However, the man who's on record as my biological father, Baron von Hessel, now gone to his reward, was not my real father. He was sterile. But he agreed to marry my mother, a Danish lady of royal lineage, so that he could boast that he had a son. What he could not brag about was that his reputed child was of nobler lineage than he. He married her shortly after she got pregnant with me. She conceived me in an illegitimate liaison with Crown Prince Frederick, who, as you know, became Emperor Frederick III of Germany.

"Thus, I'm half-brother of the Kaiser, Imperial Germany's present ruler, though I doubt he'll sit on the throne much longer. My country is doomed to defeat. My brother is not, as far as I know, aware that he has a bastard brother. Nor is anyone else now that my parents are dead."

"Get to the point," Savage said softly.

Von Hessel's voice was almost inaudible and seemed to be coming from another direction. The American, though he strove hard to pierce the mists with his gaze, still could see only a dark grayness.

"I check the state of the elixir about every four years," the baron said. "I examine a skin sample with a microscope. It shows the mutated bacteria in my flesh. Until recently, there was no change. But now . . . it seems the bacteria are dying!"

The baron was not able to keep anxiety from his voice. He was indeed near despair—unless he was a very good actor.

"I'll begin aging at the normal rate. But I lost my records of the steps necessary to make the elixir. They were in my ancestral castle in Prussia, and they were destroyed in a fire in 1893. I did not care about that then because I believed that the bacteria would thrive for as long as I was alive. I erred. And I also was stupid. I should have kept duplicate records in another place. But we can't be genuine supermen, can we? You and I, we like to believe that we are the equals of Nietzsche's *Übermensch*. But, in essence, we are not, are we?"

The baron seemed to be mocking both himself and Savage.

"I cannot remember certain very small but very vital steps in a long and complicated series of steps in the preparation of the elixir. After all, it's been thirty years since I did it, and I've been very busy with other matters.

"So, I reexperimented with my Russian POWs. And I'm happy to say that I have re-created the original steps in the procedure. My skin samples reveal that I am no longer aging normally! You can share in this elixir, if you care to!""

"You murdered all those men just to ensure a longer life for yourself!" Savage said.

"They would have died soon, anyway. As the countess says—you know her well, in more than one sense—they're just brutal, ignorant peasants who should thank you for ending their misery and stupidity!"

There was another pause. The American could hear, for a moment, a slight sound as of gravel crunching under a foot. But he could not determine its location.

"Think, Lieutenant Savage! You, too, can live as a young man far into the future, in a world which will make this one look primitive, sordid, and brutish! A Bushman's lean-to compared to the Taj Mahal! You and I will see marvels paling those of the *Arabian Nights!*"

Something clunked. This was followed at once by what sounded like something sliding down the slope of the coal pile in the tender.

A grenade!

Or was it just a stone cast by von Hessel to get the American to fire in its direction and so reveal his location by the muzzle flame?

But Savage could not take the chance, and he had leaped out from the ledge and to the right, as far away as his legs could spring him, to get all the distance possible between him and the blast—if it came.

It did. Just before he struck the ground, a night-bloom of scarlet rose from the interior of the coal-tender. It dazzled him, and it turned his eardrums to stone. It also dulled his senses for a few seconds. But the steel walls of the tender enclosed the explosion and sent its main force upward like a genie from a bottle.

The fire and the violence also roared into the cab and outlined in lightning paint the door and the windows. If he had been in the cab, he would have been killed. And if he had stayed on the ledge, he would have been plucked from it and hurled God only knew where or how far. Or else been smashed against the cliff behind him.

Particles of coal pelted him like a not-so-gentle spring

rain. He had lost his hearing—temporarily, he prayed—but he could smell the coal dust and then burning coal.

His wits came back to him suddenly, like a cartridge slammed into a rifle breech. Despite this, he found it hard to move, so he lay on his side for a moment. His right shoulder and ribs hurt.

There seemed to be only a few stones under him. He must have landed at the foot of the rail bed. Then, some gravel pieces pelted the side of his face. It happened long enough after the explosion to make him think that a passerby along the train had dislodged them and sent them down the slope.

The baron, of course. Investigating the result of the blast. He must have hoped that the hand grenade would land in the cab. The dark had caused him to miscalculate. Nevertheless, the grenade had gone off close enough to the cab to wipe out anybody there. Now, the baron was probably prowling around, though cautiously, hoping to find the American's corpse or his badly wounded body. Hoping that the blast had hurled his enemy out of the cab.

Silently, Savage groped around for his rifle. The baron would go off to get more men and lanterns. Maybe. Who knew what that fox would do?

His fingers touched cold steel. He scooted on his back toward it until his hand closed around the rifle barrel. He brought it up against his chest and checked its breech. He could not hear the clicking, but he doubted that the baron could hear it, either. Then, slowly, hoping he was making no noise, he got to his feet. He wondered when his hearing—partly, anyway—would come back. But, impatient, he went through the mists up the rail-bed slope until he could make out the bulk of the boxcar. Then he turned toward the end of the train away from the locomotive. The stench of burning coal was still in his nostrils. He hoped that all of the coal in the tender was not going to burn. He would, if his plans worked out, need the fuel.

Presently, he saw a dim glow ahead of him. By then, he could hear, but sound reached him as if he were under water. The glow, he found out, came from the combined light of several oil lanterns in the nearest passenger coach, whose electric lights were no longer working.

Stealthily, he climbed up the steps of the platform at the rear of the coach. There was no guard there. Perhaps the baron had used up all his men in the attack. He looked through the window in the door opening onto the platform. He doubted that he could be seen from its interior. This was mainly one large room, a sort of salon, with several moveable screens forming cubicles along the walls.

The countess, looking drawn and anxious and wrapped in a large white bearskin cloak, sat on a sofa by the ornately carved and golden-gilded wall. Near her, pacing back and forth, were a manservant and two maids. They looked even more apprehensive than she. There was no one else in the coach, unless they were hidden behind the screens.

He crouched, watching, until his hearing had become almost normal. He doubted that von Hessel was behind any screens. If he had returned to the coach, he would have extinguished the lanterns.

Where was the baron?

Just as Savage had decided that he should investigate the boxcars beyond the coach, he heard something, a faint rumbling. Then he realized what it was: steel wheels turning slowly on the steel tracks. He jumped down from the platform and sped toward the end of the train, guiding himself by scraping his fingertips along the sides of the cars.

There had been four boxcars beyond the coach. Now there were three.

The scrape and rumble of wheels was louder now because the car was going faster down the slope. Then it became fainter as the gondola passed out of earshot.

Doc stared into the wet darkness and said one word he almost never used. It expressed the essence of disgust and frustration.

Von Hessel had uncoupled the end boxcar and let gravity take its course. He was out of reach of his enemy.

On the way back to the locomotive, Doc cheered up somewhat. The baron had gotten away. But his flight was suicidal. He could not control the boxcar's rate of velocity down the gradient. If he stayed aboard too long, he would not be able to jump without cracking all his bones and jellying his brains. If he jumped after just a little while, he might be caught when the train came down. But, in this fog, he could easily hide.

Maybe the dawn would bring a wind strong enough to blow the mists away.

He stopped when he heard a very weak sound behind him, far behind him. For a minute, he wondered what it could have been caused by. Then he smiled and resumed walking. That noise would be from the crash as the gondola on which the baron was riding ripped through the barbed-wire gate by the guard station.

That must have startled the guards and made them wonder what was happening. But they would not leave their posts until ordered to do so.

XXI

Savage brought the train into camp. He blew the whistle and tolled the bell so that the POWs would not think that the train was manned by Germans returning to recapture the camp. Despite this, the train was surrounded by highly nervous and suspicious men. Doc quickly established his identity. After that, he was very busy.

It was not easy restoring order out of the chaos. Some of the officers, including Roberts and Renwick, had already started, but their task was demanding and, for a while, seemingly impossible.

Though the arc lights were now on and several scores of oil lanterns and electric torches were available, they helped only in small and isolated areas. The general darkness impeded the organization that might otherwise have gone fairly smoothly. Another obstacle was the great number of Russian prisoners. Many of them had been lost in the uprising, during which the machine-gunners in the watchtowers had cut down scores before being overwhelmed and killed.

There were still about seventy able-bodied Russians left. These had tried to seize the train and had been beaten off. Then they had grabbed every bit of food they could find and wolfed it down. Doc felt sorry for the starving men, but he wanted to save a certain amount for the long escape trek. There were also about fifty wounded Russians who had to have medical treatment. Added to that were about thirty Allied men and fifteen Germans who were so badly wounded they could not walk. Hans Kordtz was among them, solaced somewhat by the two chocolate bars which Savage gave him.

William Harper Littlejohn, "Johnny," was among the walking wounded. During a hand-to-hand fight with a German guard, Johnny's left eye had been badly injured by a rifle butt. Doc, taking a look at it in the POW hospital building, did not think that its sight could ever be restored. Not with the medical techniques now available.

Johnny was cheerful enough about it. He said that a black patch over his eye would make him a rather dashing and romantically sinister figure.

Monk's leg wound had been bandaged, and he was hobbling around, using a rifle barrel as a crutch. Doc was amazed that the man could walk after all the blood he had lost.

Long Tom was bruised and bunged up and bleeding from minor wounds. He had had to subdue the three Germans in the generator plant before he could throw the switches to turn off the lights. He did not look as if he could put up a good battle against a scarecrow, but his thin and anemic-looking body was deceptively strong. He was worth his weight in wildcats on a rut, as Monk said.

Though there was not much time to hear Monk's story of how he escaped from the guardhouse, Doc insisted on getting a rundown. Monk said that the building was not really a prison. It had one room, used as a cell for German military offenders during trial or for light punishment. It had one door, which was locked. Within the door frame was a swinging iron frame enclosing iron bars. This could also be locked.

"When that hooraw started in the POW camp," Monk said, "the one guard stationed to watch me went outside—I guess to see what the fuss was about. The wooden door was open. I twisted two of the bars inside the frame—they were no thicker than what you'd put outside your window for decoration, maybe a quarter-inch thick—and bent them enough to slide through the opening. Scraped me, tore my clothes, but I got through.

"When the guard came back in, I grabbed him by the neck and broke it. Hated to do it, he was an old man. But better him than me. Then I took the keys down from the hook on the wall, unlocked my manacles, and . . . you know the rest."

"How'd you get shot?"

"Trying to stop the train. A soldier in the engine cab shot me."

After speaking to Monk, Doc got the fire in the coal pile in the tender put out. The grenade had blown half the coal out of it, but it had not affected the cab controls. He put four men to work replacing the lost coal from the big stockpile in the camp. Then he went to the POW hospital, one of the few buildings that Monk had not set aflame.

The countess and her servants had been locked into a room there, despite her protests. They would be left behind, though free to roam, when the train pulled out. Then Doc had her brought out to interrogate her briefly. He had some inquiries regarding the validity of the baron's story about the age-slowing elixir.

Later, he regretted that he had not questioned her privately in her tiny room. There were many wounded in the larger room, among them a number of Russians pressed into nurse service. Doc had just started talking to her when she was attacked by one of the Russians. It took him completely by surprise. Before he could grab the man, who was wielding a bayonet while screaming at the countess, her face had been badly gashed and her right eyeball had been punctured.

There was an uproar for a while. The countess began

screaming and did not stop until Savage had found some morphine with which to sedate her. Then he bandaged her face while some men restrained the shouting and struggling Russian.

Now, that beautiful face would always be hideously disfigured. Her days as a seductress were over until plastic-surgery techniques could be perfected.

Doc was shaken by the sudden and unexpected incident. After he had made sure that the countess was asleep, he went to the man, a Sergei Khutzinov.

"Why did you do that?" he said angrily.

Khutzinov was a young man with long, wild hair and a bushy beard that covered his entire chest. His eyes still looked like those of a madman.

"You do not know that cruel, heartless bitch!" he said. "I, Sergei Khutzinov, was one of her family's peasants. I lived in one of the many villages they owned. Her father and her brothers were vicious exploiters. They ground their peasants under their heels, made them like work beasts. We had no recourse, no way to get mercy and justice. The family controlled the police and judges on their lands."

He stopped and asked for a drink of water. After he had gulped down the whole glass, he continued.

"You may not know this; I doubt you do, since it's kept from common knowledge, even from the Tsar. But the Bugov family—there are some others like them in our land—would hold manhunts. They would select a youth who was strong and a good runner, and they would let him loose in the forest, sometimes armed with a knife. And they would hunt him down as they would hunt a deer. They would shoot him and think it was great sport. Then they would hang his body in a barn as if he were an animal carcass, a trophy of the hunt, may God hurl their souls forever into burning hell!

"My brother Andrei was one of those hunted down and shot and his body strung up in a barn! My older brother, Andrei, who said that he was going to run away and go to America, where they do not do such things! He ran away, yes, he ran! But it was from men with rifles and dogs! And from the countess, who had begged her father to allow her to go along since it was her eighteenth birthday!

"She was the one who shot my brother—'bagged' him, as she bragged to her friends! And then the next day she went to Mass!

"I swore that someday I would get revenge! I thought that I would never get it when I was taken away to serve in the Tsar's army, may God blast him with lightning! I did not expect to return alive from the war! But..."

He clasped his hands, lifted them, and looked upward. "God has been good to me! He delivered the countess into my hands! He gave me the chance to kill her! But I wanted only to scar her so badly that no man would ever look upon her again except to shudder and to be sick with loathing!

"I have had my revenge, though it will not bring my beloved brother back to life!"

He burst into loud sobs and bowed his head.

Doc was almost as emotion-wracked as the young Russian. The evil that men and women did was beyond his understanding. He thought of that room in de Musard's house in Belgium, of von Hessel's fatal experiments with the Russian POWs, and of what the countess had done.

Someday, when he was ready, he was going to fight against such evils. His father was right. He should dedicate himself to such a course.

Meanwhile, he had to get free of this camp and get through enemy territory. Then, get back to the U.S. Air Service and fight in the skies until this war ended. Then, back to medical school and to the training and discipline that would make him a healer. Then... who knew about after that?

An hour and a half had passed since he had driven the train into the camp. That was far more time than he had wanted to take. If he could have had his way, he would have had the train leaving within fifteen minutes after his arrival. Speed was survival. For all he knew, von Hessel had ridden the boxcar all the way to safety. It might not have gone off the tracks and plunged over the edge of the cliff. The few curves in the tracks were slight. The car could have gotten to the long and level stretch outside the village of Königssee and finally stopped.

Also, a wire or wireless call might have been sent to the nearest German post before the transmitters were destroyed.

When the train was fully occupied, Doc gave the signal for it to start. Renny, the only experienced locomotive operator, was at the controls. Doc, Long Tom, Johnny, Monk, and Ham were all either in the cab or the coal-tender. Four of them were taking turns shoveling coal and keeping watch. Ham complained that Monk was using his wound as an excuse to goldbrick. But he did not mean it. He was just unable to keep from needling his crony.

The front boxcar lacked headlights, because von Hessel had taken the one with them. But Long Tom had rigged up a battery-powered set from the supply shed and had run a telephone line from the front car to the cab. The lookout in the car could give warnings and instructions to the cab, although he still could not see more than a few feet in the fog. Doc had decided not to turn the lights on. They might give warning to ambushers, if there were any out there.

He was heartsick that many POWs had had to be left behind. These were too wounded or sick to be moved.

The countess and her servants were in the coach, however. Some of the Russians in the hospital were not so incapacitated that they could not threaten to kill them. Doc believed that they would do it if they got the chance. Though he loathed the countess—this once-beautiful woman with whom he had once made love, an act which he bitterly regretted—he could not leave her to be murdered.

The train moved slowly at first; then Renny speeded it up when he estimated that it was getting close to the station by the gate. It shot without incident by the glows of the lanterns held by the guards and was in total darkness again. Though there might be a barricade ahead erected by the Germans, he kept the velocity at forty miles an hour for a few minutes.

The darkness paled but never became brighter than a

gray, pearly luminosity. Though the fog began to burn off, the visibility was no more than twenty feet, as reported by Deauville, the lookout in the front car. The train came to level ground, which ran for several miles before sloping downward again. Renny slowed the train to twenty miles an hour, still too fast if the stolen boxcar was abandoned on the tracks.

A mile and a half later, the slope began again. Either the boxcar had gone off the tracks while on the slope or it had had enough inertia to carry it over the level stretch and perhaps all the way to Königssee village.

Renny slowed the train to ten miles an hour. Soon, it would be near the village. Then he would stop it. So far, the boxcar on which von Hessel had fled had not been seen. If it had rolled into the village, the baron would have taken steps to amass a force to retake the camp. But he might not find another train available.

The escapees would leave the train and take off in whatever direction they thought best. Doc's group planned to separate itself from the others. This was one time when the maxim "Safety in Numbers" did not apply—at least not to *great* numbers.

Savage, who had been silent for a long time, said, "Men, if we make it to the Italian lines, we should get together after the war is over. It's true we'll all be busy for a while readjusting to civilian life and reestablishing our-selves in our careers. I have many years of school in front of me before I become, I hope, a brain surgeon. But I doubt if being a surgeon and a medical researcher is going to keep me happy. I'll miss the excitement of adventure, of which we've had more than enough lately to satisfy most men. I think you feel the same way.

"What I suggest is that, after we've all made plenty of money, maybe before then, we form a band. We set ourselves up so that we're a sort of Adventurers' Club, a very exclusive one. We all have valuable talents to com-plement each other. We'd make a hell of a good team."

"Sounds great to me," Monk said.

The others enthusiastically agreed.

"But just what do you mean by 'Adventurers' Club'?"

Monk said. "You mean we make expeditions into unknown lands?"

"No, not exactly," Doc said. "Perhaps I should have labeled it the Troubleshooters' Club. Or Crime-Fighters' Club. There are very evil people out there. The average person is helpless against them, and so is the police force. We could get engaged in the really big crimes."

"Like investigating Congress?" Monk said.

After they had quit laughing, Doc said, "If need be. But I was thinking about advertising our services. As if we were a kind of high-class detective agency. But we'll be rather choosy about taking cases. Only those threatened by really exceptional criminals or injustice will be accepted as clients. We won't charge a fee, so we can pick the case we think is important enough to spend time on. After all, we will also have to be earning a living at the same time.

"It's just an idea. Think about it. You'll have lots of time for that. Maybe it's impractical. Or you might get married and have kids and want to settle down. One thing I do know—if you're married, you can't be a member. That seems harsh, but the family comes first."

"I really like it," Monk said. "I . . ."

Renny, who was the only one looking ahead at the moment, cried, "Holy Cow! Down on the floor!"

They heard the squealing of locked wheels on the tracks. The German engineer must have seen their train just as Renny saw the dim eye of its locomotive. It, too, had been going slow in the fog, its bell and whistle silent.

Renny locked the brakes of his train, the only thing he had time to do before the collision some seconds later.

The others in the cab had dropped facedown on the floor, but the combined impact of the two trains, each going at about twenty miles an hour, slid the five forward on their faces. They slammed into the pile of coal in the tender with stunning force. Renny tried to cling to the lever, but he was hurled from his seat into the bulkhead before him.

They were aware of a great noise ahead. This, they found out later, was the sound of the crash as the German locomotive, loaded with soldiers come to chase the escapees, plowed into the boxcars of the stolen train. These were knocked off the tracks and folded into a heap like a wrecked accordion. Most of those in the cars or riding on their roofs were killed outright or injured so badly they could not move. The German engine crew and the soldiers were not injured so extensively, but they were unable to spring into action for some minutes.

Though Renny and the others were stunned and battered, they quickly came to their senses. None of their bones were broken, though some, they found out later, did have hairline fractures. They managed to get out of the locomotive and into the fog before the Germans could get to them. Some of these plunged into the mists looking for Doc and his men. But most of the able-bodied were busy dragging out the injured and trying to extricate those pinned in the twisted and crumpled cars.

The cries and screams of the badly hurt were heart-searing. But the six men could not stay to help. They would be shot if they were captured.

A month later, they got to the Italian lines. The tale of how they made it through the mountains while hundreds of men were looking for them, how they kept from starving to death, is a saga in itself.

It was a long time before Doc found out about the countess and the baron. She had not been killed in the wreck, but her back had been broken, and she was paralyzed from the waist down.

Von Hessel had gotten to the village and recruited the trainload of soldiers to go up to Camp Loki. He was not injured badly in the collision. A short time later, according to the Intelligence reports Doc got, the baron had disappeared. Both the Allied and the German authorities were looking for him. Just what the baron's own people had against him was not known to the Allies for a long time.

But Clark Savage was not certain that he would not hear from the baron again. Nor from the countess. Both had reason to hate him.

ABOUT THE AUTHOR

PHILIP JOSÉ FARMER was born in 1918 in North Terre Haute, Indiana, but has spent most of his life in Peoria, Illinois. His career began as a technical writer for the space-defense industry. Farmer's first piece of science-fiction, *The Lovers*, appeared in *Startling Stories* magazine in 1952. It was the first s-f story to deal with sex in a mature fashion in the pulp magazine field. Farmer has received three Hugos and a *Playboy* short-story award. He has written 68 novels and short-story collections in addition to his "biography" of Doc Savage, *Doc Savage: His Apocalyptic Life*.

In 1991, Farmer and his wife will celebrate their 50th wedding anniversary. They have a son and daughter, six grandchildren, and one great-grandson.

Mr. Farmer has been reading the Doc Savage series since the first one came out in 1933, and this novel fulfills a lifelong ambition to write an original Doc Savage novel.

You've just read Doc's *first* thrilling adventure.

Now continue the series written by Will Murray, writing as Kenneth Robeson, with an all-new adventure story based on a never-before published outline written by Lester Dent in 1935.

Here is the exciting first-chapter preview from **PYTHON ISLE.**

It was a diamond smuggler named "King" Hancock who was the first to sight the strange monoplane. This later proved to be extremely unfortunate. Had King Hancock not chanced to be gazing out at the Indian Ocean at that moment, it is quite probable that considerable trouble—not to mention several deaths—might have been avoided.

King Hancock did not look like a diamond smuggler. He did not even look like a crook. He was a spry, dapper-looking individual who wore his hair slicked back and his mustache thin and pointed. He wore a long Prince Albert coat, in spite of the heat. The coat was King Hancock's trademark.

Actually, King was not his given name. He had come into the world as Bartholomew Hancock, but claimed to be a descendant of John Hancock, the natty Revolutionary figure who also had sported the appellation King. The current King Hancock had made it his life's work to emulate his famous ancestor, except that he was a rogue. Not that he was evil. King Hancock hadn't an evil bone in his body. Not a good bone, either. King Hancock hadn't any particular inclinations either way, he was fond of saying. But he did like to dress and eat well, and he did like money.

This was why King Hancock was currently lounging at the rail of the tramp steamer *Mighty*, which was two days out of Durban, South Africa, with a clandestine cargo of purloined diamonds.

The plane swept out of the northern horizon. It was a small craft, built for speed. It behaved queerly. One wing dipped erratically. The drone of its motor sounded like a bumblebee with a bad case of hiccups. The queer plane angled toward the *Mighty*. It was then King Hancock snapped out of his casual pose.

"Cap'n!" he yelled. "Trouble at ten o'clock!"

At once, the decks of the decrepit steamer were aswarm with cursing, hard-faced men of varying nationalities. Rifles were brought out of hiding places. Deck plates were pried up and squat deck guns hoisted into the African sun.

"What the bloody blazes is going on?" a voice exploded. It might have come from one of the tramp's rust-scabbed funnels. The voice belonged to "Blackbird" Hinton, notorious diamond smuggler and skipper of the *Mighty*. Blackbird Hinton was a short, rangy man who walked with a pronounced rolling gait. His cold black eyes wore a perpetual sun-squint. He was dressed in black. His coat, pants, shoes, even his captain's cap, were as black as an unlucky cat. His face was brown and shiny, like a bird's beak. He was not called blackbird without reason.

"Where did that bloody-damned plane come from?" Blackbird demanded of his first mate, King Hancock, when he saw the queer plane.

"I don't know. It was just—there," Hancock explained.

Blackbird Hinton telescoped a jet-black spyglass and peered through it.

"Any markings?" Hancock inquired.

"No. Looks beat up, though." Blackbird's mahogany face was grim. His forehead was dry, in contrast to King Hancock's perspiration-streaked visage. He passed the spyglass. "What do you make of it?"

King Hancock wiped sweat from his brow, peered heavenward. "Looks to be in trouble, all right. I'd say they're running low on fuel," Hancock decided.

"Could be a trap," Blackbird said suspiciously. Behind him, the *Mighty*'s crew watched the tiny plane approach hesitantly, guns held ready.

"There's a funny gleam on one wing," Hancock remarked, "but I can't make out what it is."

The strange plane drew closer. Its bumblebee drone continued intermittently. One wing—the shiny one— dipped repeatedly, and it was plain to see the pilot was having difficulty keeping level. It continued on a direct line to the wallowing tramp steamer."

"Which way did you say it came from?" Blackbird demanded.

"Due north," Hancock replied. "Nothing but monsoons up there."

Blackbird considered, then turned to his crew. "Shoot it down!" he screamed. "It's the law."

Gunfire erupted from the rolling deck. Rifles kicked. The deck guns remained silent, because the plane was directly overhead. One crook fell over dead in the heat of the excitement. A bullet fired straight up had returned to deck after losing velocity; it stove in the top of his skull.

A thin trail of smoke grew out of one wing of the beat-up plane. The tail sprouted fiery red feathers, then oily smoke. The shiny wing heeled precariously for a long moment, then the craft plunged toward the water. Shooting ceased then.

Blackbird Hinton ran his thick hands over his dark coat front. He looked like an evil raven preening himself after a meal. "That takes care of him," he grunted.

It didn't. At the last possible moment, the plane righted, got level, and pancaked into the Indian Ocean less than a mile from the *Mighty*'s stern.

The craft did not sink, although the crew watched it like carrion birds, waiting for the waves to claim the tiny ship.

"Probably the South African authorities," King Hancock mused out loud. "They must have found that diamond mine we raided two days ago. Maybe there were survivors we didn't know about."

"That's just what I'm thinkin'," Blackbird said. He stared at the plane. One wing was entirely awash. That meant the cabin was filling. At length, the *Mighty* skipper gave his first mate orders.

"Take some men in a launch and check that bird out. Take prisoners, but make sure that plane gets the deep six. If the law is on our trail, we're better of knowin' about it."

Dapper King Hancock barked orders. Men fell to. Soon, a launch was racing toward the stricken plane.

The launch did not approach the crippled aircraft directly. At King Hancock's direction, the launch crew circled the plane, eyes alert and modern rifles handy. Hancock, standing in the bow, looked a little like Napoleon in his Prince Albert.

"Man alive!" a deck hand exclaimed when they drew close. "Did we shoot him up that bad?"

The plane was a sight. Its fuselage was a patchwork of repairs and makeshift plates covering—sometimes barely so—various rents and holes.

"Glory be!" someone ventured. "If those ain't gold plates holding that wing together!"

The scarecrow of the skies was indeed repaired with gold, it was plain to see. Fist-sized patches of the yellow metal studded one wing. What might have been golden rivets studded the craft's air surfaces. The propeller blade was gilded in spots, perhaps for strength.

Strangest of all were the designs. Almost every inch of gold had a design hammered into it. These were difficult to make out, except One. On the gold-sheathed wing, a serpent wound its coils. The sight was somehow barbaric—and sinister.

An eerie silence fell over the launch. King Hancock broke this.

"That's one of those transoceanic jobs," he said. "Like that one Lindbergh flew to Paris." His voice was strangely quiet. "Hold your fire, men. The law didn't send *that* bird after us."

It was fortunate that the natty diamond smuggler ventured his opinion at that exact moment because his men, nervous at the vision of the weird craft, were becoming trigger-happy and doubtless would have fired when the cabin door suddenly popped open.

An apparition emerged from the cabin and onto a brine-washed wing. If anything, this individual was even more remarkable than the scarecrow of a plane that had lately come, seemingly, out of nowhere.

It was a man—but a man dressed as none of the cutthroats from the *Mighty* had ever seen a man attired. He wore an odd costume. It might have been an abbreviated smoking jacket, except that it was white, edged with gold, and its skirt fell only to the man's knees. His arms and legs were completely bare.

"Is that a dress that bloke's got on?" someone wanted to know.

"Maybe it's a kilt," another laughed. "Them Scots get around."

The fantastic individual in white ignored them. He reached into the cabin door. If the astonishment aboard the launch had been great before, it now grew by yards after the second individual quitted the strange skybird.

For the second individual was a woman!

She, too, was queerly costumed, but her garb consisted of a trailing gown of purple and white. Her hair was black, glossy, and pinned high on her head with a golden ornament. She seemed very young. Her face was a nice oval. She was a vision.

"This is gettin' interestin'," a man to Hancock's left remarked, licking dry lips.

"Shut up!" Hancock barked. "Orders are to take them aboard. Hop to it!"

The launch, engine throttled, pushed toward the plane.

The black-haired vision spotted them and yelled something no one caught.

"What'd she say?"

"Never mind," King Hancock said shortly. "Watch them! They're going to swim for it!"

They tried. The odd pair jumped into the sea, surfacing together some yards distant.

"Boat hooks!" Hancock ordered. The long, hooked poles used to steady docking craft sprouted from the launch like quills. "Steady as she goes," he told the man at the engine. "We don't want to run them over. The woman first."

The launch eased toward the bobbing head of the swimming girl. She cast frightened eyes over a shoulder, redoubled her efforts. Nearby, her companion called out in a foreign tongue. The launch, engine idling, glided unerringly after her.

"Grab her, quick! You won't need the hooks."

King Hancock was correct. The launch all but bumped the girl. A big seaman reached down and pulled her out by her shoulders. She struggled violently, then subsided as it dawned on her that the big sailor was more than her match.

"Hold on to her, now," came the command. The launch, once more under power, came about and bore down on the swimming man.

The strange fugitive in white—they saw now that he had flaming red hair—abruptly ceased swimming and began treading water. He waited for the launch calmly.

"Get those hooks out," Hancock warned. "He may give us a row."

The swimmer did not start a fight—at first. He merely grasped a proffered boat hook and allowed himself to be pulled to the launch's side. Strong hands assisted him aboard. He accepted these readily.

The red-headed man stood amidships, seawater stringing off the skirt of his garment. He was tall, and gangling. His hair was the color of new rust and his eyes, in contrast to the sloe orbs of the companion, were bright blue.

King Hancock, no less out of place in his long coat than the other, approached.

"Got a name, mate?" he asked.

The redhead answered by way of a roundhouse right to the dandified diamond smuggler's pointed jaw. King Hancock's head rocked back under the powerful punch. But for a quick-witted crewman, he would have been precipitated into the drink.

They jumped the redhead. Blows fell. Men grunted. The launch rocked to the sound of men in violent combat.

"No guns!" Hancock warned. "And someone hold onto that girl!"

The strange antagonist proved himself to be a fighter. Two men fell unconscious, their jaws whacked out of shape. A boat hook *swished* by him, but missed. Another descended on his thatch of carroty hair. He heard it coming and twisted, but the pole caught him painfully in the shoulder and he went down.

The sloe-eyed girl screamed. Someone clapped a big paw over her mouth, effectively silencing her.

The red-haired man lay unmoving across a thwart.

"That settles his hash," the boat-hook wielder announced proudly.

"O.K.," King Hancock said, rubbing his bruised jaw. "He'll keep. Take us back to the ship."

The launch got under way.

King Hancock sat in the bow, facing the captured girl, who was seated between two burly ruffians. His eyes were intent upon her obvious charms. Even soaked to the skin, this vision from the sea was an entrancing creature. She held her head high, in a way that was almost regal, and perhaps a bit disdainful. King Hancock had never seen anything so fetching in his life.

"Some dish," one of the men remarked, jerking his thumb toward the girl.

"Pipe down!" the dapper crook snapped. "She can hear you."

"So what?" the worthy argued. "You heard her talk. She can't speak English, it's plain to see."

"Just shut up, then."

The other shrugged. "You're the boss, mate."

All eyes were on the enchanting girl in white as the launch beat back toward the *Mighty*. Thus, no one noticed the vanquished prisoner surreptitiously open one blue eye, extract an object from his clothes, and conceal this under a thwart.

If someone had, he would have seen that the object was a length of bamboo.

Blackbird Hinton was standing on the tramp steamer's deck like a great black crow when King Hancock clambered aboard.

"I thought I told you to scuttle that blasted plane.!" he roared.

"Take another look at it through the glass," the natty crook exhorted. "It's covered with gold plates. No wonder it was in trouble. One wing is three-quarters gold."

Blackbird looked. He shouted orders to the wheel-house.

"Get alongside that plane before it sinks!" To his first mate, he said, "Ready a crew with the boom."

"Aye, aye, Cap'n," King Hancock saluted.

By this time, the prisoners had been hauled aboard. The ravenlike diamond smuggler strode toward them with his rolling gait. Both the girl and her companion were walking under their own power.

"This one doesn't speak English," a sailor offered, indicating the girl. "We're not sure about this guy, though. He gave us a fight."

"So I noticed," Blackbird said sarcastically. "I also noticed it took most of you lubbers to bring him down. We've got almost a half million dollars in uncut diamonds aboard this tub, with the South African law apt to be breathin' down our necks most any time, and you swabs can't even handle one guy—and a guy in a dress, at that!"

The men looked sheepish. No one spoke a word.

"And what about you?" Blackbird roared, turning on the red-haired captive. "What have you to say for your bloody self?"

"What ship is this?" the prisoner asked. He spoke acceptable English.

"This is the *Mighty*, me bucko, as fine a hellship as ever prowled the seven blasted seas. I'm her skipper. Call me Blackbird."

"What destination?"

"Bombay, India, if that means anythin' to you."

The prisoner nodded. "It does. What year is this?"

Blackbird Hinton blinked button eyes. "What?" he roared.

"I asked: 'What year is this?'"

Blackbird blinked. Then he blurted, "Nineteen thirty-four. Are you daft?"

The redhead let out a long, gusty sigh. "Seven years . . . Incredible! I can't believe it's been that long."

Before the black-clad skipper could continue this conversation, the *Mighty* drifted alongside the damaged aircraft. A boom swung out, lines dropped, whizzing. Seamen slid down those lines and secured them to various points on the plane. A signal was given.

Then, the boom slowly raised the scarecrow plane. Water rushed out of its cabin. When most of it had been drained, the boom swung inward and deposited the plane in a gaping hold.

"Let's see this gilded bird," Blackbird rumbled. "Bring the prisoners along."

Most of the crew, including King Hancock, and the prisoners went below to inspect the crippled plane. It was, they saw, a metal Harlequin. It was patched and repaired with multitudinous gold plates, so that the entire craft resembled a dural and gold jigsaw puzzle. Moreover, most of the plates were cunningly wrought, as if by master artisans, and one wing—the left—was sheathed in thinly beaten gold.

Virtually every golden surface was ornamented by serpent designs, singly, in pairs, and intertwined. They were repulsive, like swollen veins.

"Snakes," someone muttered. "Gives me the creeps."

"What beats me," another put in, "is how he coulda flown this thing in the first place. Lindy himself would have had a tough time with it."

"Lindy?" The red-haired prisoner asked puzzledly.

"Yeah, Charles Lindbergh. The hotshot who flew across the Atlantic. Say—I never heard of anyone who never heard of Lindbergh!"

"So," the other said wistfully, "someone finally made a transatlantic hop."

"What are you tryin' to pull!" Blackbird snarled.

Before he could get an answer, King Hancock, who had been hovering attentively around the girl prisoner, came rushing up.

"Cap'n, that girl is talking a mile a minute in a lingo I never heard before," he reported.

"What of it?"

"She keeps repeating a name," Hancock insisted.

"What name?"

Dapper King Hancock swallowed noticeably. He was having difficulty with his words.

"Well!" Blackbird Hinton bellowed. "What name?"

King Hancock croaked two words: "Doc Savage."

A hush fell over the murky hold. All eyes turned toward the girl in white and purple. Sweat oozed from dirty foreheads. King Hancock licked his pointed mustache. Blackbird Hinton nervously commenced his preening motions, smoothing his black coat front repeatedly.

"Doc Savage," Blackbird repeated hollowly.

It would have been hard to imagine a more unsavory lot of criminals—than Blackbird Hinton and his crew. Not two days ago they had fallen upon a hapless diamond mine on the east coast of South Africa, slaughtered its workers to a man, and made off with a young fortune in uncut stones. They were bloody-handed diamond smugglers and worse. Yet every one of them visibly paled at the mention of the name Doc Savage.

Even in this out-of-the-way corner of the world, the name of Doc Savage had carried. Doc Savage was a renowned adventurer, but he was more than that. He was the supreme adventurer. Everything about the man of bronze—as the newspapers called him—was superlative. He was reputed to be a fabulous individual who had been placed in the hands of a succession of scientists at birth. These scientists had raised him to be a superman—and they had succeeded. Doc Savage had grown up to be a mental marvel and a muscular Midas. His life's work—so the story went—was to travel to the far ends of the earth, helping those in trouble and punishing evildoers.

In the silence which followed the utterance of the dreaded name of Doc Savage, each man in Blackbird's crew considered the fact that he was himself a wrongdoer, and that this was certainly one of the far corners of the world.

Blackbird Hinton swung suddenly on his red-headed prisoner. "What's your connection with Doc Savage?" he demanded.

Defiant blue eyes bored into Blackbird's own. The prisoner said nothing.

Blackbird Hinton drew a spike-nosed pistol—a black one—and waved it meaningfully. "I asked you a blasted question!"

The prisoner remained adamant.

In a rage, Blackbird pointed his pistol at the girl. "One last time," he grated. "What's your connection with Doc Savage?"

King Hancock interposed, "Wait! If this guy *is* hooked up with Savage, killing the girl is only going to get us in deeper. We can't afford that."

Blackbird hesitated. The girl stood calmly, regarding them without comprehension. It was a little eerie. She flinched not at all under the pistol's snout. It was as if she did not understand what the weapon meant.

That, more than King Hancock's words, decided the ravenlike skipper.

"Stick them in the cabin across from mine," he ordered a seaman. "We're a hundred miles out. They'd have no place to go if they tried something stupid." He said it so the red-haired prisoner would get the message.

The strange captives were taken away.

The African sun set early, but very slowly, inasmuch as the tramp *Mighty* was steaming into the sunset. Red dusk swathed the disreputable ship. No other ships or planes had been sighted since the scarecrow plane had been brought down. Ahead lay the Cape of Good Hope, where the Indian Ocean becomes the Atlantic.

A lull descended upon the smuggling vessel, one during which there was considerable discussion of the gold-plated aircraft and its weird passengers.

Currently, this discussion was centered in the ship's mess, where the crew was enjoying their supper—or enjoying it as much as they could. The *Mighty*, whose crew was composed of crooks and wharf-rats from three continents, was short-handed. Thus, the food was terrible and the cabin in which the prisoners were being held was not guarded while the crew ate.

The prisoners had proven to be quiet, and seemingly content to await developments. King Hancock had reported that all was well after personally delivering their food. Most of the crew noted the dapper first mate's interest in the captives, especially the girl. He became the butt of not a few ribald jests.

Most of the talk, however, dwelt upon the gold. Several thousand dollars' worth had been stripped from the scarecrow plane. This occasioned much speculation, the upshot of which was that anyone who would repair a plane with gold evidently had plenty to spare.

So it was that no one was about when the two prisoners eased out of their cabin and down a companionway.

"I spotted a radio room on our way in," the redhead remarked. "It may be deserted now. Everything else is."

The girl did not respond. They located the radio room.

"Empty! Now maybe I can get a message to Doc Savage."

At the name Doc Savage, the black-haired woman broke into voluble speech.

"S-h-h-h!" the redhead admonished. "Pipe down. Lha, they'll—" Then, realizing that his companion spoke no English, he shifted to another tongue. The girl quieted. Her black eyes, however, held an impatient light.

The gangling man sat down and warmed up the sending set. He began to tap out a hurried message.

Heavy feet sounded in the passageway outside. The red-haired one almost jumped out of his chair. He furiously worked the sending key.

"The hell!" a voice roared. Then Blackbird Hinton plunged into the radio room. "I'll fix you, mate!"

The other bounded out of his chair. A fist connected. The diamond smuggler bounced backward. For all his gangling looks, the redhead was a scrapper. He dragged the woman addressed as Lha out onto the deck. Behind him, Blackbird was bawling for help at the top of his leathery lungs.

When they gained the deck, the captives found it swarming with men. They raced off.

"Got to find that launch," the scrappy redhead panted. He did. It was wet from recent immersion, so he knew it was the craft they had been rescued in—if rescue was the correct term for it.

The launch hung on davits. These swung easily out. The man stepped aboard and rapped out strange words to the girl as he prepared to release the lines that would lower the boat into the sea.

Before the girl could join him, rifles started banging forward. Lead chewed the ship's rail, and made a *squeak-rip* of a sound as it tore off a vicious foot-long splinter near the girl. She jumped backward in startlement.

"Grab that girl!" King Hancock screamed.

The girl hesitated, confused. Her companion called out, "Lha!" Then a quick-thinking soul got a fishing net, gave it a quick toss, and snared her. Other seamen made for the suspended launch.

For a moment, it looked as though the red-haired fighter was about to plunge into the oncoming men. Instead, he said "Damn!" feelingly, and started the motor. The launch, released, smashed into the ocean, dug in her stern, and raced away at a high rate of speed, throwing up great sheets of brine.

Bullets *whupped* into the water, but none hit the careening craft.

Once out of range, the redhead reached under a thwart and withdrew the length of bamboo he had earlier secreted there. He examined this. It was an ordinary tube of jointed bamboo, except that it was closed at either end with blue sealing wax. Each end bore a weird design which had been pressed into the wax when it was hot. The design was that of a twisting serpent.

The seals had not been tampered with, he found.

The redhead looked back at the darksome tramp steamer, now receding in the night.

"This is all I have left now," he said to himself, "to prove to the world that the whole incredible thing really happened to me."

Now read the complete book, available in October 1991.

He never intended to be a hero.

THE ROCKETEER

1938. In Germany, Nazism reached a fever pitch. Rumors of war spread across the continent of Europe. In the calm before the storm, Hitler searches for a shortcut in his plans for world domination -- and looks to Hollywood. He sends his agents across the Atlantic to the celluloid capital of sin and glamour, on the trail of an all-powerful secret weapon.

After thugs destroy his prized GeeBee race plane during an FBI gun battle, barnstorming air race pilot Cliff Secord finds himself out of work, out of luck...and hung out to dry. For someone has saddled him with the most dangerous weapon of the war -- the Cirrus X-3 rocketpack, a flying device faster and more dangerous than any Secord has ever encountered. Now he and his starlet girlfriend are on the run, one step ahead of gangster mercenaries, federal agents, and Nazi assassins, who prowl the City of Angels looking for America's most reluctant hero.

Men have died for this weapon.

Cliff Secord is next in line.

The Rocketeer
A novel by Peter David
Based on the screenplay by Danny Bilson & Paul DeMeo
From a story by Danny Bilson
& Paul DeMeo & William Dear
Based upon the comic-book series
The Rocketeer created by Dave Stevens
Now a major motion picture from Walt Disney Pictures.

On sale wherever Bantam Falcon Books are sold.

AN311 -- 8/91

THRILLERS

Gripping suspense...explosive action...dynamic characters...international settings...these are the elements that make for great thrillers. Books guaranteed to keep you riveted to your seat.

Robert Ludlum:

☐	26256	THE AQUITAINE PROGRESSION	$5.95
☐	26011	THE BOURNE IDENTITY	$5.95
☐	26322	THE BOURNE SUPREMACY	$5.95
☐	26094	THE CHANCELLOR MANUSCRIPT	$5.95
☐	28209	THE GEMINI CONTENDERS	$5.95
☐	26019	THE HOLCROFT COVENANT	$5.95
☐	27800	THE ICARUS AGENDA	$5.95
☐	25899	THE MATERESE CIRCLE	$5.95
☐	27960	THE MATLOCK PAPER	$5.95
☐	26430	THE OSTERMAN WEEKEND	$5.95
☐	25270	THE PARSIFAL MOSAIC	$5.95
☐	28063	THE RHINEMANN EXCHANGE	$5.95
☐	27109	THE ROAD TO GANDOLOFO	$5.95
☐	27146	THE SCARLATTI INHERITANCE	$5.95
☐	28179	TREVAYNE	$5.95

Frederick Forsyth:

☐	28393	THE NEGOTIATOR	$5.95
☐	26630	DAY OF THE JACKAL	$5.95
☐	26490	THE DEVIL'S ALTERNATIE	$5.95
☐	26846	THE DOGS OF WAR	$5.95
☐	25113	THE FOURTH PROTOCOL	$5.95
☐	27673	NO COMEBACKS	$5.95
☐	27198	THE ODESSA FILE	$5.95

Buy them at your local bookstore or use this page to order.

Bantam Books, Dept. TH, 414 East Golf Road, Des Plaines, IL 60016

Please send me the items I have checked above. I am enclosing $_____
(please add $2.00 to cover postage and handling). Send check or money
order, no cash or C.O.D.s please.

Mr/Ms _____

Address _____

City/State _____ Zip _____

Please allow four to six weeks for delivery.
Prices and availability subject to change without notice.

TH–11/90